SARAH TUCKER

is a travel journalist, broadcaster and author. A presenter
and reporter for *BBC Holiday Programme* and travel
writer for the *Guardian* newspaper and the *Times,* she
is also the author of the bestselling books *Have Toddler
Will Travel* and *Have Baby Will Travel.* She has presented
award-winning documentaries for the Discovery Channel.
Formerly a travel correspondent for Classic FM and a
presenter and deviser of the award-winning weekly travel
show *The Jazz FM Travel Guide,* she lives in England and
France and has a young son, with whom she travels a lot.

The Last Year of Being Married is the follow-up story
to Sarah's wickedly honest, sexy and funny debut
Red Dress Ink novel, *The Last Year of Being Single.*

ACKNOWLEDGEMENTS

Thank you…

To my editor, Sam, who refused the first draft of this book. It wouldn't have been this funny or sexy first time 'round.

To Sarah Shurety, who has always led me in the right direction. You are a breath of fresh air, Sarah.

To friends, some of whom happen to be family: Jo, Amanda, Claire, Helen, Chris, Kim, Linda, Gina, Caroline, Fulva, Helen, Nim, Coline, Karin, Paul (not the one in the book) and Hazel. Thank you for your love and support. This book is about friendship more than anything else—and I couldn't ask or wish for better friends than you.

And to Doreen, you star.

To Thomas, who is sunshine.
And my dad, who is looking down on us
now and smiling.
Daddy, I will never ever give in.

SUMMER INTO AUTUMN

AUGUST

Sleeping with the enemy

My husband is an alien. My husband of seven years is an alien. He still looks like Paul, but it's not Paul. This person doesn't walk like Paul, talk like Paul, drink, eat, or even smell like Paul. He's like that character taken over by the hideous fire-breathing insect in *Men In Black*. He's an alien in a human suit. Only Paul is marginally better looking. And I'm worried. As in lost-a-dress-size-in-a-week worried. So I'm meeting Kim Bradshaw, thirty-eight, no-bullshit best friend and *Financial Times* columnist, in Circle, hip-happening funky restaurant in the heart of London's medialand. I know I'm worried because I'm on time for our meeting, and I am *never* on time for anything. *Ever.*

Kim—'God, Sarah, you're on time. I was hoping to catch up with work. I usually get about half an hour before you turn up. I've just interviewed some twat about an Internet scandal and Dick has given me a ridiculous deadline for tomorrow's paper. I've only just got here myself.'

Kim is a girl who calls a spade a fucking shovel. Dick, her editor, loves her because, he tells her, he's surrounded by stupid sycophants and she's brighter than him and tells him the truth. Even when it hurts.

I like her for the same reason. That and the fact I've known her for over ten years and we know each other inside out. We've agreed we'll end up as the *Golden Girls*. Or at least the *Witches of Eastwick*. As long as I'm Michelle Pfeiffer and she's Cher.

Sarah—'I know I'm on time. Sorry.'

Kim—'Don't say sorry. You're on time. That's great. Shit, girl, you look thin.'

A size eight Ghost dress is hanging off me. I look like a coat-hanger these days. I reassure myself that if I ever get a break on TV I will look fabulous.

Sarah—'I haven't eaten for, I think, a week. Maybe longer.'

Kim—'Sit down. Have something to eat. Try not to throw up. You look thinner than the models in here.'

Sarah—'I'm fine. I'll have the tuna. I always have the tuna in here.'

Waiter arrives and smiles warmly. Duncan Simpkins, tall, slim, dark and gay. Knows me. I used to work round the corner and this is a regular of mine. Light floods in even on miserable winter afternoons. The place is blessed with huge picture windows to watch the people-watchers. Large round white tables, pristine tablecloths, no centrepiece flowers to move, not too close together so the media buyers can't eavesdrop on a competitor's pitch for business. Simple yet eclectic menu, good champagne, unobtrusive service. Duncan sits us at a corner table out of ear- and eyeshot of everyone else.

Duncan—'Tuna, Sarah?'

Sarah—'Yes, please. And just some sparkling water. No ice. And a jug of lime cordial on the side. Side salad. Something different for a change.'

Duncan—'And for your guest?'

Kim likes her food. As in, she would have two of everything if she could. And in Circle she realises everything is the size of a starter even when it's not.

Kim—'Which choice has most food? Do I get more if I have the tuna or the cod?'

Duncan—'Well, the portions are about the same, madam. Would you perhaps like to order side dishes? The homemade chips are good.'

Kim—'That sounds good. Will they go with the cod?'

Duncan—'Yes, madam. Cod 'n chips. I think it has a certain ring to it.'

Duncan goes, and Kim gets up and gives me a hug.

Kim—'You look as though you need this.'

Sarah—'I do. I'm okay. I'm okay.'

Kim—'You sounded completely wired on the phone. Were you pacing, or something? You were up about four decibels on your normal pitch. Thought you would be chilled after the week's holiday in France, but sounds as though it didn't go to plan.'

Sarah—'No, it didn't. Paul's behaving very strangely.'

Kim—'He always behaves strangely, Sarah. What's he doing that's different from his norm?'

Sarah—'You know he never goes to the gym? Well, he's decided to go now. Twice a week. He has a personal trainer. The boys—well, they're not boys, they're forty-year-old men, most of them—anyway, the *boys* in the office are doing it, and now Paul's doing it. He tells me his body is a temple. A *fucking* temple. He showers for an hour each morning. Then there's the underpants…'

Kim—'What about the underpants?'

Sarah—'He has to buy new ones every week. Designer. Next, M&S, Gap won't do. Must be Gucci or Prada. Anything with a huge initial on the crotch area.'

Kim—'I didn't know Prada did underpants.'

Sarah—'Nor did I, but maybe they do. They've got a big P on them, anyway.'

Kim—'Appropriate, really.'

Sarah—'And now he wants separate holidays and thinks it's a good idea if we give each other space. I'm a travel journalist, for fuck's sake, Kim. How much more space can I give him? I spend three months each year travelling and get us free holidays together when I can. It's unnerving me.'

Kim—'Sarah, this has all the signs of a mid-life crisis. How old is he now?'

Sarah—'Thirty-five. Bit early for a mid-life crisis. But perhaps men are having them younger these days. Plus stress at work. It's been tough, and he's been a bit depressed about his weight.'

Kim—'What else is he doing and saying?'

Sarah—'He's coming back late. Often drunk. Been drinking with the *boys.*'

Kim—'Sounds as though his body is being treated more like a pub than a temple.'

Sarah—'And there's more. He keeps buying really strong-smelling aftershave. Smells like a brothel in the morning. Always humming to himself, too. And he's bought one of those—you know—soap on a rope things. But with a hole in the middle of it.'

Kim—'Wants a clean willy, then.'

Sarah—'I asked him about it and he said he'd read this article about penis hygiene. I think it was penal hygiene but he took it the wrong way.'

Kim laughs.

Kim—'Bollocks. He just wants to wank and wash and save time.'

I laugh now.

Kim—'What else has he said?'

Sarah—'Serious bit, this. He wants Ben and me to move out of the house. Wants to buy us a little house nearby—not too close, not up the road or anything. He says he doesn't want to accidentally bump into us. Just be in a neighbouring village. And he suggests I get a job as a PA somewhere local. So I'm able to prove I can look after myself. He feels I haven't put enough into the marriage and doesn't respect me anymore. Well, he says I haven't put *anything* into the marriage and doesn't respect me *at all,* actually. That's the bit that is worrying me.'

Kim—'He wants you to do fucking *what?* You're a travel journalist, Sarah. Why would you want to be a PA? You've worked so hard to get this far. Is the man nuts? Okay, he wants space. Let *him* move out. Let him get a bachelor pad in London.'

Sarah—'That's what I told him. And he said the house was *his house.* And that it's all *his money.* And he got very angry and threw a mini-size plastic Badoit bottle on the floor. And that made me laugh and he got angrier. But he looked such a prat, Kim. And, anyway, he doesn't see why he should move out.'

Kim—'Don't you dare, Sarah. You stay put. What planet is he on?'

Sarah—'As I said. He's an alien.'

Duncan returns with tuna, water, salad and lime. And no ice. Kim and I change the subject while Duncan hovers.

Sarah—'Ben's well.'

Kim—'That's good. How old is he now?'

Sarah—'Three. Four in December. He's getting to that edible age. You know—I want to bite his bottom all the time. And I can still go in the bath with him and play submarines and it's not considered indecent or unnatural.'

Kim—'That's wonderful. Give him a big kiss from me.'

Sarah—'I will.'

Duncan stops hovering and leaves. Subject reverts back to alien.

Sarah—'Paul is a sensible guy, you know. Dependable. Like a rock. Always there for me. Always putting up with me.'

Kim—'What do you mean, putting up with you? You're a wonderful, fabulous sexy woman, Sarah Giles. Okay, you look emaciated at the moment, but have a few chips and you'll be fine. And don't you forget it, because the man you've married obviously has. As for being a rock. Well, rocks may make you stable but they can also hold you down. And I think that's what he's done. Bit by bit, day by day, he's held you down. And chipped away—quite successfully too, it appears—at your confidence.'

Sarah—'Oh, he's not that bad. We've done some fun things together. You know, holidays and stuff. But what do I *bring* to the relationship, to be honest?'

Kim—'What do you *bring*? You *bring* you! Or are we talking dowry here? He married you because he loved you. Because you're fun and full of life and fire and energy. He knew you couldn't cook. He knew you weren't domesticated. But so what? He can afford a cook and a cleaner if he wants one. Christ, he can afford one for every day of the week if he wants to. He makes it sound as though he considers you a liability.'

Sarah—'He does. He says I'm a negative on his balance sheet.'

Kim—'He says you're a fucking what?'

Sarah—'That I'm a liability. That I spend all his money.'

Kim—'Sarah. This man is full of shit. You know Debbie—my next-door neighbour, helium-voiced Debbie? She's married to a city oik who earns—I think—half what Paul does. She has manicures, facials, pedicures, and lunches and does Knightsbridge most weeks. She doesn't do a thing for her man, Mike. Think she probably even charges him for a blow-job. They've got a cleaner, gardener, spiritual healer, live-in nanny—and Mike dotes on her. You, on the other hand, look after yourself, buy your own clothes, get your own holidays. You've given Paul a wonderful son. What else does he want you to *bring* to the marriage?'

Sarah—'Money.'

Kim—'I should imagine he earns well over a hundred grand a year, Sarah. Plus bonuses. What's he want with more money? This is all an excuse for something. He's deflecting you from something. Do you think he's met someone else?'

Sarah—'That's crossed my mind. Makes me feel sick. Best not to think about it. I'm a jealous woman—green-eyed monster and all that. Always have been. Remember the thirtieth birthday party I told you about when that girl was dancing with him? I was at the other side of the room and saw her flirting with him. One minute I was dancing in the corner and the next I zoomed in like a heat-seeking missile and sent her flying into the steaming wontons. And she was just dancing with him. If I thought he'd met or was sleeping with someone else it would kill me. Especially as he's not sleeping with me. And hasn't been for years.'

Kim—'How long has it been now?'

Sarah—'For most of our marriage, Kim—Ben was a wonderful blip—plus four of the five years we were going out before then.'

Kim—'What excuse does he give?'

Sarah—'Same old story. Same reason. Doesn't respect me. Doesn't feel I *bring* anything to the marriage. Doesn't trust me. He brought up all the past things I'd done when he smashed that Badoit bottle. It's as if he's kept a mental list. But he says he still loves me and all that.'

Kim—'Sounds as though he resents you, Sarah.'

Sarah—'I think so, too. But I'm no innocent, Kim. I haven't exactly been squeaky clean, have I? After all, *I had an affair.* And Paul discovered the affair by reading one of my e-mails. You know? That e-mail from Stephen from Australia.'

Kim—'Er, yes, that was a bit of a bummer. Explicit, wasn't it?'

Sarah—'Er, rather. If you have an affair with the editor-at-large of a lad mag—and he was…well, rather large—he tends to be rather eloquent with words. Especially when writing about sex. And—well, he did enjoy it. And hey, for fuck's sake, so did I. I hadn't had sex for years. I used to go to the gym and work out like crazy. The Kai Bo teacher said he didn't know where I got my energy. I got so flexible and fit I could do the box splits, and there wasn't even a face to sit on. But Stephen's e-mail… Well, it was quite poetic—about how the water trickled down my back when I bent over, and how he loved my nipples, and how he wished we could have stayed in the shower longer but the hot water ran out and then so did we, and ended up having sex on the bathroom floor. And on the dining room table, and in the garden under the apple tree. He wrote a sonnet. Think he published it in a later edition of the magazine he was so proud of it. Not nice to read. Well, I enjoyed reading it, which is why I saved it. But not nice for Paul, obviously.'

Kim—'Well, he shouldn't have been reading your e-mail, then, should he? Serves him bloody well right.'

Sarah—'He was trying to sort out my virus and was checking to see who had given it to me.'

Kim—'Yeah, really. Well, he found out, didn't he?'

Sarah—'Yes, yes, but you know what I mean. Well, he was furious—and rightly so.'

Kim—'What do you mean, *rightly so?* He wasn't fuck-ing *fucking* you, Sarah. *He hasn't been sleeping with you for years.* That's emotional cruelty or punishment or some-thing. Anyway, it's not natural, and I think he should go and see a counsellor or someone about it.'

Sarah—'Think he went to see his priest.'

Kim—'*His priest?* That's gonna screw him up even more.'

Sarah—'I know, Kim. I've got to the stage when I think Hey, my husband won't sleep with me, won't give me a sound reason why he won't sleep with me, and won't go to see anyone about why he won't sleep with me, but he doesn't want me to mention it to anyone.'

Kim—'Of course he doesn't want you to mention it to anyone. They'd think he was bonkers. You're a babe, Sarah. And with friends like his, they'd probably try and sleep with you themselves.'

Sarah—'Yes, one of his brokers did say over dinner once that if we lived in London he would have proba-bly slept with me by now.'

Kim—'Was he drunk?'

Sarah—'Think so.'

Kim—'Was Paul there at the time?'

Sarah—'The broker was taking us out for supper. At the Ivy. He was with his wife. She talked Botox all night.'

Kim—'Sounds like a lovely evening.'

Sarah—'It was interesting. Never saw them again after that. Think Paul still does business with him, but I don't ask. Anyway, I'm going slowly nuts. And along comes this guy who obviously *does* want to sleep with me. And—well, the rest is history.'

Kim—'If your husband doesn't fuck you, someone else will. If it was the other way round he would have slept with someone else. Mark my words, Sarah. He would have had an affair. Lots of them.'

Sarah—'Yes, I know it's different for men.'

Kim—'Too bloody right it is. They can do it. But you can't. Well *you* did. But *you* had a reason.'

Sarah—'Paul could argue that so does he.'

Kim—'Ah, but that's different. The no-sex thing is *his* choice, Sarah. Not yours. And it's up to him to go and see someone about it. You can't go for him.'

Silence again. We're both thinking. Then…

Kim—'I know one guy who had an affair with this other woman. But when he got divorced from his wife, and the other woman said she wanted to marry him, the bugger turned round and told her he couldn't marry someone like her because she'd gone off with a married man and he couldn't marry someone that immoral.'

Sarah—'Double standards.'

Kim—'Quite. But it happens. Anyway, have you told anyone other than me about the no-sex thing?'

Sarah—'Few people. Told Stephen in Australia. That's why he slept with me.'

Kim—'Not a good idea to tell men about that. Specially those that are a bit lecherous. Beware men who see you as vulnerable. They think it's sexy. Plus you're easy prey.'

Sarah—'Well, I wanted to. Can't seriously say he seduced me, or I was taken against my will. Think I actually seduced him. And it was the other side of the world.'

Kim—'Yeah, and it came back to haunt you. Bloody e-mails. You never know who's reading them.'

Duncan returns to ask if we are enjoying our meals.

Duncan—'Is it enough for you, madam?'

Kim—'Yes, thank you.'

Duncan—'Good. Anything else I can do, just let me know.'

Kim—'Thanks. Dessert menu after this would be good.'

Duncan smiles and leaves.

Sarah—'I think one of the problems we have is that he comes from a very traditional background. His mother did *everything* for him. He's the eldest of four boys, and his father was out working all the time, so his mum got the brunt of it. And she's a bit—well, *odd* emotionally. So he's used to having everything done for him. And getting his own way.'

Kim—'Yes, he is rather boorish. But he has to be aggressive for work. It's a dog-eat-dog environment.'

Sarah—'Absolutely, and he doesn't like most of those he works with, and trusts even fewer, so that's bound to rub off. As for my lifestyle—on the face of it, everything is fine. Big house in the suburbs, house just bought in France, fabulous child, two cars. But you know, Kim, it's not me. I feel as though I *should* be happy, but it's not me. I don't live in a house I particularly like. Actually, I hate it. I don't live in a town I like. Actually, I hate that, too. And I don't particularly like his parents. His father is okay, but his mother is—well, cold. Shit, I sound ungrateful.'

Kim—'No, you're just being true to yourself.'

Sarah—'I sometimes wish Dad were still here. He gave me really good advice. It's nearly four years since he died. Don't know if he ever knew I was pregnant with Ben. Tried to tell him in hospital, but don't think he could understand me. He would have loved his little grandson so much.'

I'm fighting back tears. I don't want to cry. Not now. Not about that. Not in public. I've got too much else to worry about. Kim senses it and leans over the fish 'n chips to hug me. I think—Don't cry. Don't cry. Think of something that will stop you from crying. Someone that makes you anaemic emotionally. I know, Tony Blair. Visualise Tony Blair sitting on the toilet. Great, that's done the trick. Tears stop immediately.

Kim tucks into her cod and chips. I don't have an appetite. I think my stomach has shrunk, so after two mouthfuls I'm full. Then…

Kim—'Sarah, *I think he's got someone else.* I've been thinking. It's obvious. He wants space suddenly. Clean underpants. Coming back late and drunk. No sex. Bringing up things from the past. Why bring them up now? The things he says—they all say the same things. I've heard this all before, with other friends. It's fucking spooky, really. As though men have all read the same books. You'd think they'd be smarter, but they're not.'

I redden. And start to feel very hot. Because deep down I know she's right, but don't want to believe it. I don't think even visualising Tony Blair on the toilet will work this time.

Sarah—'Perhaps.'

Kim—'Sarah, women run *from* a relationship they're

unhappy with, but men tend to run *to* another woman. Men don't leave—emotionally or literally—until they've found someone else to look after them. Someone to lean on. It's in their nature. They're weak; they need the support. Paul is like any other. Just out of interest, how much time do you spend with Ben and how much with Paul?'

Sarah—'More with Ben, of course.'

Kim—'Well, then. Paul's even further down the pecking order.'

Sarah—'That's obvious. Ben is three. Paul is thirty-five. Slight difference.'

Kim—'The more I get to know men, the more I think they're just like toddlers. They want to be looked after. Paul just has more grown-up toys. And probably likes dollies.'

Sarah—'He knew what he was getting when he married me.'

Kim—'Perhaps he thought he could change you.'

Sarah—'You can't change people.'

Kim—'Paul is so arrogant he thinks he can do anything.'

Sarah—'People can mellow.'

Kim—'No. Their traits usually get stronger as they grow older.'

Sarah—'Think so?'

Kim—'Yep. If they're mean, they get meaner. Generous, they become more generous. Seen it in all my parents' friends. They just go round in circles. Don't learn.'

Sarah—'Do you think I should start cooking for him?'

Kim—'God, you're *that* worried, Sarah? No, if I were you, I'd just stay the same. Play cool and focus on Ben. And get some food inside you, girl. Sounds as though he's got someone, but wait until he's drunk or something. He may tell you then. They usually do.'

And, looking at my untouched tuna…

Kim—'Are you going to eat that?'

With that, she swaps plates and scoffs the lot.

Duncan returns.

Duncan—'Have you finished, ladies?'

Sarah—'Yes, that was wonderful, Duncan.'

We start talking puff while Duncan clears the plates.

Kim—'So, what are you doing this afternoon?'

Sarah—'I've got to make a deadline, too. I've been asked to write a feature for a women's magazine, and it's the first break I've had with them so I don't want to screw up. "*Where to go for a romantic weekend break.*" I've got to collect Ben from nursery, and then play with his new bike and stuff for a few hours.'

Duncan goes.

Sarah—'Then welcome Paul home. If he comes home. I'm very worried, Kim. You know, I think you're right. I think he may have met someone else.'

Realising I'm about to sob hard, and probably rather loudly, in the middle of a restaurant full of people-watchers, Kim lightens up.

Kim—'I was joking, Sarah. Fuck Paul. Who the fuck would fuck him?'

Sarah—'I know, I know. But you know what I'm like.'

Duncan returns with the dessert menu. Smiling at me, then turning to Kim.

Duncan—'The apple pie dish has most volume, just in case you're interested.'

Kim—'Thank you. Apple pie, then. And Sarah will have the same.'

Duncan—'We do ice cream on the side.'

Kim—'Dollop on top will do nicely. Thank you.'

Duncan goes. Think he's starting to warm to Kim. We start talking again.

Kim—'Why have you stayed with this guy for so long, Sarah? Under these conditions? A girl like you? You don't have to put up with this crap. He's been bullying you so long now and you just take it. Do you enjoy that sort of thing?'

Sarah—'I've got used to it. I've become conditioned to it. It's easy.'

Kim—'It doesn't sound easy to me. It sounds bloody horrendous. You can't respect this man, Sarah.'

Kim leans over and holds my hand.

Kim—'Sarah, this is no life. You deserve better. You always have. You're not a trophy wife. You're more than that. And you're cheating yourself by staying with this man. You know it and I think he knows it. He's doing you a favour, Sarah.'

Sarah—'I shouldn't have married him, should I? I shouldn't have married him.'

Kim sighs and looks up at Duncan, who's just arrived with two double-sized portions of apple pie.

Duncan—'There we are, ladies.'

I think he knows Kim's going to eat both, because I don't get a spoon.

Kim—'Well, no, I don't think you should have married him. And I *definitely* don't think you should have told him on the third day of your honeymoon that you were having an affair while you were engaged to him, and had an abortion by this other guy. Think that was a bad move.'

Sarah—'Er, yes. That probably was a bad move.'

Kim—'No *probably* about it, Sarah. Bad move. No man can take that. Why the hell did you tell him then? Why not before you got married? Why ever?'

Sarah—'I wanted to wipe the slate clean. I wanted him to know that if he ever tried to withhold sex from me again I would betray him. I also wanted to tell him just in case John turned up on our doorstep when we got back from honeymoon and said, "Oh, hello, you must be Paul. Well, I'm John, and I've been fucking your fiancée. Just thought you should know." You know— that sort of thing.'

Kim—'So you wanted to save his pride? And sacrificed yourself and your chance of happiness to do that?'

Sarah—'Yes. I didn't want John to have the satisfaction of humiliating Paul.'

Kim—'So you did it instead?'

Sarah—'Yes. But at least it was one on one.'

Kim—'At Raffles? In Singapore?'

Sarah—'Yes, over a candlelit dinner.'

Kim—'On the third night of your honeymoon?'

Sarah—'Yes.'

Kim—'You told him about John?'

Sarah—'Yes.'

Kim—'And the abortion?'

Sarah—'Yes. But I also gave him the opt-out clause. I told him if he wanted to annul the marriage then and there he could do so.'

Kim—'You wanted out *then,* Sarah. That's why you told him. You wanted out then. You just couldn't do it yourself. Problem was, neither could he. Not then, anyway.'

Sarah—'I realise I've betrayed him, Kim.'

Kim—'Yes, but what's more important is that by staying with him, Sarah, by marrying him, having his child, you've betrayed yourself.'

We sit in silence again. I think about what Kim's just said. I love her clarity of thought. My thoughts are clouded by my feelings. When I'm with her I realise how much my anger, my fear, my pride have clouded my reason for such a long time. How I've become immune to the hurt, as though the emotional bruises are now an integral part of me. They have been there for such a long time. My feelings of self-contempt and wanting to do the right thing are so strong. I've always thought staying with Paul is the right thing to do—when I know, have always known, it's not. But now there's Ben. Little Ben. And it's not his fault that this has happened. And I've got to protect him. And think of him. And think of myself.

Sarah—'You're right, Kim. Of course you're right. But you're not on the inside. I am. And I can't see this the way you can. Without the emotion.'

Kim—'Without what emotion? You can't think straight because you're angry and upset and perhaps a bit guilty, but also probably because you're not eating enough and can't think straight. You don't love this man, Sarah.'

Sarah—'I think I do.'

Kim—'Well, I think you *think* you do, if you get me. But I don't think you do. I think you're proud and jealous and want to do the right thing, even if it's not the right thing for you. And Paul has never been the right thing for you. Paul treats you like a child. He's become your daddy and he just wants to control you. And now he resents *you* for it. He's a controlling bugger, Sarah. Get out of this marriage now. He's done you a favour. And if there is a *she,* which there may be, I think she's done you a favour, too.'

Sarah—'I've got to try to save the marriage, Kim. Even if it's just for Ben's sake.'

Kim—'You should only try for *your* sake, so at least

you can look back and say you did try and won't always wonder if perhaps, maybe, it could have worked. Ultimately, you must make your own decisions and your own mistakes. That's the way everyone learns in life. Not through other people's mistakes. But take it from me, as a friend who knows and loves you for all your faults, you married a man who *doesn't* know and love you for all your faults, Sarah. And he isn't your friend anymore.'

We don't talk through dessert. I sit and think. Kim lets me while she eats both apple pies and then complains of indigestion.

Duncan walks over to our table with the bill. Kim grabs it.

Kim—'I think I should pay for this one. I've eaten most of it.'

Sarah—'Thank you, Kim. I'm very lucky to have you as a friend.'

Kim—'Bollocks. We're lucky to have each other as friends. You've helped me through shit in the past. Perhaps this is my time to pay back. I've seen this coming for a long time. It's what you need.'

Sarah—'I haven't asked a thing about you. How is Jamie?'

Kim—'Oh, Jamie is fine. He's working on a merger. He's floating the company and it's taking up all his energy and time, and I wish he could spend more time with me. But he can't. You know. The usual.'

Sarah—'He's lucky to have you. You're wonderful and special.'

Kim—'I know. I tell him that all the time—usually just before I go down on him. He always agrees. Usually because I threaten to bite if he doesn't.'

Sarah—'I haven't gone down on Paul for years. Forgotten what it looks like. Well, erect anyway.'

Kim—'Probably small. He has a big house, big car, oversized ego and bank account. Say no more.'

Sarah—'It always was small. But having a child doesn't help. I'm not as, well, tight as I used to be. I've been doing those exercises. The ones with the pencil. But I don't want to get lead poisoning.'

Kim laughs.

Kim—'His penis is about the size of a pencil, is it? Oh, well. You're missing nothing, then.'

We get up. Duncan comes over to say goodbye and gives me a hug, whispering.

Duncan—'You look thin, Sarah. Hope everything is okay. Your friend is a pig.'

And smiles.

Duncan—'Thank you. Lovely to see you.'

Kim—'I don't think your waiter friend likes me.'

Sarah—'He likes your appreciation of his food. And your curly pink tail.'

Kim—'Hug, then.'

We stand outside Circle and hug for five seconds. I start to sob again, very quietly, so my body shakes and aches. I have this feeling of dread, of something being just round the corner, that makes me feel faint and ill. And I can't fast-forward this bit of my life. I've got to live through it and learn from it and grow. And standing there, with my friend, I feel terrified. And alone.

Kim—'I'm here for you, Sarah. Your friends are here for you. And the one good thing about this whole mess is that you'll find out who your friends are. And that's worth a lot. Some people go through life and never find out. And another thing. If you don't listen to anything else I've said today, listen to this. Don't leave the house, and if you find out he has got someone else call me. Any time. Day or night. E-mail, if you like. Text. Anything. Paul sounds like he's being a mean bugger. He's arrogant, so will be self-righteous in anything he does— even when it is suggesting his wife and child leave the house. He'll validate his behaviour somehow, so you'll look bad and he won't. Because that's the way his mind works. He's always been a good liar. He's manipulative, mean, insensitive and self-obsessed. You just wait. You'll see him for what he is soon enough. He'll make himself out to be the injured party. Don't let the bastard get you down any more than he already has.'

Sarah—'I love you, Kim. Why can't men be more like women?'

Kim—'Because they have willies, darling. Because they have willies. And that's where they keep their ego and their brains. Give Ben a big kiss from me. And *call* me. Now, I've got to get this twat's article done.'

Journey back to Chelmsford takes an hour, but somehow it seems shorter this time. My mind is not on the journey, but buzzing with everything Kim's said to me. Her insight into the situation, which I can't see because I'm living it.

I collect Ben from nursery. His little face when he sees me and calls out 'Mummy' moves me to tears. He sings the *Teletubbies* theme tune in the back seat. I've got to try to make it work for his sake. I've got to try. But I'm tired emotionally. I'm tired of living in a house I hate, in a relationship I hate, with a man I think I'm growing to hate. And I think I hate myself. Kim's right. I've got to deal with this head-on. But Paul and I have never been able to talk about the big issues—and it's even worse now. So what can I do?

Back at the house, I let Ben play in the garden with his new bike, then give him tea—salmon in white wine and garlic. It's really for his daddy, but somehow I don't think Paul will turn up tonight. Ben is eating more than I do at the moment. I bathe him and read him a bed-time story. The one about the witch—*Room on the Broom*. He likes that one.

Ben—'I lub you, Mummy.'

Sarah—'I lub you too, Ben.'

Ben—'Are you okay, Mummy?'

Sarah—'Yes, I'm okay, Ben.'

Perhaps he senses something is wrong. They say children can sense things clearly at this age. They're like animals; they know when something is wrong. No hiding anything from them. I feel very protective towards this little boy.

I work on the *She* feature, but don't feel in the mood to write about romantic breaks, somehow. I switch off the computer. Perhaps Paul *will* make it home tonight. Perhaps not. So I wait in the sitting room and watch reality TV, which has absolutely nothing to do with anything *real* at all. Sets are fake. Situations are fake. People are fake.

The front door opens. The alien returns. It's nearly eleven.

I get up and walk over to greet him. He looks morose and drunk.

Sarah—'Hi, would you like something to eat?'

Paul—'No, thanks. Had something on the train. Think I'll just go to bed.'

Sarah—'Okay. You do that. Say night-night to Ben.'

Paul—'Will do.'

I hear Ben's bedroom door open and a faint, *'How's my best boy, then?'* And a kiss. And a quiet *'I lub you, Daddy.'* And, *'Can I have a dog?'*

Then I hear him go into our bedroom and close the door. I stay downstairs for ten more minutes. Watching blankly as a couple tear each other apart emotionally on *Temptation Island*.

I check on Ben, who is snoring happily in his mini-bed which has just been converted from his mini-cot. Our son is now a fully-fledged little boy, with Buzz Lightyear duvet and pillows. His room is the nicest in the house. Bright yellow walls, now almost covered with his drawings and paintings, and scribblings of his name and what he did for the holiday and what he likes to eat and what his favourite television programme is. Carpet deep blue, hiding all the baby sick and mess that comes as part of the package with children, especially boys. Because I'm told little girls are so much tidier and more mature.

But I'm so very pleased I had Ben—that I had a little boy. I remember clearly how I felt when I was in the labour ward and this little red and puffy bundle squished out and looked around as if to say, 'Where am I now, then?' And Paul was there to see his son come into the world, and he beamed with pride and love that day. And I remember the midwife took Ben away and quickly cleaned him. I said I wanted Ben straight on the breast, and he immediately hooked onto my left nipple and never liked the right as much. And he travelled with me wherever I went, and awoke every two hours for the first three months, and I didn't mind one bit. I knew then he had a lovely nature. A gentle and kind nature. My sunshine.

Just a pity my dad never saw him. I was five months pregnant at his funeral. Hope he's looking down now and smiling on us both. He would have loved this little bundle of joy. Ben's a cuddler, and the best thing in the world is when he wraps his little arms around me and looks me in the eyes and says, 'You're very beautiful, Mummy.' Because for that brief moment I feel I am.

Paul is fast asleep. Snoring loudly. Farting silently. Must open windows. Last time I didn't, and almost threw up when I woke up. Don't want to be gassed in my sleep.

Paul still an alien in the morning. Perhaps he thinks I'm one, too.

Paul—'God, it's bloody freezing in here. Why are all the windows open?'

Sarah—'Thought we could do with some fresh air.'

Paul—'I'm going to be late tonight. Work to do. Don't wait up.'

Sarah—'Okay. Is everything okay?'

Paul—'Yes. Have you thought about what I said? About moving out?'

Sarah—'No. Don't think it's a good idea. I work from here, and this is Ben's home. It's easier for you to move into London and get yourself a flat if you need the space.'

Paul—'Told you how I feel about that.'

Sarah—'Told you how I feel about that.'

Paul—'We'll talk tonight.'

Sarah—'We won't, because you won't be back till late.'

Paul—'The night after that, then. But we need to talk. I need space.'

Sarah—'I know you do.'

Paul—'I don't like it when I'm around you.'

Sarah—'I know. At the moment I don't like it when you are around me either.'

Paul—'Look, why don't I give you an allowance of, say, thirty thousand a year, and you can look after Ben and yourself. I'll even find you a house.'

Sarah—'This is madness, Paul. What the fuck is going on?'

Paul—'I told you, Sarah. I just need space. Don't hassle me. Got to go now. Going to be late.'

Paul—alien, former lover, former friend—leaves bedroom. Prada underpants, smelling of something spicy. Soap on a rope worn out.

Confused, I get up and see if Ben is awake, so he can wave goodbye to Daddy. Ben is toddling towards me, big smile. 'Hello, Mummy, hello, Mummy. Can I watch *Teletubbies?*'

Sarah—'Say goodbye to Daddy, Ben.'

I pick him up and hand him to Paul. Paul's face warms and softens and he smiles at this little boy and cuddles him, and I think, Hey, these moments are worth fighting for.

Twelve-thirty. Half an hour early. Circle again with Kim one week later. Half a stone lighter. Looking like someone out of a concentration camp. Distraught. Corner table.

Sarah—'He's got someone else.'

Kim's face screams *I told you so.* Her lips don't move. I continue.

'He came home the other night, drunk as usual, and suggested we sleep in separate rooms. Don't mind about that one little bit. He's become really farty—so at least the bedroom smelt okay in the morning. Anyway, he was more morose than usual. Kept asking me when I was moving out. Got so bad over the past week I actually agreed to it at one point. And that seemed to please him. He actually hugged me and looked into my eyes and said that we could still be friends. *His friend.* What happened to being his wife! I asked if he was okay, said I was his wife, not just his friend, and didn't feel he was being particularly friendly to me at the moment. In fact, I told him I thought he was a prat. And that he was neglecting Ben as well. Who's had chicken pox all this week. And he hasn't come home until after midnight each night. Then he said because I had failed to move out, to give him space when he had asked so nicely, he thought the only way forward now was a divorce. A *divorce.*

'I was stunned. I asked if he'd met someone. His exact words were—I can remember them so clearly—*"There is someone else."* As though this someone else was in the room with us at that moment. Like a ghost. I froze. Then collapsed. Then screamed. Completely lost it. Couldn't really take in what he said to me after that. Crying. Ran into the other bedroom to get away from him. Didn't want to be in the same room as him. I'd wanted to talk to him for such a long time about so many things, but at that moment, Kim, I didn't want to talk to him or see him or know him. He followed me. And tried to hug me. But now I think about it, it was more like restraining me.

'I thought, Fuck you. I think I *said* fuck you, actually. Well, screamed fuck you. But that's understandable in the situation. I asked him if he loved her. He laughed and said of course not. I asked where they'd met. He said in a bar. I wanted to know so much—but didn't want to know anything, if you know what I mean. Because it made it worse.

'Paul then said that he thought it best if we slept in the same bed that night after all. He said he was worried about me. I didn't want to, Kim. I really didn't want to. But I did sleep in the bed. I couldn't sleep. He was so drunk he went straight to sleep. Farting and snoring. Thought about lighting a match and blowing him up in his own gas.

'I couldn't sleep. At about 1 a.m. I got up. Got in the car half-dressed and headed for Samantha's house. Rang

on her bell. She looked confused, but woke up fully
when I told her what had happened. She looked
shocked. Couldn't believe it. Not Paul. Not lovely, cud-
dly, butter-wouldn't-melt-in-his-mouth, devoted Paul.
Told her devoted Paul had found a new model and
wanted a divorce. She said it was probably the woman's
doing. That she'd probably given him an ultimatum.

'I stayed for about an hour. Then drove back. I'd
sobbed a lot. Hard. And it was good to be hugged by
a friend. When I got back the prat was still fast asleep,
and next morning he said he hadn't realised I'd gone.
I had to drop Ben off to nursery, and asked Paul if he
could call in sick today at work. He said he was too
upset to go in, but wanted to be by himself. He said he
was confused. I remember sitting on the bottom stair
with him by my side, telling me he was confused. Then
watching him from the bedroom as he walked down
the street towards the centre of town. Listening to his
Sony Walkman.

'He didn't come home that night. He'd told me he
was due to see *her* that night. That they always met on
Friday nights. But I asked him not to meet her this Friday night as it would be different this time. I would
know where he was, what he was doing. And that would
be particularly cruel.'

Kim—'He stayed out, didn't he?'

Sarah—'Yes. He stayed out. All night. And I was de-
stroyed, Kim. And it's been nearly a week now. And I
can't talk and I couldn't talk. You're the first person
other than Samantha that I've told. Because I think,
hopefully, it's a blip. But this has been going on for
nearly a week, and I'm being strong for Ben but I'm
weeping inside.'

Kim leans over and hugs me. I don't know how long

she hugs me. But Duncan usually welcomes us with the menus in the first five minutes, especially as he now knows the extent of Kim's appetite, but I think the man has a sixth sense. Either that or he's shocked by my size.

Kim—'So you haven't told anyone else about this?'

Sarah—'Samantha has been there for me, but she's just got engaged and I don't want to burden her too much with this nightmare. The girl's full of hope and love at the moment. She has no time for reality.'

Sarah—'What about your mum and his parents?'

Sarah—'My mum's on holiday in Australia, visiting friends. His parents don't want to get involved. They live two minutes away and haven't been round once. They're scared of losing contact with their grandson, of course, so they've got to be nice. But they're siding with their son—which is, of course, natural.'

Kim—'Yes. Shortsighted, small-minded, but natural.'

Sarah—'Do you think Paul still loves me?'

Kim—'I don't think he fell out of love with you suddenly. But I don't think he's in love with you now. No. But it isn't a sudden thing. It's a gradual process. But he didn't have the courage to just leave you. He had to have someone to move on to. He probably thinks you'll crumble and he'll get out of this losing very little.'

Sarah—'I am crumbling.'

Kim—'You are now. But you just wait. You'll be fine, Sarah. Has he been to a solicitor?'

Sarah—'He says no, but I think he has.'

Kim—'What makes you think that?'

Sarah—'I opened his post.'

Kim—'Good girl. Have you been through his pockets, too?'

Sarah—'Of course. I found receipts. That restaurant

Tuffnells—you know, the romantic one round the corner from here where you can't see what you're eating?
He took her there. And he's taken her to Cambridge.
Think he took her there when I was away on that trip
to Brazil.'

Kim—'Keep the receipts somewhere safe. How long
does he say he's known this girl?'

Sarah—'He says it's only recent, but I think it started
in June.'

Kim—'Methinks so, too. Rule of thumb is always
double what they say. If they say three, it will be six.
They think it will hurt less. Hurt *them* less. He'll feel
less guilty about hurting you, that is. Anyway, think of
the positives, Sarah. You can have guilt-free sex with
who you like now. Form a new relationship or not, as
you choose. Have your own home. And you'll probably see more of Paul's money than when you were
married to him.'

Sarah—'I still am married to him, Kim.'

Kim—'He wants a divorce. He's told you *there's someone else,* as he so coyly puts it. He's a fool for telling you,
of course, but at least you know the situation now. You
know why he asked you to move out. You know his
motivation—that he's a devious little bugger. And now
it's a case of *What Sarah does next.* It's your call now.'

Sarah—'So much has been going through my head.
Do I stay with him? Do I agree to the divorce? I've written a list of his good and bad points. I wanted to weigh
up the pros and cons of trying to make it work or let-
ting go. It's here somewhere…'

I delve into my handbag, which is a mess of old receipts—some of which are Paul's—train tickets, credit
cards and used handkerchiefs.

Sarah—'Here it is.'

Kim reads.

Arsehole tendencies:

Picks nose and eats bogies
Toxic farting during nights
Snores very loudly
Mean with money
Mean with me
Large car syndrome, small willy
Likes me to stick my finger up his bottom
Arrogant and boorish qualities becoming more apparent
Controlling with sexual favours—i.e. gives none—to me anyway
Has lousy taste in furnishings—soft or otherwise (house looks like gentlemen's club)
Criticises the way I drive (unsurprising, perhaps, as crashed his Lotus two years ago)
Criticises the way I talk
Criticises the fact I don't earn enough money
Criticises the way I don't spend enough time with him (perhaps not include this one, as not relevant anymore)
Doesn't praise me when I do something well
Doesn't support me in my work
Has boring friends
Always leads when dancing and has lousy timing
Don't like his family
Fussy with food
Hypocritical
Untidy and lazy in the house

Good tendencies:

Good when on holiday—fun to be with and funny

Good dad to Ben—gives lots of cuddles—except recently when very drunk. Ben would never go without

Have never loved anyone as much as I loved him. No, doesn't count. These are my feelings for him. Not his qualities

Used to be considerate lover—doesn't count. Not anymore. Delete this one. Only now counts, not past

Would never have money worries as controls all finances

Lovely eyes

Lovely hands

Good dancer when not being held by him

Good cook if cooking without dairy or wheat

Tries hard in the garden

Sarah—'I kept wanting to write things down that were in the past. His kindness. His sense of fun and romance. His spontaneity. But they aren't relevant any more. Haven't been for a long time. I always felt safe with him. I knew I could always trust him. But I couldn't write those things down. Not now. Because they aren't true now. Good stuff in the past doesn't rectify what is happening now, and the arsehole tendencies outweigh the good almost two to one.'

Kim—'Does he really eat his bogies? How disgusting. Finger up the bum thing, I understand. Jamie likes that, too.'

Sarah—'Why the fuck did this man marry me, Kim?'

Kim—'Well, the romantic view is that he loved you. Cynical view is that he thought he could change you and you were a good catch and he knew it.'

Sarah—'To be fair, I thought I could change him, too. Our sexual relationship was never great even before we got married. I told you about the abortion I had when we'd been going out for nine months? Well, he never really recovered from that.'

Kim—'So perhaps it wasn't such a clever thing to do to tell him about the abortion you had with John, was it?'

Sarah—'Okay. I know. But it was clean slate time, and it was also a possible opt-out for me.'

Kim—'Why do you still want to be with him?'

Sarah—'I don't know. As I said, perhaps it's a combination of guilt, the fact that I'm fundamentally loyal, and that there is still love there. Or perhaps it's fear of the unknown.'

Kim—'Not because of Ben, then?'

Sarah—'Ben will be happiest if his parents have a happy marriage. If it's not happy, he will sense it. So I don't want to stay together for his sake. Paul will always see Ben—not as much as he thinks he will, but I will never stop him from seeing his son. Unless he starts to behave towards Ben the same way he does towards me. That's different. But this issue is to do with Paul and me.'

Kim—'You really think you still love him, don't you?'

Sarah—'I think it's love. I fell in love with his soul when we first met, and the feeling's still there. Would be so much easier to say it's not, but it is.'

Kim—'You've forgotten that he's selfish and opinionated and boorish.'

Sarah—'And, of course, there's my jealousy. The *other woman* syndrome. Want to wring her neck.'

Kim—'Sounds as though he's punishing you. Tit for tat. Bet she's nothing like you. From what you've said, sounds as though he's done this more out of anger and lust than anything. And relationships that start that way aren't built on firm foundations.'

Sarah—'Perhaps. But that's not my problem. Wonder if she's good at gardening and cooking and stuff?'

Kim—'Who gives a fuck? Do you want to be good at those things?'

Sarah—'Well, no.'

Kim—'Then why worry? Let her prune his roses and mend his slippers.'

Sarah—'Mmm, suppose so.'

Kim—'What have you planned this week?'

Sarah—'Well, this past week Ben's had chicken pox, so I've been looking after him. Paul has been home occasionally. Of course acting strangely. It's sort of like sleeping with the enemy.'

Kim—'Hasn't started to line things up in the cupboards, has he?'

Sarah—'No, not that bad yet. But, you know—watching me when he's here. Bit like the way Jack Nicholson got with Shelley Duvall post-axe scene in *The Shining.*'

Kim—'You've got to get him to move out, then, Sarah. You can't move out—nor can Ben. *He's* got to move out.'

Sarah—'He won't.'

Kim—'Then its going to end up like *War of the Roses.* Must admit when I first watched that film I thought it was overdoing it. But the more I learn about this divorce thing, the more I'm amazed most divorcing couples don't kill each other.'

Sarah—'Thanks for the cheery thought, Kim.'

Kim—'I'm sorry, Sarah. But I can't help thinking that Paul—love him though you think you do at the moment—has done you a huge favour. So has this other woman. Fuck, she's got a man who's a baby—a rich baby, but a baby nonetheless. With emotional baggage.

You don't need that. You've got your life to lead and—fuck it, girl—you're thirty-seven and look ten years younger. Even if this girl is years younger than you she'll have to go some way to look as good as you. You've come a long way, despite little support from your husband, family or his family, and you've given him a wonderful son. Where did that *blip* occur? You obviously had sex once.'

Sarah—'During a week in Mauritius.'

Kim—'How the fuck did he expect to have children if he didn't sleep with you, for Christ's sake?'

Sarah—'I know, I know. But he claimed I made him impotent. The abortions. Telling him about John on our honeymoon. Then finding out about Stephen and the shower. He struggled to deal with it and he couldn't.'

Kim—'All this is supposition, Sarah.'

Sarah—'It has to be. The guy won't talk to me. He tells me not to talk to him. Not to e-mail him at work. Not to text him. He hides his mobile phone, which makes me think he's sending and receiving intimate love messages from this girl, and it's driving me nuts.'

Kim—'That's jealousy. That's pride speaking, not love.'

Sarah—'I know, and I have to deal with it.'

Kim—'You don't want him, Sarah. You just wish it hadn't happened this way.'

Sarah—'Maybe. But at the moment I'm reeling, Kim, and I don't know where I stand legally about leaving the house. Should I stay or go?'

Kim—'Then find out. Go and see bloody good solicitors and listen to what they say. They strip the emotion and look at the facts, which is what the court will do. And they can be as ruthless as Paul—at this moment you can't. I could be wrong, but I think from the sound of it Paul is on a mission, and he wants out. He's a banker, a trader, and they're compulsive about getting closure quickly. Just surprises me he hasn't got the papers for a divorce signed up already.'

Sarah—'Perhaps he wants to wear me down emotionally first. I don't know, perhaps you're right. Only I don't know any good solicitors. I know—I'll contact Jane. She's been through all of this recently with her ex—Pierce. He works with Paul. It's a bit incestuous, but Jane knows her business, knows Paul, and thinks straight. Perhaps I can use her solicitor.'

Kim—'Sounds good to me. Well, my love, I've been here for fifteen minutes and they haven't asked what we want to eat and I'm fucking starving. Where's this Duncan, then? Where's my chips?'

SEPTEMBER

Leaning on the wrong shoulder

Café Nero. Liverpool Street Station. Three p.m. Watching all the bankers go by with their secretaries, or maybe their work colleagues. Wonder if one of them will be Paul. And *her*.

Waiting for Jane, thirty-six, buzzy, brilliant, beautiful, and ex-wife of Pierce. Always has a mobile in her hand. Pierce told Paul she even took calls while he was going down on her. Chief accountant at Malvern & Duff, merchant bank. Not a conventional banker's wife, either. Hence divorce a year before. She lost two stone, if I remember rightly. Pierce had to take a month's leave with a suspected nervous breakdown. She's met someone else. Getting married next year. Pierce was always meeting someone else, but probably won't ever again—get married, that is.

Paul and I got Pierce's side of the story. Never knew hers. But, knowing Pierce, hers is probably a more honest version. Perhaps will find out now. She's agreed to meet me between meetings. I've got fifteen minutes. I've briefed her already about Paul. About the affair. About the history. And about the divorce.

I'm early again. Sit and order a black coffee, waiting until Jane arrives.

She's on time, smiling, striding towards me, turning heads in her tight white cotton Paul Smith blouse, just—above-the-knee skirt and kitten heels. Legs up to armpits. Mobile in one hand. Purse in the other.

She hugs me, and looks me up and down a few times.

Jane—'Hello, Sarah. See you're feeling it, then? Can't eat anything?'

Sarah—'No. Bit like you were.'

Jane—'It will pass. You'll look back on this in two years' time and think, Hey, wish I could lose weight like that when I want to. You will put it back on; don't worry. But I think you should look healthier and be healthier for Ben. You've got to look after him, and to do that well you've got to look after yourself well. And, more importantly, be *seen* to be looking after yourself well.'

Sarah—'What do you mean—be *seen* to be looking after myself?'

Jane—'If it goes to court, you will need to show you're responsible enough to look after Ben. Fit mentally, financially *and* physically. Looking like someone who's just come out of a concentration camp is not a good look. The mother usually gets custody, but I know Paul, and he sees everything as a possession. It's not just *his* house and *his* money, but it's also *his* son. So he may fight for custody at some stage.'

Sarah—'Well, Ben *is* his son. But Ben is *my* son too.'

Jane—'Quite. But he doesn't see it like that, Sarah. And it's not his house or his money. It's your money and your house as well. Remember that. Because the court will remind him of that. The fact he suggested you leave the house makes me think he's done his research, but you need to see a solicitor to give you all the details, Sarah. Try my solicitor. She's good.'

Sarah—'I don't want to divorce him, Jane. I love him.'

Jane—'Do you think you can salvage the marriage?'

Sarah—'Don't know. I've been strong for Ben.'

Jane—'Well, you have to make your own decision about that, Sarah. And you're going to hear this from a lot of people, but let me be the first to tell you. *You've got to move on*. For your sake. For Ben's sake. And for your own sanity.

'The only role of importance Paul has in your life now is to be a good father to Ben. He's not been a good husband. Well, he has in some ways. Not in others. And you're not faultless. But that's past. You must deal with the present and future. You can do something about those two.

'Bottom line—he's admitted he wants out. And, again, I know Paul. He's stubborn, and once on track he won't sway from his course. He must provide for you as carer of Ben, and for Ben's future. That simple. And by suggesting you leave the house it seems to me he wants to short-change you. You know what you're dealing with. It's understandable, but ruthless. I need a coffee. I'll get you a chocolate brownie.'

Jane goes to order coffee and calories while I sit, stunned by the thought Paul might try to take Ben away from me. It makes me feel physically sick.

Jane returns with coffee and no cake.

Jane—'Ran out of cakes. You would probably throw it up anyway.'

Sarah—'Do you think he will take Ben away from me?'

Jane—'He will think about it. But he won't succeed unless he can prove you're emotionally unstable and therefore unfit to care for Ben yourself. Of course, he could try to *make* you emotionally unstable. Or lower your confidence to such a level you feel you can't look after Ben. Wouldn't put that past him, Sarah.'

I think I'm going to throw up. Jane continues.

'I'll be frank. I like Paul. I like both of you. But it made me very angry when you told me he suggested you move out of the house with Ben. That's under-handed. That's mean. That's a shitty thing to do. I don't like that. Expect a call from Felicity Shindley-Hinde. She's my solicitor. Dreadful name, wonderful lady. She did good for me, and may have a recommendation for you. She's an ace divorce lawyer and you'll need one. Because Paul's attitude to money is the same as Pierce's. He will ruthlessly protect every last penny of his salary. Paul considers the money in the bank to be *his* money.

'Felicity managed to squeeze £300,000 out of a marriage that lasted less than a year. Something unheard of in the industry. Pierce was happy as he had over three million in the bank, so a mere £300k was peanuts to him. But he didn't think of it that way at the time. And, from what I hear, crashed a few cars and a few parties for a few months. I didn't get my hands on the offshore funds, non-listed American stocks and miscellaneous works of art he bought for cash. I knew about them, of course, because I managed his books while we were married. But I didn't care. I wanted to keep on good terms with Pierce post-divorce.

'You see, Sarah, Pierce has a lovely, gentle side to him, and if I'd gone for everything—well, he would have hated me till the day he died. Anyway, I have enough. Money doesn't make you happy. Too much and it ulti-mately makes you greedy for more.'

Jane drinks her coffee in one. And stands to leave.

Jane—'I'll get Pierce to call you. He's always had a soft

spot for you and he may be able to reach Paul on an emotional level. He might be able to reason with Paul. It might not be too late.'

Sarah—'Thank you. Everything will be all right, won't it?'

Jane—'Yes, everything will be all right. But not immediately. You will go through denial, regret, anger, sadness, joy—the lot. It takes time. Sometimes years, sometimes decades. Some people—both men and women—never get over it.'

Jane's mobile rings.

Jane—'Sorry, Sarah—got to take this one. It's important. Buying a house.'

To phone…

Jane—Hi, there. Yes. Yes. No. Tell them no. Don't care what they say. Tell them no. Tell them that's the offer or we walk away. Tell them for every week they refuse the offer we will drop by £5k. We'll do that for four weeks and then walk away. Tell them to fuck off, then.'

Click.

Sarah—'You don't want the house, then?'

Jane—''Course I do. But don't want them to know that. All a game, Sarah, all a game. Bit like divorce, really. If you can't convince the opposition of your motives, confuse them. Got to go now, Sarah. Text Pierce. That's the best way to reach him these days. And expect a call from Felicity. She's good.'

Interesting character, Pierce. Equity salesman in the city. Earning, according to Paul, 'a fucking fortune'. I met him through Paul. When he was still married to Jane. Paul invited them both for Sunday lunch. They came one Sunday in August. We ate outside. One of those rare hot summer days.

Paul cooked trout on the barbecue. I'd done the stuffed peppers dish from Delia Smith's book that looks wonderful and is impossible to mess up. Paul had retrieved his guitar from the guest bedroom and had started to play his edgy rendition of 'Stairway to Heaven.'

Pierce said he played a bit, and then proceeded to play Led Zeppelin. John Williams. Elton John. Brilliantly. Then he started to sing. Beautifully. He was amazingly multitalented. There was nothing that Pierce could not do with ease. With grace. Style. Flair. Tall, dark, handsome, brooding, he looked at me when I first met him at our front door as though he wanted to devour me. Paul reassured me he looked at all women that way. Disconcerting for Jane, I thought at the time.

But if anyone could handle Pierce it was Jane. She was amazing in her own right. She was incredibly talented, well-travelled, English degree at Oxford, and spoke five languages fluently—but unfortunately not even she could understand Pierce sometimes. Jane had boundless energy and enthusiasm for life, and she was still only thirty-four when I met her.

Only problem was, Jane was wife number three. And Pierce was then just thirty-six. Paul said Pierce had a dark side. Which I'd never seen. Pierce had seen counsellors, psychotherapists, spiritual healers, and none had worked. He talked in consultant-speak when he talked about relationships. He knew all the theory, but somehow couldn't put it into practice.

He also had a reputation in the Square Mile for being rather sexually kinky and masochistic. Exploring the little shops in Soho for that must-have latest dildo or nipple clamp. Hey, whatever turns him on, I thought. He's not harming anyone—except himself, of course. I ignored all this. It was all irrelevant. Jane said he would be a good contact, so I made contact. And anyway, he could keep me informed on how Paul was in the office, or if he had turned up in the office at all.

I sent a text message.

Message sent:
Hi Pierce. It's Sarah, Paul's wife. Jane suggested I should call you. Can you talk?
Message received:
Yep.
Message sent:
Can you call me?

Phone rings.
'Hi, Sarah, it's Pierce.'
Sarah—'Hi, Pierce. Thanks for calling. Jane suggested I contact you. Has Jane told you?'
Pierce—'Yes. Not all of it, just the gist. I couldn't believe it. Paul having an affair. Thought he would be the last person to ever have an affair. He dotes on you and Ben.'
Sarah—'Well, I've had an affair, and we haven't been happily married for some time. But I love him and don't want to end the marriage. But he seems determined, and now—well, now he's suggested Ben and I move out of the house.'
Pierce—'Sarah, Paul is my friend, but I'm your friend, too. My advice is not to do that. Go and see a solicitor.'
Sarah—'Yes, Jane has already said I should do that. And I will. But I want to save the marriage.'
Pierce—'Moving out won't save the marriage. I think this has gone too far. Can I ask, why did you have the affair?'

Sarah—'It's been a sexless marriage. And we didn't have sex for most of the time we were going out.'

Pierce—'It's a personal question, but why?'

Sarah—'Because I had an abortion early in our relationship, and Paul couldn't cope with that. Then he couldn't cope with an affair I had before we got married, and then—well, he couldn't cope with an affair I had while we were married, and then he just couldn't cope.'

Pierce—'Sounds as though you both couldn't cope. But if you didn't have sex, how come you had Ben?'

Sarah—'A one-off. A wonderful one-off on holiday.'

Pierce—'How did he find out about the affair? Did you tell him?'

Sarah—'Told him on our honeymoon.'

Pierce—'Not the best way to start a marriage.'

Sarah—'I know. I know. I know. And then I had another affair with a journalist, two years ago, when I was away travelling.'

Pierce—'And you told him about that, too?'

Sarah—'No, he found that one out. Reading my e-mail.'

Pierce—'So that broke him?'

Sarah—'Yes, I suppose it did.'

Pierce—'Very sad, then, isn't it? For Ben?'

Sarah—'Yes. But I've said sorry, and Paul said at the time he forgave me, and that was years back and now this. Now a new woman and he wants out.'

Pierce—'Well, I understand why he wants out. But I also understand why you had the affairs. No one can live in a completely sexless relationship. Not as far as I'm concerned. I couldn't. But you need to protect yourself, Sarah. And Ben. Get a solicitor and listen to what she says. Paul's a nice guy, but he shouldn't have suggested you leave the house. Especially not with Ben.

He's got to be fair. I gave Jane £300,000 as part of the settlement, and we were married for only a year. Plus, we don't have children. You have Ben, and he needs to be looked after, and then there is your future. You won't be able to work as much when he's at school. Won't be able to travel as much. So you'll have to change or give up your career. There's lots to think about.'

Sarah—'I know. I know. I wake up in cold sweats a lot these days. And my feelings for Paul change by the minute. Sometimes I wake up in the morning and think I love him. Then I hate him. Then I love him. Then I hate him. Then I love him. It's freaky. But Jane tells me this is natural, and will get better as time goes on.'

Pierce—'Yes, it will. Jane told me she used to play one particular song at full blast in her car when we were breaking up. You know the one about hating someone so much? It worked for her. You'll get your own theme tune.'

Sarah—'Yeah, I have loads of songs. But the ones I'm playing at the moment are mostly by David Gray and Dido.'

Pierce—'Real wrist-slitters, then. Try to listen to something more upbeat.'

Sarah—'Such as?'

Pierce—'"I Will Survive"—Gloria Gaynor. "Stronger"—Sugababes. "My Way"—Frank Sinatra. "I'm Not in Love"—10CC. That sort of thing. Nothing about heartache. Or one-night stands.'

Sarah—'Thanks.'

Pierce—'Have you given yourself a break recently?'

Sarah—'No—been looking after Ben. He's not been well. And there's plenty of work, which is good. Because it's something else to focus on.'

Pierce—'Jane says you're thin and need fattening up.'

Sarah—'So I'm told.'

Pierce—'Fancy dinner? Have you been taken to dinner lately?'

Sarah—'Paul took Ben and me to Pizza Express two weeks ago.'

Pierce—'And you haven't been out since then?'

Sarah—'No. I've been looking after Ben. I think right now he needs to see one of his parents, if not both. And I need friends right now.'

Pierce—'I could do this Friday night. Can you get a babysitter?'

Sarah—'Yes. Tina can do it.'

Pierce—'The Waterhole Restaurant, round your way. Is that okay?'

Sarah—'Fine. Upstairs is posh; downstairs bistro.'

Pierce—'Think you deserve posh. Book upstairs. Say about seven?'

Sarah—'Fine—and thank you, Pierce. I'm not a bad person. I've just made bad decisions.'

Pierce—'We all have. It's part of life. But you can't change the way someone feels, and Paul feels very angry at the moment. You've just got to let him chill. He may see reason eventually. But it will take some time.'

Sarah—'I can't change the way I feel either, Pierce. And I still love him.'

Pierce—'Perhaps. Perhaps you only want what you haven't got. You sound as though you need a hug.'

Sarah—'I do.'

Pierce—'See you Friday, then.'

Sarah—'Okay. Bye.'

Click.

Paul isn't coming home before midnight each weekday. And he never returns home on a Friday, usually arriving about three in the afternoon on Saturday to take Ben to the park for an hour or two. I don't know if he's with *the girl* or with *the boys*. I'm finding more receipts in his pockets. He is completely useless at hiding his trail. But perhaps he wants me to find them. Anyway, I am finding them. Lots of restaurant receipts. An eclectic mix. Thai, Indian, French, a few Italian, lots of sushi bars and Tuffnells once a week. Must be their favourite. I'm trying to work out if she's a vegetarian. Think so. She likes chardonnay. Feel a bit like Miss Marple. Don't think she's a drinker. Well, not when she's with him anyway. No champagne on the list ever, so perhaps she's not *that* special. Or perhaps he pays with cash. The heart-breaking receipts are the hotels. When I see a receipt saying how many guests to a room.

And then there's the extras. The videos they send up for. The receipts list if they ordered room service or videos, but not what videos they were. Wonder if they were pornographic. Or funny. Or romantic. Wonder if he's made her watch *Highlander I, II* and *III,* like he made me watch them when I first met him. Hope so. Serve her right.

Then there's usually a cinema receipt or two a week. I can tell if he's seen a film with her already. He always makes a comment.

Paul—'*One of my friends* said they enjoyed this.'

Or:

Paul—'*One of my friends* said they didn't think much of this. Found it boring.'

Or, worse:

Paul—'I know *someone* who would really enjoy this film.'

When have any of his friends ever been *one of his friends?*

When did Paul start to have nameless friends?

It's Friday already. Six p.m. Time has no meaning at the moment. Probably why I'm on time or early these days.

Babysitter has arrived. Tina is busy running around after Ben. Getting him bathed, bedtime story then lights out. Kiss for Mummy. Then night-night. Thankfully Ben seems not to notice Daddy hasn't been about much these days. Occasionally he asks where Daddy is, but he spends most days in the nursery, and I keep him busy with games and fun in the evenings.

I've briefed the staff at the nursery about what I've come to call *the situation at home.* Sat down with the principal nursery nurse for half an hour, managing not to cry. She reassured me divorce and separation are becoming the norm, not the exception. There are four other children in Ben's class where the parents are experiencing what she called *similar problems.* I didn't go into too much detail. I doubt if these other couples have quite the same story to tell.

I try not to cry in front of Ben. When I do he tells me to, 'Brush those tears away, Mummy. Brush those tears away.'

And I do. And I tell him I love him. And that Daddy loves him and that Mummy and Daddy love each other. And that calms him and me both.

Babysitter Tina also knows about *the situation at home.* She's been looking after Ben since he was a baby. She's extremely sensible and efficient, and Ben loves her and is terrified of her. Paul is terrified of her, too, which is good. Her advice is a little drastic. She tells me I should kill Paul in his sleep. I tell her this would ruin my social life and that I look lousy in stripes.

Doorbell rings. Too early. Can't be Pierce.

It is.

Sarah—'Hi, Pierce. Didn't expect you this early.'

Pierce—'Hi, just came from the gym. The showers weren't working properly there. Can I use your shower?'

Sarah—'Er, yes, of course.'

Bit confused. Not the usual way to start an evening. I've never had someone come to take me out to dinner and ask to shower at the house. And he goes to the same gym as me. The showers were working perfectly all right when I went there yesterday. Perhaps he's had sex at the gym or at lunch or something. And wants to get the smell of the other woman off his body. Whatever, it's a bit weird.

I've got to shower, too, so I take a shower in the en suite bathroom off the main bedroom. He takes a shower in the main bathroom. So I suppose we're sort of taking a shower together.

Half an hour later, both finished. He's wearing something Armani and black and looks—well, gorgeous. I'm wearing something feminine and tight, but not short. Having lost so much weight, I now want to wear things that add weight rather than take it off. This outfit does.

Pierce—'You look lovely. Paul is silly. You're a babe, Sarah.'

Sarah—'Thank you, Pierce. Nice to feel I'm a woman again.'

Pierce drives a BMW 5 series convertible. Dark blue. Black and tan leather interior. He mixes his own CDs. While we drive to the restaurant we listen to Norah Jones, Prodigy and Vaughan Williams. Pierce has eclectic tastes.

Sarah—'Do you see much of Jane these days?'

Pierce—'We talk on the phone. She's met someone. I haven't. But I'm happy for her. I still love her, but couldn't live with her. Nor her me. I know our divorce was for the best, and I'm sure you will feel the same about Paul.'

Sarah—'At the moment I don't. I've known Paul for twelve years. I've been through a lot with him and I still believe I love him and want to try to make it work. I think he's tried to make the relationship work in the past, mainly through trying to change me rather than himself. But we've both avoided the issues in our own way. Now we've got to confront them. For Ben's sake if not our own.'

We turn into the restaurant car park. The car purrs to a halt.

Pierce—'You are a very beautiful woman, Sarah—(holding my hand)—very beautiful. And you deserve a lot. And Paul wasn't able to give it to you. I know you're feeling vulnerable at the moment, and you've got to be careful at this time. You're feeling vulnerable, and you may just hook up with any man to get rid of those pent-up sexual frustrations that have been building up inside you over the years. The longing you must feel… It must be terrible. Just make sure you only confide in those you trust. Someone you trust and respect and who is here for you.'

I look at Pierce. And think, Yes, I am distraught and vulnerable. And haven't been made love to for ages. And I do feel unloved and unwanted and unconfident and bruised. But I'm not stupid. And I'm not desperate. And I think that was a chat-up line.

'I can get rid of those sexual frustrations the same way I've always got rid of them. I work out. A lot.'

Pierce—'Yes, you're in good shape. I can see you're very toned. You know I've always found you attractive.'

Sarah—'You find a lot of women attractive, Pierce.'

I think, Is this a good idea? Dinner with Pierce? It's

just dinner, after all. Nothing wrong with that. I need a friend now, not a lover. Not just yet anyway and not him. Too close. He works with Paul and I know Jane. Too soon. Still want to try and make it work with Paul. And he's possibly kinky. *Kinky* not good for me at the moment.

The Waterhole is full of the upper crust of Chelmsford society—the senior back office boys. The settlement clerks of the City. The wannabes of the Square Mile. Then there are the made-good second-hand car dealers, jewellery dealers, drug dealers. Loud watch hanging from one wrist. Louder wife hanging from the other.

Pierce ignores the flirtatious glances of these women as we walk to the table. He turns more heads than I do—which I expect. We order. He looks good.

We order something with salad to start. Then fish. Tuna, grilled, with soy-something. I'm not hungry, but I think I can eat tuna. Nothing tastes of anything these days. It's just good to be out of the house.

Pierce—'You realise you'll be perceived as a predator now? You won't hear from many of your so-called friends because they'll suspect you will pinch their husbands.'

Sarah—'You think so?'

Pierce—'Yes. I know so. I know some of the brokers Paul works with have the hots for you. They've told me as much.'

Sarah—'Er, right. Don't like any of them. Quite liked Wills, but Paul doesn't work with him anymore. I wouldn't go for any of them, even if they made a pass at me.'

Pierce—'I think you're just stressed. You need to relax. I remember when I was going through the divorce with Jane I was very stressed, and just needed to chill and relax. You need a good, long, slow, sensual massage.'

Sarah—'I probably do. And I'll have to book one sometime. When I have time. My main concern is Ben and that he is okay and that he still knows his daddy loves him—despite the fact his daddy reeks of beer and stale aftershave these days.'

Pierce—'Others in the office have noticed Paul's started to take longer lunches and not come back, and he looks—well, like shit in the mornings.'

Sarah—'Nothing to do with me. Wish it were, but it's not.'

Pierce—'You can't change his mind. I've had a word, Sarah, and he just says that you had affairs and he can't deal with it, and it's sad but it's over. One thing my relationship with Jane taught me is that you can't change the way people feel.'

Sarah—'I know. You said before.'

Pierce—'Do you know how I feel about you?'

Sarah—'Am I going to find out?'

Pierce—'I like you Sarah. You're a very sexy woman.'

Sarah—'I don't feel particularly sexy or sexual at the moment, but thank you, Pierce. But I think you and I have enough on our plates at the moment without making life even more complicated. For a start, you work with Paul. Despite the fact he's bonking another woman, he won't like it that someone in his office is bonking his wife. Even if she may be his soon-to-be-ex wife.

'And then there's Jane. Although she's now your ex-wife, it would also complicate matters.

'Then there's Ben. He is my priority, and I don't have time for a relationship—sexual or otherwise. I need friends now. Level-headed, genuine friends. And simplicity in my life. And, lastly, I think you have enough sex kittens. I get some of your text messages occasionally, meant for other women, and think you have your hands full already.'

Pierce smiles.

Pierce—'Nice brush-off. Eloquently done. Okay. But you *are* a babe and don't forget that—whatever happens over the next twelve months.'

Sarah—'I won't.'

Rest of conversation revolves around sex kittens. How he once had three in a bed and it wasn't as good as he thought it was going to be, because they tied him up and stole his money and left him naked and penniless in the Charleston Hotel, just round the corner from the office. And how the maid had to call the police. And his boss. And then we talk books, and where you can buy the best range of self-help guides and works on erotic bondage and self-flagellation.

After the tuna, which I didn't touch but was getting really rather good at playing with, Pierce takes me home.

Tina's watching *A Room with a View.*

Tina—'This film is lovely.'

Sarah—'I know. It's my favourite.'

Tina—'Very romantic.'

Sarah—'I know. I'm not watching it at the moment.'

Tina—'Oops. Sorry.'

Sarah—'No worries.'

I pay Tina, say goodbye to her at the door, and go upstairs to check on Ben. He's asleep. Curled in a foetal position sucking his thumb. Giggling quietly. Hopefully dreaming about Buzz or Woody or perhaps even his daddy.

Coffee in hand, I return to the sitting room and to Pierce, who is now sitting on my sofa. Shirt off. Firm, muscular and tanned torso on display. No signs of flagellation.

Pierce—'Hope you don't mind. Bit hot.'

Sarah—'I'll turn the heating up, then.'

Pierce—'I do a mean massage.'

I think, Do I let Pierce massage me? What's the harm? I'm in control. Hey, go for it, girl. Perhaps I'll release some tension without getting hurt.

Sarah says—'Okay. Give me a massage, then.'

Pierce looks surprised.

Pierce—'Okay.'

Sarah—'I'm keeping my clothes on.'

Pierce—'That's fine. And probably wise, in the circumstances.'

Sarah—'And no being tied up.'

Pierce—'No being tied up.'

I lie down in the middle of the sitting room floor. Make sure door is closed. Ben is upstairs asleep. I don't want him to open the sitting room door to see Mummy on the floor with a tall, dark handsome stranger straddling her between his rather well-toned and probably—though I can't see them—bronzed thighs. Stroking her back. Can imagine his conversation with Paul next time he sees his daddy.

Ben—Hello, Daddy. Mummy was with this man on the floor downstairs and he was tickling her back. And he wasn't wearing any clothes.

Yeah, right. So, door firmly closed. I lie on the carpet in the centre of the room. Lights are dimmed. I feel Pierce leaning over me and starting to massage my shoulders. Then running his fingers over my shoulderblades. Then down the middle of my spine, right to the base of my back, and then swirling motions with his palms all the way up to the top of my shoulders. He starts on the legs, then the arms, and finally runs his fingers through my hair, pulling gently. It's very good. Genuinely very relaxing. And ever so slightly sexual, and somehow, with clothes on, even more sexy.

After what I think is about fifteen minutes, he stops.

Sarah—'Ah. Thank you, Pierce.'

Pierce—'Now *I'm* feeling stressed.'

Sarah—'Can I massage you?'

Pierce—'That may stress me out even more.'

Sarah—'I will be gentle with you. Keep your trousers on. You've got your shirt off already. So leave it at that.'

Pierce—'Okay. But can I take my shoes and socks off?'

Sarah—'Fine.'

Pierce takes off shoes and socks. He lies on the floor exactly where I've just been lying.

Pierce—'I can smell you.'

Sarah—'Can you?'

Pierce—'I can smell your perfume.'

Sarah—'Oh, yes. Right.'

Pierce—'What is it?'

Sarah—'Sure antiperspirant. Won't let you down.'

Pierce—'Ah. Right.'

I straddle him and start massaging in a similar way to the way he massaged me, but with longer, harder, firmer strokes—across the back—up and down—side to side. I'd learnt how to massage on a gulet holiday in Turkey, where one of the girls in the crew was a sexual masseuse. I watched her like a hawk to learn the art. It's served me well ever since. It was always wonderful pre-coitus.

The muscles in his back are more relaxed than those in his legs, and I need to be firm and push deeply, which Pierce seems to like. He lets out the occasional sigh, but we don't speak. There is no music in the background, so I'm able to hear him breathing quite clearly. I move down his legs slowly and start to massage his feet. And then, for some reason, start to blow between his toes.

I think I'm teasing him. Or am I teasing myself? Toying with the idea of having sex with him? Shall I? Shan't I? Shall I? Shan't I? Imagining the what ifs. What would the harm be if I did suddenly start to kiss or lick or stroke? I haven't had sex for years. Perhaps I've forgotten how to do it. How to feel again. Feel sexual again. Give and receive pleasure. Feel lust. That lust I last felt with Stephen. With John. And a long time ago—a very long time ago—with Paul. Feel that energy. That release. Feel like a woman. Behave like a woman. Use that bloody box splits position and really give Pierce something to talk about in the office the next day. And make everyone jealous. Even Paul.

Perhaps I should move my hands more provocatively. I know he wouldn't resist. I know he would take the opportunity. But this is not the right man. I realise this now. On the verge, I realise this. At this moment. This is not the right man. Not the right time. Not the right place. Too soon. Someone not suitable. And Ben is in bed upstairs. Three strikes, and he doesn't know it but he's out.

Pierce—'Ohh. That's different. That's nice, Sarah. Blowing between the toes. That's really feels good.'

Sarah—'Sort of refreshes the parts other strokes can't reach. It should give you quite a good sensation.'

Pierce—'It does. This is almost better than sex.'

Sarah—'I don't think so, somehow. But it's safer. Better to blow than suck or whip or beat. That's what I say.'

Pierce laughs.

Pierce—'Mmm, well…'

I move from the feet to the hands and massage his palms and each finger. Sucking the fingers will be a bit too suggestive. So I stop there.

As I finish I lift my legs over his body and he coils round, smiling broadly.

Pierce—'Thank you, Sarah. That was lovely. Unexpected and lovely.'

Then:

Pierce—'I understand how you feel. But I know how I feel, too. And, well, I find you very sexy—that's all I can say. You will be fine. You're a babe, and you'll find another man who will love you. And will treat you the way you want and deserve to be treated.'

Sarah—'Yes, I know. But at this moment in time I just want Paul back. Funny, that. Wish I could be cold-blooded about it. But I can't. And while I still have this love for him I want to try to make it work. Because I realise once the love has disappeared—that's it. That's it with me. I don't look back. I'm not that sort of person.'

Pierce—'I feel sorry for you both, Sarah. But he's so stubborn.'

Sarah—'I know. Want a cup of tea?'

Pierce—'That would be good.'

I feel more relaxed with Pierce, somehow. As though the tension has been released. I don't feel threatened by his presence in the house any more.

Pierce—'Do you like poetry?'

Sarah—'I love poetry. I had a thing about Keats at school. Read all his odes. *Nightingale* was wonderful. Depressing as hell, but wonderful. Think I've got a book of his poems upstairs. Do you want me to read you one?'

Pierce—'That would be wonderful.'

I run upstairs and get the little black book John gave me as a present the first time we went away for a whole romantic weekend. I always keep it by my bedside. Well-thumbed, the pages fall open at *Ode to a Nightingale* naturally, and I read it as I walk down the stairs.

A drowsy numbness pains my sense, As though of hemlock I had drunk.

Wonderfully depressing. Keats was indeed the Dido of his time.

I recite the poem to Pierce. He listens quietly and patiently, sipping coffee, which should have been tea because I forgot what I'd suggested and made coffee anyway.

And then he recites poem after poem by Wordsworth. The most beautiful poetry, beautifully spoken. Probably word-perfect. Eloquent. He doesn't lift his gaze from mine and his deep voice resonates over every vowel, every syllable, with just the right inflection. It's magical. And then he stops.

Pierce—'I have to go now.'

Sarah—'Okay, then. That was wonderful. You are very talented, Pierce. Where did you learn that?'

Pierce—'Oh, at school. The dregs of an expensive education. And I love poetry, too, which helps.'

Sarah—'And I expect it helps to pull the sex kittens.'

Pierce—'They're not interested in poetry, Sarah. They're interested in this.'

He grabs his crotch and jiggles his balls about as though they are worry beads.

Sarah—'I wonder? I think if you recited more poetry you'd attract a different sort of pussycat.'

Pierce—'Perhaps. Jane was the closest I've met to my match. She's sexy and brilliant, and I love her energy and attitude.'

Sarah—'But you couldn't live with her.'

Pierce—'No. Couldn't live with her.'

Sarah—'Do you know why?'

Pierce—'Perhaps we're too much alike. Perhaps. We went to counselling, but it didn't help much.'

Sarah—'Have *you* had much counselling?'

Pierce—'Yes. It helps me. But it depends how open your mind is to it. And what you want to learn about yourself. You've got to make yourself very vulnerable.'

Sarah—'What sort of things did you and Jane do?'

Pierce—'Oh, we had to write a list of things we liked about each other. I think I got mine wrong about Jane.'

Sarah—'How can you get it wrong?'

Pierce—'Well, I put all stuff about how she made me look good, and what she did for me that was good, rather than anything about her in her own right. And the counsellor said that said a lot about me.'

Sarah—'Paul won't go to see a counsellor. I know he won't. I've tried, but he's refused. By himself or with me. At least you went.'

Pierce—'Don't worry, Sarah. Everything will be fine.'

Methinks Pierce has a very sweet side to him. I understand why Jane wants to keep in touch with him, despite his sexual pecadilloes. Perhaps he's exorcised the demons. Perhaps the rumours about his aggressiveness and kinky sexuality are wildly exaggerated. The rumours that he ties women up at lunchtime in their bedrooms naked and doesn't untie them till he leaves work in the evening and then fucks them senseless. Which actually doesn't sound perverted to me at all. With the right person it sounds a turn-on. If rather boring for the person tied up. But then there's the practicalities. What if they wanted to go for a pee? Or they had a deadline to meet in the office? Or something? *Oh, sorry, boss, I got tied up.* Yep, could work, I suppose.

Pierce hugs me in the hallway. Long hug. He keeps hold of me a bit too long, but I make it obvious it's not going to end up in a tongue-in-the-mouth clinch. He holds me so that we are face to face with each other. I know what he wants to do so I say:

Sarah—'No kissing. Thank you for a lovely evening, but no.'

Pierce—'Okay, then. And thank you. If you want to talk you know where I am.'

Sarah—'I do.'

I wave him goodbye. And as I close the door I feel as though I've passed some sort of test.

Five minutes later my mobile buzzes with a text message.

Message received:
I loved you in those trousers Sarah. U looked wonderful. And thanks for the massage. Px

So I send one back.

Message sent:
My pleasure. And thank you for a lovely evening.

As I walk up to bed…

Message received:
Can I tell you what I'm thinking?
Message sent:
Only if it's decent.
Message received 1/3:
I want to rip your clothes off. I had such a hard-on and wanted to fuck you hard up the
Message received 2/3:
Butt. I wanted to make you bleed. You have an amazing bum Sarah. I want to rip off your dress and push you up against the wall and

Mr Hyde has obviously come out to play. I sooo made the right choice. I'm playing with fire here, and I deal with it straight away.

Message sent:
Stop sending me these messages Pierce. Stop it. This is for your sex kittens. Not me. This is Sarah. Paul's wife. I'm not interested.
Message received 3/3:
Come all over your face.
Message sent:
Goodnite Pierce.
Message received:
I'm very very sorry Sarah. I should have known you weren't that sort of girl.

I think, Hey, I may be. Just not with you.

OCTOBER

Leaning on the right arm

Felicity Shindley-Hinde is a *grande dame* of the legal world. And a partner of Wearing, Shindley and Strutt. She presides over offices in Drummonds Close, on the edge of the City of London.

Sarah—'Hello, can I speak to Felicity Shindley-Hinde, please?'

Felicity's snotty-sounding PA—'Yarse, I'll just put you through. Who shall I say eeze calling?'

Sarah—'Sarah Giles.'

Felicity's snotty-sounding PA—'Sarah Geeles. Thank you.'

Felicity—'Hello—Felicity Shindley-Hinde.'

Sarah—'Hello, this is Sarah Giles. I think Jane Harris contacted you about my case.'

Felicity—'Oh, yes, hello.'

Her voice warms with the recognition of a potential client.

Felicity—'Yes, she told me you were rather stressed. Jane's given me the background to most of the case already. You will need to come in and tell me everything. You understand this? It will be quite painful. We will need to know details. But if you want us to represent you and do a good job you will need to be completely honest. Warts and all. No storytelling. Because we don't want to be surprised in court—do we, now? And we want to tell you realistically what you can hope to expect in terms of financial settlement. We charge £300 an hour. Do you have access to that sort of money at the moment, or has your husband frozen the accounts?'

Sarah—'Paul and I have separate accounts. And yes I do have the money.'

Felicity—'That excludes VAT. When can you come in? How about Friday? Say, eleven.'

Sarah—'Yes, that will be fine.'

Felicity—'Do you have any of his financial details?'

Sarah—'I know where he keeps his files. But I don't know how much money he earns or his bonuses.'

Felicity—'Do you know who your husband has hired as his counsel?'

Sarah—'No, don't think he's hired anyone.'

Felicity—'But he will have spoken to someone, I'm sure. He knows enough to realise the impact of you leaving the house and earning a wage to support yourself and possibly your son.'

Sarah—'I wouldn't know.'

Felicity—'I will see you on Friday.'

As I put the phone down I realise my hands are shaking. That my body is shaking. I sit down on the floor in the middle of my study. I'm not cold or shivery. I'm shaking. I suddenly feel this is all going too fast for me. My emotions are having to play catch-up in a process which doesn't wait for tears or grief or sadness or regret.

I've got a husband I don't know or trust anymore. I've got friends and strangers suddenly giving me advice about grown-up stuff. Life-changing stuff that matters. I'm trying to be strong and alert and happy for Ben. Be a good mum and also stay true to my values and what's left of my self-esteem. I want to protect Ben and myself. And I wonder about this other woman. The vegetarian teetotaller who likes being taken to Tuffnells. And I feel very alone.

Sitting in my study, I realise it's the only room of my house that has anything really to do with me. Other than Ben's yellow and blue bedroom. The study has all my books, my computer, my phones and faxes. The walls are filled with my awards, and numerous photographs of Ben and me on our travels. Strange now, looking round. There's nothing of Paul here. No photos of him. As though he doesn't exist in my little corner of the house. The rest of the house is his. But this little corner is my bit. My home. And I sit on the floor and feel I am about to sob, and suddenly I stop because Ben toddles in with his Buzz Lightyear, beaming. 'Buzz Lightyear to the rescue.' And he zaps me with his laser gun.

Friday arrives. I turn up promptly at ten forty-five at the immaculate Georgian offices of Wearing, Shindley and Strutt. This is my first journey into central London since Paul told me *'There's someone else.'*

Jane suggested I photocopy all the files I could find concerning our joint accounts. So I arrive by taxi from the station with a large cardboard box of statements and receipts dating back years.

I had sobbed uncontrollably in the cab.

Driver—'Want a handkerchief, darling?'

Taxi driver obviously distracted by very loud, very ugly-sounding sobs.

Sarah—'Er, yes, please. Thank you.'

Driver—'What's the matter? Man trouble?'

Sarah—'Um, yes, it is. I'm probably getting divorced, and we have a little boy and it's all very sad. I'm going to the solicitors now.'

Driver—'What's this chap do?'

Sarah—'Works in the City.'

Driver—'Wanker, then.'

Don't know if I heard right.

Sarah—'Banker—yes.'

Driver—'Take him for every fucking penny. Not fucking worth it, them lot. Absolute pigs.'

Sarah—'Well, it's not all his fault. And I don't want a divorce, but I think that's what he wants. So I'm going to find out about the implications and where I stand financially and how I can protect both my son and myself.'

Driver—'You do that, darling. And, mark my words, you take him for every penny—because if you don't you'll regret it. My daughter was married to a banker. She thought she'd be nice and just take a small piece of the action. And take care of the kids. Well, you know what? The bugger just took advantage and decided he didn't want to see the kids anymore, or pay her any money. He's married again, with more kids, and she's had to go to court so many times to get that bugger to pay up. Mark my words, you take him for every penny—you hear?'

Sarah—'You know bankers well, then?'

Driver—'Been driving the City for nearly twenty years, and they've changed. Used to be gentleman bankers. Now just a bunch of people who want to make money fast. Get-rich-quick merchants. Well, you can do that, but you pay a price—and they do, these guys. What I hear in this cab is no one's business. Lots of unfaithful bastards, they are. And the women who work with them are no better. Don't give a toss if there's a ring on their finger or anything. Anyway, good luck to them, that's what I say. And better luck to you. You take every penny. Do you hear? Every penny.'

Methinks I wouldn't like to be a banker in his cab.

I arrive at Drummonds Close and offer to pay.

Driver—'Don't worry. Good luck. God bless.'

And with that he drives off.

Wow. A London cabbie who gives a free ride. And gives *me* a tip. Perhaps my luck is changing after all.

Felicity has a reputation for being formidable. As in winning every case she handles and leaving the opposing counsel hating her and never wishing to have her opposing them again. This is the girl for me, I think. The girl in question is midforties, dark, short, and reminds me of my French teacher, who wouldn't take any crap from anyone. Some children would be so nervous about going to her lessons they would be physically sick beforehand. I could never understand the subjunctive tense. Or was it subjective? Anyway, there was one tense I couldn't get the hang of, and I remember her hovering over my book and banging me on the head with the ruler every time I got something wrong in an essay. I got a lot wrong. Of course she wouldn't be allowed to hit children now, but at least I learnt that bloody tense.

I feel the same about Felicity. I feel if I don't agree with what she says she will lean over the table and whack me with a ruler. I am shown to an all white room, with a white table, six white chairs and an amazing view over Drummonds Close. There is nothing else in the room except a large box of tissues on the table. Nice touch, I think.

Receptionist—'Would you like a cup of tea?'

Sarah—'No, I'm fine, thank you.'

Felicity—'Ms Giles will have tea.' Then, to me—'Ms

Giles, tea will help. You will want tea, I assure you. Sweet and hot.'

Sarah—'Er, right. I'll have tea. No milk. Thank you.'

Felicity—'And biscuits, too. Please.' Then to me— 'You look as though you've lost weight, or are you always that thin?'

Sarah—'I've lost weight, but I'm naturally thin.'

Felicity—'You need to put on weight. The opposing counsel may suggest you're too weak and feeble to look after your son.'

Sitting next to Felicity is a girl who introduces herself as Gemma. Gemma looks about twenty-nine, with blond hair and a round face. I'm sure she has a broad smile—when she does smile.

Felicity—'Gemma is here to take notes. She is my assistant. She will be here to support the case, should you wish to take this further. Do you understand?'

Sarah—'I understand.'

Gemma promptly picks up her pen, poised to take aforementioned notes.

Felicity—'What are all these papers for?'

She has noticed the large cardboard box of copies of accounts and bills I've brought into the meeting room.

Sarah—'Paul's accounts.'

Felicity—'Ah, you don't trust him? Well, we will see. We've got to find out about the case first. Before we start, I need to remind you I charge £300 per hour. Gemma here—' she nods to Gemma, who half smiles at this point '—costs £200, so she's good value. That means that you should seriously think about what you tell us. You should not waffle. You should tell us everything. If you don't, we can't give you good advice and you won't receive best counsel. Do you understand?'

Sarah—'I understand.'

I feel I'm being spoken to the way I speak to Ben when I tell him if he eats too much chocolate he will be sick. *Do you understand? Yes, Mummy, I understand.*

Felicity—'Rather than ask you to go through the whole of your relationship and life, I will ask you direct questions. This will save time and money. Are you okay with this?'

Sarah—'Yes.'

Felicity—'If at the end of the meeting you feel you want to hire us, or there is anything you have not said you wish to say and has relevance to the case, you must tell me. Okay?'

Sarah—'Yes.'

Felicity—'You've been married for seven years?'

Sarah—'Yes, seven years. And now he's scratched.'

Felicity looked up. 'They can scratch after any amount of time. When did you discover he was unfaithful?'

Sarah—'Last month.'

Felicity—'Why did he tell you?'

Sarah—'He was drunk and I asked him outright.'

Felicity—'Have you ever been unfaithful?'

Sarah—'Yes. Once before we got married, while engaged, and once when we were married—about two years ago.'

Felicity—'So you weren't happy?'

Sarah—'Well, I loved him, but we weren't having sex.'

Felicity—'How long did you not have sex?'

Sarah—'For the duration of the marriage.'

Felicity—'So your son—Ben, is it?'

Sarah—'Yes, Ben.'

Felicity—'Ben is not Paul's?'

Sarah—'Yes, he is. We had sex on a holiday one time.'

Felicity, noticing I may need those tissues, pushes them to me.

Felicity—'If you want to cry just do it. That is what they're here for, and you will do a lot more over the next year. Try not to waste too much time crying in this hour as it's expensive. Try to compose yourself. Next question. Why did you not have sex?'

Methinks I've got to tell a complete stranger the story of my life with Paul. I don't want to do this, but I've got to do it to move forward. It seems I've been telling the same story over and over and over again for the past month now. And I'm growing tired of it. But I mustn't miss anything out this time. So here goes.

Sarah—'Long story cut short: nine months into our relationship I fell pregnant. We both agreed I should have an abortion. It had an impact on him. He couldn't sleep with me or wouldn't sleep with me.'

Felicity—'How long did this last?'

Sarah—'Four years.'

Felicity looks surprised.

Felicity—'So you stayed with him for four years with no sex and then you got married?'

Sarah—'Yes.'

Felicity—'Did he have sex with you then?'

Sarah—'No.'

Felicity—'Why not?'

Sarah—'I had an affair with someone called John before I married Paul. I also had an abortion by this man. I confessed to Paul on our honeymoon, third day, that I had had an affair. He said he couldn't deal with that.'

Felicity looks surprised again.

Felicity—'Apart from no sex, was the marriage basically what you would call a happy one?

Sarah—'There was love there. No sex, but there was love. I travelled a lot. I'm a travel journalist, and I just travelled more and worked out more at the gym to get rid of the tension on my part. Paul worked late. We saw increasingly less of each other.'

Felicity—'Do you believe he was faithful?'

Sarah—'To my knowledge.'

Felicity—'But he could have been unfaithful? He had opportunity?'

Sarah—'As much as I did. Yes.'

Felicity—'And you were eventually unfaithful during the marriage?'

Sarah—'Yes. Two years ago, with a journalist in Australia.'

Felicity—'Did you tell Paul?

Sarah—'No, he found out by reading my e-mail.'

Felicity—'When was that?'

Sarah—'A year ago.'

Felicity—'How much does he own? What is he worth?'

Sarah—'I don't know. That's why I've brought the files. I was looking through, but I think he must have a few million in the bank. And there's no mortgage on the house.'

Felicity—'The marital home?'

Sarah—'Yes, and then there's the house in France we bought earlier this year.'

Felicity—'How much is that worth?'

Sarah—'About £200k, but it needs some renovation.'

Felicity—'Are both houses in both your names?'

Sarah—'French house, yes, English in his. And we have two flats we rent out. Both close to our house in England.'

Felicity—'Do they have mortgages on them?'

Sarah—'Yes—only small ones. The rent covers both easily.'

Felicity—'And he's made most of his money during the marriage?'

Sarah—'Yes, most of it.'

Felicity—'What does he do for a living?'

Sarah—'He's a banker—a trader.'

Felicity—'What are his earnings?'

Sarah—'I think he earns about £80k a year, and this year expects to earn over £800k in bonuses.'

Felicity—'And when did he ask for a divorce?'

Sarah—'Well, he mentioned it last month, but he hasn't given me any papers or done anything about it.'

Felicity—'And he's asked you to leave the house?'

Sarah—'Yes, with Ben—my son.'

Felicity smiles for the first time in our meeting.

Felicity—'With your son? That's good.'

Sarah—'No, it's not.'

Felicity—'Yes, it is. It's good for the case. Most preposterous thing. Wealthy banker kicking mother and child out of marital home. Anyway—next. Do you know anything about this girl?'

Sarah—'No, but I think she works in the City.'

Felicity—'She has money, then?'

Sarah—'Don't know.'

Felicity—'If you can find out if she has money this is good. If he moves in with her, or she with him, if they have a house, this is good. If he buys her any jewellery or gives her money or goes on expensive holidays with her this is good.'

Sarah—'No, it's not. It's awful.'

Methinks, Where are those handkerchiefs?

Felicity—'It is good, Sarah. Anything that shows he is spending money elsewhere and not on his family, and is therefore behaving irresponsibly, is good. Does he come home late? Or not come home at all? Or come home drunk?'

Sarah—'Yes, yes and yes.'

Felicity—'This is also good.'

For some reason, I feel suddenly very defensive of Paul. He sounds rather sad and lost and pathetic as I explain his behaviour very coldly to a complete stranger who's intent on getting as much money out of him and—realistically—me as possible.

Sarah—'Paul has always behaved very responsibly. In many ways it's me who's been the irresponsible one over the years. We've both ignored emotional issues we should have dealt with head-on. But that's the past. I have to deal with the present. And he *is* behaving irresponsibly *now*. He isn't giving me any money for food now, and we have separate bank accounts, and I don't earn as much money now, since having Ben.'

Felicity—'In order to get an interim maintenance order you must petition for divorce.'

Sarah—'So I've got to get divorced to get any money for food, even if I don't want to get divorced?'

Felicity—'In short, yes. Unless you can negotiate with Paul. But by the sound of it he doesn't seem to be around enough for you to negotiate with him. And when he is he's drunk or angry or both.'

Gemma stops writing. Felicity takes in breath. I grab a tissue and blow my nose.

Felicity—'Sarah, believe it or not, this is common. This happens in a lot of marriages, and men—especially men who work with money day in, day out—react in very similar ways. However, from what I gather he has accumulated most of his money during the marriage. This is bad for him, good for you. You have contributed to the marriage in the eyes of the law, whether he thinks you have or not. You have provided him with a son, whom you look after. Dependent on how much he has in stocks and shares, as a director of a company he has to show his assets, his earnings and bonuses. You should get the marital home, perhaps with some of his investments, as your settlement.'

Sarah—'I would like the French house.'

Felicity—'I doubt if you will get that, Sarah.'

Sarah—'I would rather have that than the English house.'

Felicity—'There's Ben to consider. Unless Paul agrees you can't take him out of the country. You can move anywhere in England and Wales. Not Scotland. How old is your son?'

Sarah—'Ben is three.'

Felicity—'Then he is young enough to start any new school and you are able to move. It's when they are older it's more difficult, with changing schools and unsettling the child. You also have to decide on who is to have Ben for holidays. I think you should agree that Paul sees Ben every other weekend and perhaps midweek after work.'

Sarah—'Is this the norm?'

Felicity—'Some fathers see their children less. Some more. It's up to you. Plus, you want a life as well.'

Sarah—'I know. I don't feel I have one at the moment.'

Felicity—'Anyway, you should, from looking at these figures, get the marital home. I don't think you can save the marriage. It sounds from what you've told me as if too much has happened. He sounds angry and vengeful, and he now has another woman and that adds impetus to the action. She will act as a catalyst and be the strength he doesn't have. This happens a lot. The man will not leave unless there is another carer in place. You both sound damaged emotionally. Let me know if you want to hire us. Gemma will send you our invoice.'

Felicity and Gemma stand up, shake hands and leave

me with tepid tea, tears and tissues. Wow. Three hundred quid. Twenty pence a word.

Nothing changes over the next two weeks. Paul continues not to return home. When he does, he's drunk and morose. He is trying to wear me down emotionally. I see that now. He tries to get me to leave the house. He tells me how good the other woman is in bed, compared to me. How would he remember how good we were? It's been such a long time.

Paul—'She's an amazing fuck. Gives me what I need.'

Sarah—'That's good. I can't remember—it's such a long time since we had sex.'

Paul—'Yeah, and we don't just have sex, Sarah. We make love. Long, tender, slow, passionate love.'

Sarah—'That's nice for you.'

Paul—'She gives amazing head.'

Sarah—'Good.'

Paul—'It is. It's fucking amazing. You were crap in bed. Fucking awful. And, what's more, I need a holiday. I'd like to go on holiday with her. I'm not asking your permission. Just want to know how you feel about it.'

Sarah—'Well, I feel dreadful about it, actually, but as you're going already why bother asking?'

I don't try to find out any more about her than I know, which is very little—although Paul insists she's better at everything than me. And has more maturity in her little finger than I have in my whole body. A body which is growing thinner by the day.

Each day, after nursery, Ben and I go to the seaside or the zoo, or play on the swings and slides, and in the late-summer sunshine we sing songs and nursery rhymes over picnics in the park. And we chase the squirrels. And hunt for imaginary bears. Each night, after bath and bedtime story, I sit at my computer and write about fly-drives to Florida and cruising in Alaska. Usually till about midnight. Then I stare for ten minutes, sometimes longer, into nothingness. And fall into bed. Alone. And wake up. Alone.

I take Ben to the theatre in London. I take him to see *Chitty Chitty Bang Bang.* He claps to all the songs, but sleeps through the second half. He knows all the words to 'Chu-Chi Face.'

Paul loses these moments. The bathtimes. The trips to the theatre. To the park and the seaside. The bedtime stories and morning hugs. But this is his choice. He chose this. He also loses a lot of the hassle and sleepless nights. Well, he probably doesn't lose the sleepless nights—but he's having them for different reasons. I'm sure he's having fun times with whoever he's having fun times with, but I can't believe they are better than being with Ben.

One week later and the money situation is bad. There is no food in the house for Ben and myself. I contact Felicity to ask to petition for a divorce. I get Gemma on the phone.

Sarah—'Hi, Gemma. I would like to petition for divorce.'

Gemma—'Are you sure?'

Sarah—'Yes. I'm sure.'

Gemma—'Then we will go ahead. Do you have any money?'

Sarah—'I have some savings. And I have friends who can help.'

Gemma—'Then we will proceed.'

Three days later Paul receives a letter petitioning him for divorce.

I'm surprised when Paul is shocked. And furious.

Paul—'Why have you done this?'

Sarah—'You said you wanted a divorce. So I'm giving you one.'

Paul—'But I thought we would be able to handle this amicably. Without lawyers.'

Sarah—'We can't. You don't come home. How can we discuss anything amicably when I don't see you to discuss things? You have spent little time with Ben. And you don't give us money for food. When you are at home, you are drunk and morose. Discussing anything amicably is not on your agenda.'

Paul—'This is ridiculous.'

Sarah—'No, Paul, this is your choice. You've got what you wanted. You've got a divorce.'

For the first time in months, Paul looks suddenly very sober.

Events now take on a new pace.

Paul still doesn't come home. When he does, he keeps asking me to leave the house. And he continues to taunt me with references to his sexual prowess—which, the more he mentions it, has less impact. I refuse to leave the house as Felicity suggests I try to remain there as long as possible—unless he becomes physically abusive, in which case I can get a restraining order.

Paul hires a solicitor—ironically, the same solicitor Pierce used in his divorce from Jane. So it's becoming very incestuous.

Then Felicity introduces me to my barrister.

I always imagine barristers short and dumpy, like Rumpole of the Bailey. Rotund. But as I sit in the chambers of Netherton & Sons, nervous, numb and painfully thin—still reeling from the pace of the divorce proceedings—a tall, dark, handsome man in his forties walks into the room. My immediate thought is that Paul will hate him. My second is I hope he is as good at his job as he is good-looking.

He smiles at me warmly and walks quickly to our table. Felicity and Gemma sit on one side, I on the other. He sits in the middle. Silks flying.

'Just come from a case. May I introduce myself? My name is Jeremy Fielding.'

Sarah—'Very nice to meet you.'

Methinks, This is interesting. I am still, I believe, in love with my husband. When Paul taunts me about his lovemaking with her, it still destroys me inside. Paul still has the ability to make me feel angry and guilty. But I'm starting to get my feelings back. To find other men attractive again. And, perhaps I'm imagining it, but I sense this Jeremy guy likes me. I sense it instinctively. Probably imagining it. Get real, Sarah. This guy is charging you hundreds of pounds an hour. Of course he fucking likes you.

Jeremy—'Right, I've been given the details of the case, and they seem pretty straightforward to me. Married seven years. He's earnt most of his income during marriage. You work. Travel writer. Travel with your son, Ben, three years old.'

While he is talking he scans a file of letters and notes and papers and photos. Ben's photo is on the top. Where is that tissue box?

He continues…

Jeremy—'You own a house in England. No mortgage, worth about half a million. And one in France, near Toulouse. Mmm, I have one near there, actually. Gaillac. Very nice area, isn't it?'

Sarah—'Er, yes. very nice. Only had it six months, but I have a closer affinity to it than the one in England.'

Jeremy—'I understand that. I feel the same way about my French home.'

Sarah—'It has a romance about the place.'

Jeremy—'Yes. I find that, too.'

He pauses. Stares at me for a few seconds—contemplating the statement, I suppose—and then continues.

Jeremy—'Anyway, house in France. Two properties. Two flats in England. Renting out. Small mortgages. And he is expecting a large bonus this year. And savings. Well, Sarah, I think we should go for about forty to forty-five per cent of his gross assets. Maintenance we'll deal with separately. Have you worked out what you need a month?'

Felicity—'Yes, I have the papers here.'

Felicity hands Jeremy more papers. He reads further.

Jeremy—'Mmm, interesting case. No sex, eh? For years? Mmm. Emotionally controlling, perhaps?'

Sarah—'Mmm.'

Where are those tissues? Think Tony Blair. Tony Blair. Tony Blair.

Jeremy—'Yes, we can go for that. When will we have access to his files?'

He turns to Felicity.

Felicity—'We've already asked for them. We should get them in a week or so.'

Jeremy—'And he's a director, so he can't hide his income. Not to say he can't hide a lot of other things.'

Felicity—'Quite.'

Felicity—'But I think you will be fine, Sarah. You won't be destitute, anyway.'

Sarah—'Good to know.'

Jeremy smiles.

Jeremy—'You will be fine, Sarah. We will make sure of that.'

AUTUMN INTO WINTER

NOVEMBER

Meeting the new Sarah

Paul is still living in the house. Still insisting he needs space. It's now a mantra. Paul 'I need space' O'Brian is officially driving me nuts. Sometimes I'm upset the marriage is coming to an end. Think wistfully of all the good times. Sometimes I think, Thank God another silly cow's going to take this guy on. Good luck to her.

There's even an upside to being as thin as I am. I now have cheekbones. Wonderful cheekbones. Okay, I also have shoulderblades that stick out and legs that are straight where they should be curvy, but I like the cheekbones. And it's winter, so I can do baggy clothes without anyone noticing too much. Only my friends.

I've also become very creative. I remember my English teacher telling me artists and poets and writers are usually at their best when they are miserable. T.S. Eliot wrote brilliant stuff, but as soon as he married his secretary and got all loved up he couldn't write a single thing. I'm writing loads of articles at the moment. Really good stuff that isn't being altered by the commissioning editors. Some of them are even e-mailing back and *saying* 'good stuff', which is unheard of in the industry. They don't have time to respond in such a lengthy fashion usually, or give such unbounded praise.

And poetry. I'm writing lovely poetry.

Paul is now refusing to talk to me at all. Apart from saying, 'I need space,' he says little else of any note.

Paul—'I don't want to talk to you. I don't want you to talk to me. I don't want you to write to me. I don't want you to e-mail me. Do you understand?'

Sarah—'Yes, I understand, Paul. But this is different. I've written a poem about Ben.'

I hand him a framed poem.

Sarah—'I've framed it, and I give it to you, Paul, because it isn't about you or about me or about us. It's about Ben. Who at this time needs us both. And I give it to you to remind you of the fact that this little boy is the only remaining symbol of our love.'

Paul reads.

The most beautiful face in the world
Beckons me each morning with cries of 'Mummy'
Wow, this unbroken voice of unconditional love
Nature's wake-up call to the meaning of life
Heavier by the moment, no longer a babe in my arms
That used to be so fragile, I could graze with a cuddle
Now he is walking, talking, laughing and questioning
In sequence
Words of
Why and more and please and thank you
Trickle daily
My sweetpea and cuddle bunny and lightness of my life
Is my light and my love
Is the sunshine and the stars and all that is good and
wonderful in me

And my husband. Without the sin and the questioning
and the guilt
And the nonsense we call responsibility
Tight in my arms and my heart and my head and spirit
I am stronger with him and for him and he for me and
I will never let that go
Everything is new and wonderful in his better eyes
And now it is in mine.

I think if that can't touch his heart, nothing will.
He reads it blankly. Looks up at me.
Paul—'That's nice.'
Oh, well. I tried.

Monday morning. One of my newspaper editors,
Jack, calls me with an urgent commission. Jack is
wonderful, and on the verge of a nervous breakdown. Always doing ten things when he needs to do
one. Very patient and open to ideas, and doesn't
change my copy.

Jack—'Deadline. Urgent. As in yesterday. Need someone to write a piece—actually three pieces—on trips for
kids. Must be something local. Something on the con-
tinent. You know—Spain. Somewhere in Spain. And I
need a piece on Disneyland Paris. Someone's let me
down. Can you help, Sarah?'

Sarah—'Love to. When do you need it by?'

Jack—'Got to do this within the next three weeks,
Sarah. Can you help? I've contacted all the PRs and
they've said they will work around us.'

Sarah—'Fine. Can I bring Ben?'

Jack—'Of course. That's what it's about. And I'll pay
extra, as it's late notice and you're saving my neck.
Okay?'

Sarah—'Okay. So can I do, say, Legoland in the UK? There's a place called La Manga in Spain which is good, and then a few days in Disney?'

Jack—'Perfect. Perfect. Got to go—got to go. Bye.'

So I decide to give Paul the space he so desperately craves and take a break, care of the newspaper feature and several public relations offices.

I explain this to Paul.

Paul—'I will miss Ben. But I won't miss you.'

Sarah—'I know. He can call you every day if you like.'

Paul—'As long as I don't have to hear your voice.'

Sarah—'You won't. And perhaps it will give you time and space to think about what's happening. And the way you're handling it.'

Paul—'I'm handling it fine. We're getting divorced. That's for the best. You've got to move on, Sarah. Emotionally.'

Sarah—'I know, Paul. I will. In my own time. As you will. In your own time.'

Paul—'I have.'

Sarah—'We will see, won't we?'

Two days later. Sunday morning. Luggage in the car, I watch Paul hug Ben. I don't look Paul in the face, focusing on his neckline. I haven't looked him direct in the eyes for months now.

Day at Legoland. Ben and I ride dragons, swirl round giant spiderwebs, interview a few families and are blessed with good, if rather nippy, weather.

Then drive to Gatwick Airport. I get lost. Feel as though I'm the character in *The Blair Witch Project,* as it's dark and the country roads are getting narrower and there's no streetlights. And I think, How the fuck can I get lost in Slough? Is this really Slough?

I eventually find my way back to the main road, and reach the airport in time to catch a plane to Spain. Where it's raining.

For a week Ben learns to play soft tennis and I have personal tennis lessons with Johann, who comes from Denmark and is tall and slim and blond and very good-looking—and has a girlfriend called Saffron, who is a yoga instructor. And who can get her legs round her neck.

Sarah—'I used to be able to do that. I can do the box splits, though.' I say this as I practise my forehand.

Johann—'*Das ist gut.* That is good. Let me see.'

So I do the box splits in the middle of Court 54 and make a young Danish tennis player smile.

Johann—'Mm. Must get Saffron to try that.'

At the end of the week my tennis swing has improved—both fore- and backhand. And my lobs aren't bad either. Ben is playing soft tennis with style. I'm told he has good hand-eye coordination and think of my dad, who was good at tennis. Perhaps Ben will be the next Wimbledon champion? Well, they missed a generation with me.

Then on to Disneyland, where I spend a fortune on plastic toys and swirly sticks that light up and look and act like vibrators but have Winnie the Pooh stuck on top.

On the last day Ben looks at me, surrounded by his collection of various cartoon toys, brown with his Spanish suntan, and says, 'This is lovely, Mummy. Thank you. This is lovely.'

Paul doesn't ring my mobile for the duration. He doesn't ring the hotels. He's got the numbers. So perhaps he lost them and perhaps he didn't. I leave a few messages on our home answer-machine.

Hi, there, this is Sarah, Ben is having a wonderful time. Speak to Daddy, Ben.

Hello, Daddy, I'm having a wonderful time. I've seen Mickey Mouse and been on a dragon and I can play tennis. And I'm very good at it, Mummy, aren't I?

Yes, you're very good at it. Now, say bye.

Bye, Daddy. Love you.

Bye, Paul.

Click.

Arrive home on a Monday evening, straight from the Eurostar. Expectant and nervous. Has my alien changed? Has the nasty fire-breathing insect evolved and will greet me with lilies and oral sex?

No.

In the hallway Paul, looking guilty, greets Ben and then turns to me

Paul—'I had a very good time while you were away. Missed Ben lots, but I don't like myself when I'm around you.'

No change, then. But perhaps it's the holiday, or the break, but I'm feeling stronger. I'm even able to look him in the eye without wanting to cry or punch him. Or both.

Sarah—'I've given you time to think. If you've decided to use the rope to hang yourself, that's your problem. I've also done some thinking. No way are Ben and I moving out. We're staying put. If you want to go, that's your move. We're not chucking you out. But you go if you want to. As for giving you space—I've looked after Ben for the past three months single-handedly while you've been out pissed and shagging your girlfriend. Well, I'm out tomorrow. Theatre with Jane and Kim. Play with Dawn French. *My Brilliant Divorce.* Somehow thought it appropriate, and perhaps I can learn a thing or two. So you can stay in with Ben. He's forgotten what you look like.'

Theatre is good, and Jane and Kim are on form.

Kim—'You look good, Sarah. Much better. Still too thin. But better.'

Sarah—'I'm not over it yet, you know. But much better. Less angry.'

Jane—'It takes time. It takes about a year to two years from the time he moves out or you divorce—whichever is soonest. For your sake I hope he moves out. You both being in the same house—I can see fireworks starting to happen.'

Dawn French is funny. The play is poignant and funny. And I cry.

Kim—'Perhaps not a good play to see after all.'

Jane—'Bit soon, perhaps. But it was either this one or *Tell Me on a Sunday*, and that's all about a girl continually getting dumped by arseholes—one of whom I think is a married man—and losing her self-worth, where this is about someone gaining it. Sort of.'

I get home after eleven. Lights still on in sitting room. Ah. He's left his mobile on the sofa. It's still on. He hasn't locked it. Let's see if there are any messages…

Click.

One from Pierce. To do with work. Prices.

One from a girl called Kirstie.

One from a girl called Sarah. Not me. Surname Fry.

Another one from a girl called Sarah.

And another one.

And another.

And…

Her name is Sarah.

He's chosen someone with the same fucking name as me. He's fucking a Sarah.

What do the messages say? What do they *say?* I can feel my blood start to boil. All the relaxing tennis and the Disney and Legoland experience disappear. All the anger is back with a vengeance.

Message received 20:05:
Thinking of you. Xx
Message received 21:10:
I wish you were in my bed tonight.xxxxx
Message received 21:30:
Ben is so lucky to cuddle up to you when he wants.
Message received 22:59:
That was wonderful. Thinking of you big boy.

Red. I see red. Big boy. *Big boy. He's small. He's a nee-dle-dick.* And how *dare* she text my son's name? *How dare she?* And *wonderful. That was wonderful.* I'll fucking kill him. I try to ring the number. But it's an answer-machine. And what do I say to her? Why do I need to speak to her? So I put the phone down. Best to say nothing.

I stop to think. Must calm down because I might just do it. *Crime of passion.* Avoid kitchen. Yes, avoid kitchen and call Kim. Call Jane. They will calm me down. It's nearly midnight, but I call Kim.

I get the answer-machine.

Hi, this is Kim and Jamie. We can't get to the phone at the moment, but please leave a message and we'll get back to you as soon as possible. Beep.

Sarah—Kim. *Kim!* It's Sarah. *It's Sarah.* Pick up the phone if you're there. It's Sarah. It's urgent. Pick up the phone. *Please* pick up the phone. Please.'

Kim—'Hi. Hi—hi, I'm here. I'm here. I'm here, girl. What's up? What's up?'

Sarah—'Her name is fucking Sarah. Her fucking name is Sarah. He's chosen someone called Sarah. He's fucking a Sarah. A Sarah is fucking my husband. Sarah and Paul. Paul and Sarah. It's *fucking* ridiculous! How the fuck could he choose someone with the same fucking name? Always knew he was lazy, but this is fucking ridiculous. Found out reading the text messages on his phone. She's even got an *h* in her fucking name. Fuck her. Fuck him, the fucking fucker. Why not Emma or Lucy or Felicity or Natasha or Natalie or Jo or any other fucking fuck-off name? There aren't that many Sarahs in the world, surely?'

Kim—Wow. Pace, girl. Deep breaths. In we go, and out we go, and in we go, and out we go. Breathe… Got that?'

Sarah—'Yes, I've got that. In I go. And out I go. In I go. And out I go.'

Kim—'Feel better?'

Sarah—'No. *Still want to rip his fucking heart out.*'

Kim—'Imagine how he felt when he read Stephen's e-mail to you, then.'

I stop.

And think.

Sarah—'Yeah, you're right. He was furious. But it wasn't my choice. The sexless relationship wasn't my choice.'

Kim—'Putting up with the marriage was. Staying in the marriage was.'

Sarah—'I was being loyal. I loved him.'

Kim—'You weren't that loyal.'

Sarah—'Considering the circumstances I was.'

Kim—'You can't do anything about that now. You know what he's like. You know he won't change. You know you can't change. If you burst in on him now and scream at him, what's he going to do? What do you expect him to do? Deny it? Say, *Well done, you've found out?* He's admitted it and, hey, you know her name now. And, hey, you know her number now. And, hey, you know she texts him, which you probably expected anyway. And, hey, you know she lies about the size of his dick. So she's pandering to the size of his ego already. So what's the use of waking him up at—what time is it?— twelve-thirty in the morning to tell him you've found out who she is?

'I know you're dying to know what she's like. Who she is. Where she works. I know that. You're a journalist. That's your fucking job, for Christ's sake. But it won't help you. And that's what you've got to think about. Think about *you*. What will help *you*. Because you haven't thought about *you* for a long time. Not about you and Paul, because there is no you and Paul anymore. There's you and Ben. That's it. Think of you and Ben.

'Whoever she is, this *new Sarah*, she's not you. And will never be you. And that's what's important. And it's fucking ironic he's chosen or got landed with another Sarah—because perhaps he's trying to find another you, or the old you. I don't know. Anyway, it is a bit freaky. But then I've always thought he was strange.

'Calm down. Go for a drive. Sit and scream in the car. Cut up his old teddy bear. Leave it, Sarah. Leave it.'

I sit on the sitting room sofa and weep down the phone. I know Kim's still there because I can hear her breathe. I cry for about five minutes. And then gradually calm down. Crying less noisily and getting my breath back.

Kim—'I love you, Sarah. Jane loves you. Ben loves you. And Paul probably still loves you. But he doesn't think he loves you that way any more. And this *Sarah*— well, this Sarah doesn't know you and doesn't owe you anything. And she has probably been told a load of stuff by Paul. And she's got Paul. With all that baggage. So you should feel sorry for the poor cow. She's a lesser model. You're the original.

'And she's having to deal with all his crap, and the fact he's getting drunk and the fact that he's torn about Ben and about the family and about so many things, and all his demons, and she's probably getting the brunt of that. And she's baggage for him, too, and she'll want to marry him and settle down and may get pregnant, and he can't cope by himself so he'll jump from the frying pan into the fire. Sarah, you're best out of it. Hey, he's even chosen a girl with the same name. How fucking unoriginal can you get? I bet that bugs the fuck out of her.'

Sarah—'Don't give a fuck.'

I start to cry.

Kim—'You'll be okay, Sarah. You're a beautiful, sexy woman, and there's a lot of anorexics out there that would love to be your dress size right now. You have friends who love you, a wonderful little boy who adores you, and a bloody good solicitor, by the sounds of it. Like the sound of your barrister, too. Very horny. Does he have a brother?'

Sarah—'Dunno.'

Kim—'Look, you're getting rid of someone you may have loved once but who's treated you badly and is closing the door. *He's* closing it, Sarah—not you. And *he* has to live with that. Not you. His history tells me he's not very good at living with or dealing with guilt.'

Sarah—'That's not my problem.'

Kim—'It's not anymore. Well, I've got some news which will take your mind off this. I'm pregnant.'

Sarah—'Oh, Kim. Well done. It's Jamie's?'

Kim—''Course it's Jamie's, you silly cow!'

Sarah—'Well done, well *done*. Does Jamie know?'

Kim—'Called him in New York. And e-mailed. He's getting smashed on champagne and behaving like a twit, buying everyone cigars.'

Sarah—'Sounds like Jamie. Very Jamie. Well done, well done. I'll give you loads of tips, of course I will. You'll get them from everyone. But remember these two—two most important things to remember. First— have an epidural. Forget all this natural childbirth crap. The pain is nothing like a period pain. Well, not one I've had anyway. If my periods were that painful I think I'd top myself. You gain sanity and the ability to love your baby when it comes out of you rather than scream- ing like some harpy "Get the fucking thing out of me!"

'Second—as soon as the baby comes out of you, whether it's Caesarean or natural, get the midwife to put him or her on your nipple. Worked for Ben and me. I fed him for eight months and it was wonderful. Just him and me—every two hours, every night for the first three months, in my rocking chair in his room. He fed and I rocked in the silence. No traffic, no TV. No hassle from Paul or my mother to do it this way or care for him that way. Just Ben and me. In a funny sort of way I've never been happier, and I'd like you to have that magic. Bottle is not quite the same. And I'm not a mumsy mum, but that is magic. Plus, it makes getting around so much easier. I remember going on the train to meet Paul one lunchtime, and Ben sucking away happily at me while I had him in the baby carrier, and people on the carriage wondering where the sucking noises were coming from. He was so small; his head was no bigger than a tennis ball. And Paul was so happy to see him and—well, and…'

Kim—'And he's never going to have a brother or sister?'

Sarah—'Yeah. That's what I'm thinking. He won't have a brother or sister now. Perhaps it would have made it easier if we'd had two before this happened. Or perhaps harder. One is easier to cope with than two. And Ben's at a good age for it to happen. He won't remember his mum and dad ever being together. That's good for him, I think. But sad. Because we were happy. Once.'

Kim—'And you will be again. He might have a stepbrother or stepsister.'

Sarah—'Didn't want him to be an only child, like his mummy. It's quite lonely, you know.'

Kim—'Yes, I know. But he will have loads of friends, and a family that loves him, and he is unique—just like his mum. Now, get some rest. Why don't you sleep in Ben's bedroom tonight? With the new man in your life rather than the old?'

Sarah—'You know what? I will. Night-night Kim. And well done. You will be a wonderful mother.'

Kim—'I know. Just like you.'

I get a sleeping bag out of the cupboard, lay it by the cot-bed and fall asleep listening to the sound of Ben snoring and giggling and pretending to be Buzz Lightyear. Rescuing again.

Next morning I wake to the sound of the front door slamming. The man has left the building.

My mobile rings. I don't recognise the number.

Sarah—'Hello?'

'Hello.'

It's a female voice. I don't recognise it.

Sarah—'Hello…?'

'Hi. You called me. Last night.'

Sarah—'Oh. Is this Sarah Fry?'

Sarah Fry—'Yes.'

Sarah Giles—'Ah.'

I think, Say you got the wrong number. But I can't say that now because I've just said her name. Fuck. Okay. Here goes.

Sarah Giles—'Hello, I think you know my husband. Paul O'Brian?'

Silence. Thirty seconds of it. Then:

Sarah Fry—'I do.'

Find out what she knows.

Sarah Giles—'And you obviously know he is still married?'

Sarah Fry—'I do.'

Sarah Giles—'And that he has a three-year-old little boy?'

Sarah Fry—'I do. I have never been out with a married man with children before.'

Didn't expect that answer. Think it irrelevant, but hey-ho, this is such a weird conversation anyway, why not go for it completely?

Sarah Giles—'Well, as you know he is married, and that he has a little boy, I think you should also know that I love my husband very much and that I want my family back. You have the opportunity to walk away now.'

Sarah Fry—'*You* had an affair.'

Didn't expect that either. She's rehearsed this conversation in her head a million times over. Satisfy myself with the fact that she's creating such dreadful karma for herself that she might drop dead sometime soon and I won't have to lift a finger.

Sarah Giles—'That's none of your business. But as you seem to know you're going out with a married man, that his wife still wants him back and he has a family, then that's all I need to know about you.'

Sarah Fry—'It's up to Paul what he does. It's his decision.'

Sarah Giles—'I agree. But it's up to you, too. Goodbye.'

Click.

Phone Kim.

Sarah—'Hi, Kim. If ever there was a conversation to prove Sarah Giles can't do nasty it's this one. I've just spoken to *her*. She called me. She checked up on her phone and just called me back. Why didn't I scream down the phone "You fucking bitch"?'

Kim—'Because it wouldn't have done any good whatsoever. What did she say?'

I repeated to Kim what she'd said. Verbatim.

Kim—'Mmm. Well, as you say, she'd rehearsed it in her mind many times before. It's serious stuff. She's created her own karma. She owes you nothing. Paul's the one who made you the promises. Leave them to it. And don't call her again. She's not worth it. Walk tall. Taller than her and him. And think of Ben and yourself. I'm suffering from the most bloody awful morning sickness.'

Sarah—'Dry biscuits. Try water biscuits. They're the best. It usually only lasts the first eight weeks.'

Kim—'First eight weeks! You mean I've got another month of this? Oh, well—Waitrose, here I come. I've got to go now, Sarah, but remember—don't phone her again. She'll probably call Paul immediately and tell him what's happened. He'll go nuts. But that's his problem, not yours. Just think of it this way: his problems are not your concern any more. All that free time to focus on yourself and Ben.'

Phone rings. I expect it's Paul.

Sarah—'Hello?'

'Hello, it's Simon.'

Sarah—'Does not compute. Simon who?'

Simon—'The gardener.'

Simon the gardener is twenty-seven, intense, Libra with Scorpio rising (he tells me), and bursting with hormones. Prunes the roses, mows the lawn, tries to shape the hedges in the form of vaginas. Well, he may not be doing it intentionally, but they all look like vaginas. He never does what Paul tells him to do, even when he shows him exactly. But at least he's a better gardener than me. I used to help Paul in the garden, but could never tell a weed from a plant. And how the hell was I supposed to know the plant was a euphorbia? Okay, I pulled it up by mistake. But we have hundreds of the ruddy things.

So why is Simon the gardener calling me?

Simon—'Hello, Mrs O'Brian.'

I hate being called Mrs O'Brian. Oh, well, not for much longer. Simon is the *only* person who's ever called me Mrs O'Brian. I think he's read *Lady Chatterley's Lover.* He keeps asking if I want any forget-me-nots in the garden. Er, no. I'm not going to entwine them in your pubic hair, Simon.

Sarah—'Hello Simon. How are you?'

Simon—'Fine, Mrs O'Brian. Just wondered how you are and all that?'

Sarah—'I'm fine. I'm fine.'

Simon—'Only, I heard from my mum, who heard

from my aunt, that your old man is having it off with some girl. Is that true?'

Sarah—'Er, well, yes. But how did your aunt know?'

Simon—'She knows Paul's neighbour. And Paul's mum has been telling her neighbour stuff—you know, quiet, like. And she—well, she sort of told my aunt at a Women's Institute meeting, and that's how my mum knows. We were talking last night, the family, and it came up, like.'

Sarah—'Oh.'

Simon—'So that's how I know.'

Sarah—'Er, right.'

Simon—'So I was wondering if you would fancy going out one evening?'

Sarah—'That would be lovely. Ben would love that.'

Simon—'Oh right. Ben. Yes, Ben. We could go to the cinema.'

Sarah—'Well, we're actually going to the cinema this evening. To see *Treasure Planet*. Would you like to come?'

I think, What am I saying? But, hey, why not. Ben always gets on with Simon. He loves jumping on his back while he's digging and pruning and shaping the hedges. And Simon's very patient with him. Very thoughtful and kind and extremely generous.

Simon—'Okay. Shall I come round later?'

Sarah—'Yes. We're leaving about six.'

Simon—'Will Paul be back today?'

Sarah—'Doubt it. He never returns home these days.'

Simon—'Shagging the bird, then?'

Sarah—'Er, yes, probably.'

Simon—'Okay. Be round later. See yer then.'

Sarah—'Okay. Bye.'

★ ★ ★

This is ever so slightly nuts. But then nothing is ordinary at the moment. Everything feels slightly extraordinary, and going to the cinema with the gardener and my three-year-old doesn't seem such a strange idea. After all, my husband of seven years, who I thought would always be there for me, who had written the sweetest love poems and looked into my eyes so many times and told me I was his angel and the love of his life and how he would never leave me, is now happily bonking another, lesser Sarah. Nothing seems impossible or improbable now. So why not this?

At six on the dot the doorbell rings.

Simon is dressed in something resembling a tux. I think it could be a tux, but it's brown. So perhaps you can get brown tuxedos in Essex. Anyway, he looks a bit like Worzel Gummidge meets Liberace. Weird. Ben thinks he is absolutely brilliant.

Ben—'You are brilliant, Simon. You are very pretty.'

Simon—'Don't you mean handsome?'

I think, No, he got it right first time.

Ben—'No—pretty.'

Simon—'Er, thank you, Ben.' Looking at me—'Your mum is very pretty, too.'

Ben—Looking at me then at Simon—'Mummy is beautiful. You are pretty. I like brown. It's the colour of poo. All soft and squidgy.'

After Ben's critique of Simon's squidgy-coloured suit, we go to the cinema. I drive, in the little green Golf GTi, and we manage to park with ease and get good seats. Simon kindly buys Ben lots of Maltesers and popcorn. Which I proceed to confiscate as chocolate makes Ben tetchy and hyper. Film is very good. Keep trying to remember the names of the actors playing the characters. Recognise the voices but don't remember the names. The guy who plays Niles in *Frasier* is one character, and that Shakespearean actress is another. But can't for the life of me remember who they are.

My memory and brain are obviously going. Simon tries to furtively put his hand on mine during the film, but I put Ben between us so it makes it very difficult for him to reach me or drop something and accidentally lean over into my crotch to pick it up. Afterwards I think, I'm not doing this again. But he is rather sweet.

Simon—'Thank you for a lovely evening, Mrs O'Brian.'

Sarah—'Call me Sarah.'

As I say my name I realise it's not mine anymore. After all, *she's* called Sarah, too. But I think, Hey, I'm probably older than her. I had it first, and I like my name. So sod it.

Sarah—'Yes, call me Sarah.'

Simon—'I will. Thank you. And thank you, Ben.'

Ben—'Thank you, Simon. Can I jump on your back? Can I have a piggyback?'

Simon—'Okay, Ben.'

Ten p.m., pitch-black, and Simon is willing and able to run round the front lawn with Ben on his back. The neighbours' curtains are twitching. I can sense it. They will have something to talk about next day. Week. Month. Year…

As he goes, he turns.

Simon—'Can I just say I think your husband has got rocks in his head? You're a lovely lady.'

Sarah—'I'm no angel, Simon. I'm not the victim here. And it's my responsibility to not make Ben one either. As for Paul—if he wants to play the victim, the injured party, I will let him.'

Simon—'I know you're not an angel, Sarah. But I know what I see when you're with Ben. I don't see you when you're with Paul. He's always, in my mind, been completely up his own arse, if I can say so. But you're one cool lady. I've watched how he's talked to you when he's around while I've been working in the garden. Sometimes I've thought the guy needs a right good kick up the arse, he's so full of shit. If you don't mind me saying, Sarah.'

Sarah—'No, I don't mind you saying.'

Simon—'And, well, his mum said you went off and bonked lots of reporters when you were travelling. That you spent most of your time on your back. Horizontal, like.'

Sarah—'Did she? Well, it's not true, Simon.'

Simon—'No, knew it. *Knew* it. I told Mum I knew it. And that you probably need company. Well, I'm just saying that if you want company I will be very happy to take you out. To the cinema or Pizza Express or anywhere you'd like to go, really. With Ben, of course. Or just by yourself.'

Sarah—'That's very thoughtful of you, Simon.'

Simon—'Phew, I'm hot in this suit. Do you think I could take a shower?'

I think, What is it with men and showering in this house? Do I make them feel dirty or something?

Sarah—'Yes, that's fine. Upstairs at the top of the stairs. There are clean towels in the bathroom already.'

Simon—'Thanks, Sarah.'

I go into the kitchen and make tea while my gardener takes a shower in my bathroom. I wonder… Should I go up to the bathroom and join him? Is that what these guys expect me to do by showering in my house? Is it some tip from a *'How to fuck a woman'* bible men read?

Or do they just feel an insatiable need to be clean? But Ben is here, awake and alert, and the timing is not right. So I let the moment pass. And Simon showers without disturbance this time.

Half an hour later he comes down the stairs, smelling of my soaps and shower gels and smiling.

Simon—'Thank you, Sarah. That was lovely. I'd better go. It's late now. I'll say night-night to Ben.'

Ben runs to hug him and runs straight into his crotch. Simon looks pained.

Simon—'Bye, Ben. Did you have a lovely time tonight?'

Ben—'Yes, I did. And thank you for taking us and thank you for the Maltesers. Mummy doesn't let me eat them, but thank you anyway.'

Simon—'My pleasure.'

He puts Ben down and turns to me.

Simon—'Thank you for a lovely evening, Sarah. Remember what I said. If you ever need me. Pruning roses, kicking husbands up the arse, taking sons to the cinema—let me know.'

Sarah—'Thank you, Simon. You're a star.'

He goes to peck me a kiss on the cheek, but I pull him to me and give him a hug. Not a sexual hug. Just a hug of recognition and thanks for his unexpected kindness, because it's made me feel extremely humbled and happy.

As we wave him goodbye Ben says, 'I really like Simon, Mummy. I even like his pooey clothes.'

Saturday morning—post arrives, but I don't have time to open it. Ben has a birthday party to get dressed up for (Peter Pan costume ready), and I'm meeting Jane for lunch. Paul won't be back this weekend, I'm sure. He hasn't called since I spoke to Sarah No 2 on the phone, so I suspect he's angry and feels he's punishing me by not calling, not telling me where he is, and leaving me to speculate whether he's having sex with her round the clock. I don't care. I'm too busy. And looking forward to seeing Jane again.

I take Ben to see his friend Torin from nursery. He is celebrating his fourth birthday at home with Mickey the Clown, a bouncy castle, lots of food and non-sweetened and non-fizzy drinks and friends. For three hours. Thank you, Torin's mum, for organising this. Three hours of girlie chat at Café Rouge with Jane. Starting to get the old Sarah back now. Or is it the new?

I'm early for lunch, so decide to open my post there. Letter from Felicity saying Paul has agreed to pay interim maintenance. Well, he's been forced to pay interim maintenance. I think that is how she words it. Another one is from Linden Priory—which, if I remember rightly, is where Paul and I had our wedding reception. Wonder why they're contacting me? Open it, but don't have time to read it as Jane arrives.

Jane is late and looking a little harassed, in a short red dress with violet jacket and mobile attached to right earlobe.

She clicks off as soon as she sits down at our table.

Jane—'Hi, Sarah. You look nice. How's everything going?'

Sarah—'Fine. You look smashing, too. It was lovely to see you at the theatre the other day.'

Jane—'Yes, that was good. We didn't have much time to speak, but are you getting on okay with Felicity?'

Sarah—'Yes, I think she knows her stuff. Very efficient. I have a rather handsome barrister called Jeremy.'

Jane—'That's good. Don't fuck him. You're not allowed to fuck him while he represents you. Think you can after the case. So keep his number, or something.'

Sarah—'Well, sleeping with my counsel wasn't at the forefront of my mind.'

Jane—'It was, or you wouldn't have mentioned him.'

Sarah—'Anyway, seems I have a new admirer in my gardener.'

Jane—'The gardener? That's good. Simple men always give the best sex. Uncomplicated, earthy sex. Why don't you start a relationship with him? A fling amongst the flowers and all that?'

Sarah—'I might do. He's very sweet with Ben.'

Jane—'That's good. But irrelevant for the short term. What's he like with you?'

Sarah—'Sweet. No dress sense, but sweet. And he took a shower in my house.'

Jane—'Ha. Oldest trick. You know that one, surely, Sarah? They expect you to slip into the shower and then to slip into you. Pierce used that trick to seduce me. Worked, of course. I think there must be some book somewhere that suggests the trick works.'

Sarah—'*Gardener's Digest,* perhaps? I did think about it. After all, if Paul is having all this sex, why can't I?'

Jane—'You can, Sarah. You can have gratuitous, guilt-free sex. Only issue is Ben. You've got to focus on Ben, and in many ways another man would add problems. If you can just take it as fucking a friend—that's fine. But I think you're still a bit confused about your feelings for Paul—so perhaps best to hold off on bonking the gardener. For a few months anyway. As for lousy dress sense—you can do something about that; it's all the other stuff that's difficult. Talking of difficult, how has Paul been?'

Sarah—'The same. I spoke to his girlfriend. She's called Sarah, too.'

Jane—'Silly thing to do, Sarah. What did you want to speak to her for?'

Sarah—'Oh, it wasn't intentional. Rang her number and she called back. Dull conversation. She knows everything.'

Jane—'You think so? I think she probably knows nothing. Okay, she knows he's married with a child. But, Sarah, you will have been painted in such a way that she'll feel as though she's releasing him from some form of living hell. When in fact she's released you from it. She's allowing you to be you. *A new you.* And she has created a cage of her own. Did you thank her?'

Sarah—'Don't think I came across as particularly grateful.'

Jane—'If you speak to her again, thank her. She'll *hate* that.'

Sarah—'Well, she keeps Paul off my back. He's happy now.'

Jane—'Do you think he's happy? I don't. How can he be happy? He's always wanted a family, he loves Ben, and he wanted a very conventional lifestyle—and, hey, now this. He's angry and miserable and pissed all the time.'

Sarah—'Do you think he'll marry this girl?'

Jane—'Probably. He can't live without someone to look after him. If he does, he's a fool. But then I think he is behaving like a fool at the moment, so I wouldn't put it past him. Pierce told me he'd met her.'

Sarah—'Met who?'

Jane—'The other Sarah. Before you ask what she's like, I will tell you how Pierce described her—which I found quite hilarious. I think his words were: *"Nothing*

special. Unremarkable. Unsophisticated. Normal. Very short
and curvy. Like Miss Piggy. But skinnier version. Short arms,
as though she needs arm extensions, and her mouth is too small.
As in you'd have trouble getting a Brussel sprout in her mouth.
She'd manage a pea, but would have trouble with a Brussel
sprout. Oh, and she's ambitious."* That's about it.'

Sarah—'Looks like me, then.'

Jane—'Nothing like you. Don't give her thinking
space. You've got a lot on your plate. And, as I say, she's
done you a favour. The likelihood is, if she's seen a
photo of you, she'll wonder what the fuck is going on.
Anyway, what have you got there?'

She points to the papers I've got on my lap.

Sarah—'Oh, this one is from Felicity, saying Paul's got
to give me some money—which he'll hate. And this
one is from Linden Priory and is about…'

I start to read the letter aloud.

Dear Paul and Sarah

I am writing to inform you of a new service that
our local register office has announced. In addition
to our licence for marriages, we are now able to
hold renewal of wedding vows and baby-naming
ceremonies here at Linden Priory. From our rec-
ords we note that you held your wedding here, we
are therefore delighted to offer you the opportunity to renew your vows in the venue where your
special day was originally held. I hope this service
is of interest to you, as a way of reliving and celebrating your magical day. I look forward to hearing from you shortly.

Jane's speechless, which is rare for her.

Sarah—'Mmm. Wonder how many other couples

have received the letter and are still married? And want to relive *their magical and special day.*'

Jane—'Think the statistics are one in two these days. One in two.'

DECEMBER

Mistletoe, misery, and an awful lot of wine

Two weeks before Christmas. Paul goes on holiday to the Caribbean. He won't confirm if he's going with Sarah.

Paul—'I need a break.'

Sarah—'I know.'

Paul—'So I'm going on holiday.'

Sarah—'Are you going with Sarah?'

Paul—'None of your business.'

Sarah—'Any other time and it would be none of my business. But it's Christmas. It will be our last Christmas together as a family, and for Ben's sake it's important we make it as special as possible. It will also be our last Christmas together, and we've had good times, Paul—this may be the last opportunity we have to look back and perhaps remember those times. Going on holiday just before Christmas with Sarah is unnecessary. You need a break, I agree. But go by yourself.'

Paul—'I need a break, and she's fun and funny and sexy, and good to be with.'

Sarah—'Well, you have the rest of your life to be with her. Just this once, couldn't you hold back? It's Ben's fourth birthday you will be missing if you go. It's only this one time.'

Paul—'That's emotional blackmail.'

Sarah—'No, it's Ben's fourth birthday party. See it for what it is.'

Paul—'He will have many more.'

Sarah—'If that's really how you think, then go. But in years to come you may regret it.'

Paul—'Okay, fine. I'll go on my own.'

He storms off. My instinct is he will ignore me. And go with Sarah.

Three days later his suitcase is packed. Ben kisses him goodbye.

Ben—'Bye, Daddy. Have a nice time. Bring me back a present, please.'

Paul—'I will. And you have a lovely birthday party. I think Mummy has something very nice arranged for you.'

Sarah—'Bye, Paul. Try to chill out. And think about things.'

Paul—'I will try.'

Two days into the holiday bank statement arrives. Statement confirms he's booked a holiday for two. Could be one of his mates, of course, or one of his brothers. But I don't think so. Just to make sure I call Sarah's mobile number, which I still keep.

Hi, there, can't get to the phone at the moment. I'm away for two weeks and won't be contactable. Please leave a message and I'll get back to you.

Of course, she could be on holiday somewhere else, but I don't think so. I choose not to leave a message. And choose to delete Sarah's mobile number from my phone and my memory.

I don't have time to think about them on holiday to-gether. That's a lie. I do have time. But usually only in the five minutes before I go to bed. And I have time to think about what could have been if I'd confronted sit-uations earlier and differently.

During the day I'm too busy for what ifs. I have pres-ents to buy and decorations to hang. I've decided to go shopping with Samantha, as I haven't seen much of her, mainly because she's been busy organising her wedding to Edward.

Edward is finance director at Simmonson and Sons. He clinched the deal that got the account that made the award-winning condom advertisement. I can't remem-ber it, but Samantha assures me it was amazing. She's to-tally loved up and due to get married. I don't know much about Edward, but as long as he's good to Saman-tha that's fine by me. I also haven't seen much of Saman-tha because I don't want to depress her. She's full of hope and bubbling with Christmas spirit and goodwill to all men. Except Paul, that is.

By contrast, I'm getting divorced and I'm full of a combination of things. Sometimes anger, sometimes fear, sometimes self-loathing, sometimes sadness, some-times all four at the same time and in rapid succession. It's like having continual pre-menstrual tension and postnatal depression all wrapped into one.

So Samantha and I are going to shop, lunch and chat about all things festive at Redwater Shopping Centre, while Ben is looked after by Simon the gardener, who's going to help in the garden—probably with those bushes.

I arrive at her flat twenty minutes early.

Samantha—'Sarah—you're early!'

Sarah—'I know. It's the new me.'

Samantha—'You're never early. Well, this is good. I'll just be a minute. Come in, come in.'

Samantha lives in a first-floor flat with very high ceilings and a very large mortgage. One and a bit bedrooms. She's very happy there. Her sitting room floor is a carpet of wall-to-wall cuttings from magazines. Pictures of wedding dresses, wedding cakes, exotic honeymoon destinations, wedding invitation sample cards and little bags of pink and blue sugar almonds are strewn across the floor.

Samantha—'Oh, don't mind that. If you can find a space, sit in it—or stand in it. But we're not staying long.'

Sarah—'Looks as though you're in full swing with the wedding.'

Samantha—'I am, I am. Edward can't do much as he's working so hard. Sometimes he has to work all night. I completely understand, of course. Sometimes he's due to come here on Friday night and doesn't turn up till Saturday evening.'

Sarah—'Oh, that's a bummer. He always tells you, of course.'

Samantha—'Yes. We've had words about that. He's busy. Just told him to be a bit more thoughtful as I prepare dinner and myself for dessert and all that stuff. Very frustrating, and I get very annoyed.'

Sarah—'Bet you do.'

Samantha—'Plus, he's had a problem with his ex-girl-friend contacting him and he has to deal with that.'

Sarah—'Does she know he's getting married?'

Samantha—'Think so. That's the problem. Still loves him. She called me and introduced herself. I don't know much about her. Only what Edward's told me. But she wasn't married to him or anything. Didn't have his baby. It's not like you and…'

Sarah—'Mmm. Well, Edward has got to deal with that issue, Samantha. It's nothing to do with you. But the fact she contacted you may mean he's not dealing with it very well.'

Samantha—'Oh, Edward can deal with it. He's very strong.'

Sarah—'Maybe. Don't confuse being strong with being selfish. Or being strong-minded. I used to do that—think I was going for strong men when really they weren't strong at all. Just selfish and used to getting their own way.'

Samantha—'Women can be selfish, too.'

Sarah—'Of course they can. And I wasn't particularly strong in my relationship with Paul. But I'm getting there now.'

Samantha—'You have changed, Sarah. You're a bit more—well, chilled. You seem—let me get the word—*grounded*.'

Sarah—'Getting there. Lots to tell. You ready yet?'

Samantha—'Yes, almost. Bag. Check. Keys. Check. Money. Check. Present list. Check. Make-up. Check. Yes—ready.'

We're going in my car. My mobile rings just as I'm driving out of the drive.

Sarah—'Hi, there.'

Kim—'Hello, it's Kim.'

Sarah—'Hi, Kim. What's up? How are you?'

Kim—'Not good, Sarah. I've got to go into hospital. There have been complications, and I want to know if you can come in with me. Jamie's still in New York, and my sister will be on holiday, and I need some support. Bit worried about the baby. I'm ten weeks now.'

Sarah—'No problem. When do you want me to come?'

Kim—'It's actually this Thursday. Eleven a.m. at St Wolford's in Kensington. Would be really good if you could.'

Sarah—'No problem. I'll come to your flat, pick you up and we'll go together.'

Kim—'That would be good—thanks.'

Sarah—'What are you doing today? Do you need some company if everyone is away?'

Kim—'I'm fine. Some friends are over, and my sister is here before she goes away. I'm fine. Have you got Christmas sorted?'

Sarah—'I'm just doing the shopping now. Got my list. Getting the tree and stuff with Ben and the gardener tomorrow. There will probably just be the three of us, Paul, Ben and myself, on Christmas Day. Don't know if that is for the best. Whatever—it will be tough. I just think if my mum's there and Paul's family are there it's going to be even worse. So we're keeping it small.'

Kim—'Is Paul around?'

Sarah—'He's on holiday with Sarah.'

Kim—'Thoughtful of him. Isn't it Ben's birthday next week?'

Sarah—'Yes.'

Kim—'And he's missing that?'

Sarah—'Yes.'

Kim—'He's lost the plot, Sarah. His anger is at you, not at Ben. Anyway, see you on Thursday and thank you for coming.'

Sarah—'I will be there. Big kiss—love you lots.'

I'm worried about Kim. She always sounds so strong and sure of herself, and she says fuck a lot, and today she sounded edgy and—well, almost polite. As I'm telling Samantha about what's been happening in my life it all sounds so unimportant compared to Kim's situation.

The fact there might be complications with the baby. But I'm positive. Just a check-up. Sure she will be fine.

Samantha—'So, what have you got Paul for Christmas?'

Sarah—'A poem.'

Samantha—'You bought him a poem?'

Sarah—'No, I wrote him a poem. He said he didn't want me to *buy* anything for him as it was all *his fucking money* anyway. So I thought I'd be creative and make him a present. It's in my bag. In the black file. I want to get it framed. Read it, if you like.'

Samantha opens my bag, takes out the file and reads.

'I need space' is where it starts.
'I don't love you' where it ends.
So let's please be nice about this blip
After all, we are best friends.
Divorce is such a grown-up word
And so final, don't you think?
So let's just separate for now
And go heavy on the drink.
He can come back late and party
While I stay inside and muse
How this loving caring man
Could now be so confused
About how and why he loves her and feels he does no more
Perhaps the girl he's screwing is why he feels so sore
Of course, the little boy he's being forgets the little boy outside
Who's wondering where his daddy is and why the love has died
For the mummy who adores him
And still adores his dad
Who fails to recognise the man who's gone quite mad

*Who comes home late and wilting, full of anger beer
and bile
For the woman he adored once, now for whom there is
no smile
He fails to hear her voice pleading, fails to see the pain
and sadness in her face
Intent on destroying everything and putting something
in its place
The guests who stood there proudly as the wedding vows
were made
Stand incompetent, conspiring how the death throes can
be played
She's all alone and knows it
She'll be stronger for the day
And so much sadder in the knowledge her truest love has
gone away*

Samantha—'That's very good, but rather sad. Do you think it's appropriate as a Christmas present?'

Sarah—'For *this* Christmas, I think it's highly appropriate.'

Redwater is buzzing, but we get a space near to the main shops. I get a simple frame for the poem, a train set for Ben (it's on his Christmas list to Santa Claus this year), and some books on meditation and health spas for Jane and Kim, because I think they both need them. A watch for my mum, because she recently lost hers, and some DVDs for my cousins. *My Cousin Vinny* and *Groundhog Day.* More decorations for the tree, as some of the old ones are looking rather tired now. Then I get food. Four sorts of vegetables, a turkey, pudding and mince pies. Some candles, some wine, and a magnum of champagne. I haven't drunk any alcohol since September. I didn't think it was a good idea. But it's Christmas, so let's party!

After a hard morning's shopping, Samantha and I take a break at a spa that's just opened there.

It's supposed to represent a Thai spa, so we walk over planks with pebbles underneath into these little wooden cabins. Dimmed lights, rooms smelling of incense and water features at every corner. I feel it's been completely Feng Shui-ed.

I have a massage and reflexology. Samantha a manicure. I can't have a manicure because, as I argue, I have no nails at the moment.

Samantha—'Why don't you have a manicure, too, Sarah?'

Sarah—'I have no nails.'

Samantha—'That's why you should have one. It will encourage you not to pick.'

As I'm being massaged and pummelled, I feel a little more relaxed. A little more chilled. I think about Samantha and her wedding plans, and hope Edward is being straight with her about the ex-girlfriend. Perhaps I'm overly suspicious these days because of what I'm experiencing. It's probably nothing—and, as Samantha says, Edward is dealing with it. And Kim will be fine. I say a little prayer for her as the masseuse pushes into my sciatic nerve and I scream blue murder.

Two days later Kim loses the baby. She is devastated.

I spend the day with her in a private ward of a hospital in Kensington. Ben stays with my mum. I call her sister and Jamie and let them know. She cries a lot.

Kim—'I was too active. Wasn't I? I didn't slow down as much as I should.'

Sarah—'I don't think that was the cause, Kim. The

doctor would have told you. It sounds more complicated than that.'

Kim—'I know. I know. You're right. Who's looking after Ben?'

Sarah—'Ben's fine. He's with my mum—running rings round her, probably. Just think of yourself. Can I get you anything? I've called your sister and Jamie, and they're on their way now. Jamie's got the first flight out from New York and your sister's driving everyone nuts getting a flight back.'

Kim smiles.

Kim—'She's like me. She'll give them hell if they don't get her on a plane. She name-drops as much as I say fuck.'

I sit by Kim's bed for hours. Reading and talking to her. Sometimes she sleeps. Sometimes she cries. Sometimes we talk about life and the fact both of us are approaching forty—and don't we look fucking amazing for our age? I tell her about Simon and about Pierce. She says she knows the book they must have read for the shower trick, and how they must have both got very frustrated with me.

Sarah—'I don't give a fuck, Kim. I just thought they felt dirty.'

Kim—'That's the point. They *did*.'

Sitting with Kim, I realise my pain and loss is insignificant. Irrelevant. Loss of life. Bad health. Divorce pales into insignificance by comparison.

And it's Christmas. Why do the most dreadful things always seem to happen at Christmas, when everything is supposed to be so happy-smiley-smiley? Everyone feels pressure to be happy, and it doesn't happen like that. Life is not like that. I've learnt that the hard way. Nothing stays the same—not even Christmas—if you don't work at it.

And why Kim—who will make a fabulous mum? God, I know you work in mysterious ways, but I can't work this one out. What good will come of this?

I stay until Jamie arrives. He looks drawn and red in the face.

Sarah—'Hi, Jamie—I'll let you be with Kim now. Call me if you need me. You have my number.'

Jamie—'Thanks, Sarah.'

I hug Jamie. I hug Kim without saying anything. And I leave them both to their tears.

Ben's birthday goes well. I organise a fancy dress party for him and ten of his nursery friends at my health club—which, for £15 per head, does food, entertainment and going-away presents. None of the children of our mutual friends can come. Party games. Bouncy castle. Lots of jelly and sausage rolls and E-numbers making the children bounce violently off each other as well as the castle. Lots of the parents send only one grown-up representative—either the mum or the dad, but not both, as one has to do Christmas shopping or care for the other children in the family. So there's a lot of one-parent families and I don't feel so left out on the day. And no one asks where Paul is because they think he's doing the shopping.

In the afternoon, Simon, Ben and I go to the local tree nursery and buy a Christmas tree fit for a king. Well, a four-year-old boy at least. Ten foot tall, it touches the living room ceiling. I get down the Christmas decorations from the attic, and bring out the new ones I bought at Redwater with Samantha. Ben helps us decorate with baubles and bells, and eats some of the chocolate decorations before they make it to the tree.

Then we all put up the Christmas cards. There's some

to Ben and Sarah. Some to Ben and Paul, but only a few for Paul, Sarah and Ben. I suppose friends and family do feel they need to take sides, but it's when I look at the cards it becomes most transparent.

Simon stays for the evening, and takes us out to see *Mickey Mouse's Scrooge* and for a pizza at the local Italian. And he gives Ben a huge birthday present and leaves an even larger one for Christmas.

Paul arrives home three days before Christmas. Tanned and relaxed. I want to be chilled out when I see him. He still doesn't know I know he's been away with Sarah. And he hasn't called once or left a message to wish Ben a happy birthday. And that I'm really annoyed about.

I've kept Felicity informed of his behaviour with a diary.

Felicity—'This is all good stuff, Sarah. Good for future reference. The fact he is neglecting his son is not good for Ben, but if he suggests you are a bad mother we can refer to this holiday and the court will identify by his actions where his priorities lie.'

Sarah—'I know he loves Ben, and this is out of character.'

Felicity—'It's typical. In a year or two he'll look back and wonder what he was doing. He might even blame you for pushing him away. The fact you haven't is good. Stay calm if you can.'

Sarah—'I will try.'

At ten a.m. on the twenty-second he opens the door.

Paul—'Hi, Sarah.'

Sarah—'Hi, Paul.'

Paul—'How are you?'

Sarah—'Fine. Have a good holiday?'

Paul—'Yes. Weather not too good. That's why I'm not really tanned. But very relaxing.'

Sarah—'That's good. Where did you go?'

Paul—'Caribbean. St Thomas.'

Pause.

Sarah—'So, did Sarah enjoy herself, too?'

Silence.

Sarah—'Did Sarah enjoy herself, too? Did she have a good time?'

Paul—'Don't know what you're talking about.'

Sarah—'You went on holiday with her, didn't you?'

I was being *sooo* calm. Was starting to freak myself out with how calm I was being.

Paul—'I didn't go with Sarah. I said I wouldn't.'

Sarah—'Yes, you fucking did. What the fuck is this?' Shove statement in front of his now traumatised face. 'Yes, you fucking did, you lying little shit. You complete and utter shit. Holiday—yes, fine. But not with her. And not so close to Christmas *and* missing Ben's birthday. You didn't even call to wish your son a happy birthday.'

Paul—'What can I say? I'm sorry.'

Sarah—'Say sorry to Ben.'

Paul—'You're only angry because I went on holiday with Sarah.'

Sarah—'I'm disappointed.'

Paul—'If you attack me I will call the police.'

Sarah—'Sorry?'

Paul—'My solicitor has advised me that if you hit me or verbally abuse me I can call the police.'

Sarah—'Oh, really? Well, you're not worth wasting good energy on. Have you bought Ben a birthday present?'

Paul—'There was nothing in the Caribbean. And anyway, you probably spoiled him.'

Sarah—'Ben had a nice birthday. He got some nice presents. His friends had a lovely time. I've tried to organise as much as I can for Christmas. I suggest you collect Ben from nursery this afternoon. He will be pleased to see his daddy. Are you still planning to spend Christmas with us at home?'

Paul—'Yes, at the moment.'

Sarah—'There's no *at the moment* about it, Paul. You are or you aren't. If you aren't we will invite others round. If you aren't it will be your loss and also Ben's. I am more concerned about Ben. This is your choice.'

I look at Paul. Despite being tanned, he still looks a prat. I look at this man and the word 'pathetic' comes to mind. I feel pity for him more than anything. And I leave him to his thoughts and fantasies.

Twenty-third of December and Paul's gone Christmas shopping. With Sarah. To Redwater.

In the evening I call Jane.

'Hi, Sarah—what's up?'

Sarah—'Oh, the latest in the *Paul and the Two Sarahs Show.* Paul went shopping with Sarah for my Christmas present. They bought me a teapot. It wouldn't have been so bad if it had been a nice one. But it was an ugly earthenware thing. I know I'm very ungrateful, but I smashed it. It's on the doorstep.'

Jane—'That's for the best, Sarah. I don't think you should exchange any gifts with Paul this Christmas. Not the mood he's in. He sounds an emotional mess. You've got to try to keep it together for Ben's sake and for your own, and let Paul dig his own hole.'

Sarah—'I know. It's just—well, I used to have such lovely Christmases, and this is going to be tough.'

Jane—'And that's half the battle. Knowing it will be

and preparing for it. Don't drink anything. Just stay chilled and make it special for Ben. And yourself.'

Christmas Eve Paul stays out till midnight with *the boys*. Ben goes early to bed, if not to sleep.

I stay up till four, making a Lego castle, sprinkling fairy dust, filling the stocking, preparing the vegetables, making everything nice and happy.

Paul comes in at one a.m. Smiles a drunken smile, farts loudly, burps loudly and goes to bed.

Eight a.m. Ben up.

Ben—'Mummy, has he come? Has he come?'

Sarah—'Think so. Look—the stocking's full.'

Ben—'It's full, it's full! Where's Daddy? Can I show Daddy?'

Daddy is still in bed.

Sarah—'Daddy's still in bed, Ben. He had a very hard day at work yesterday.'

Ben—'But he'll miss my presents.'

Sarah—'You open your presents and I'll see if Daddy will wake up.'

I knock on the door of the guest bedroom. I almost feel it's enemy territory now. I hear a voice saying to come in. So I do. He's dressed, with a camcorder in his hand.

Paul—'Ready for the day? Happy Christmas, Sarah.'

I think, Go fuck yourself. And I know he's probably thinking the same.

Sarah says—'Happy Christmas, Paul.'

Paul —'Daddy wants to take some pictures of you, Ben.'

Ben smiles and runs up to Paul and hugs his calves—with a bear hug. His little arms just reach round one.

Ben—'Can I show you my presents?'

Paul—''Course you can, Ben. What did Santa bring you?'

I think, *You don't know what Santa brought your son be-cause you didn't buy any of it.*

Ben takes two hours to open his stocking presents. Then I get him dressed and we go downstairs to the tree, where ninety per cent of the presents are his anyway.

Paul—whispering—'I haven't bought you anything because you're going to get all my money anyway in the settlement, you greedy bitch.'

I hand him a parcel with the framed poem and a lit-tle present from Ben. A Gant ski hat.

Paul opens both. Puts on the hat, hugs Ben. Then reads the poem in silence. And then suddenly goes up-stairs for fifteen minutes. I think I can hear sobbing. I leave him alone and play trains with Ben.

Lunch is at two. All Ben's presents are finally open. Our plates are full to bursting. I break my no alcohol rule. After all, it's Christmas Day.

Three glasses of champagne. Three glasses too many. I break down in tears over the Brussels sprouts. I'm half laughing and half crying because I look at the sprouts and remember what Pierce said about how small her mouth was and I keep visualising Sarah—*the other Sarah*—having difficulty getting them through her lips.

But the pain of the past months overwhelms me. I get in the car and drive. Drive to Southend on Christmas Day. By the time I arrive at the pier I've run out of petrol and run out of tears and am emotionally exhausted.

I can hear my mobile going off but I don't answer. When I finally reach the sea I stop and answer the call.

Paul—'Where are you, Sarah?'

Sarah—'I'm in Southend. I'm fine. I just want to be alone for a while. You spend time with Ben. I'll be back some time this evening. In a few hours.'

Paul—'I was worried about you. You've been drinking.'

Sarah—'I'm fine. Just upset. You have fun with Ben. Bye.'

I call Kim on the mobile.

Sarah—'Hi, Kim, just calling to see how you are on this happy Christmas Day.'

Kim—'Yes, not happy for either of us, is it? But the next one will be better for both of us. I know that. Where are you?'

Sarah—'Southend, looking at the sea. Listening to the sound of the sea. And feeling alone. But calm. Think it was the champagne. Only three glasses, but I started to cry and then couldn't stay in the same house as him anymore. I'm the one who needs space now.'

Kim—'I always go to the sea when I'm feeling stressed. That's probably where you're meant to be.'

Sarah—'I would like Ben to be here with me, but at least it gives Paul some time with him by himself. I feel very lonely. But I felt very lonely when I was *with* Paul, even before all this started.'

Kim—'You were. You're just more aware of it now. Take care of yourself, Sarah.'

Sarah—'You, too. Love you.'

Kim—'Love you, too.'

I call Jane and Samantha, and wish them well. And they wish me well. And somehow I don't feel so alone anymore.

I don't want to spend New Year with Paul. So I spend it with Ben in a cosy hotel in Surrey called Pennyhill Park.

Large Victorian house, with four-poster beds and real fires in each room. Staff who remember you and call

you by your first name—without prompting. There
will be just the two of us on New Year's Eve. Paul says
he would rather be with Sarah than us. And I think, hey,
if that's the way he feels then that is best. I don't know
what he is doing or where he is. There are a lot of other
families there, some single-parent, some with both parents and grandparents, and Ben has lots of children to
run from and after.

At midnight I get a dozen text messages. *Happy New
Years* from Kim, Jane, Samantha, Simon, Gemma, Mum,
Pierce, my cousins and a few workmates. Even one from
Jeremy the barrister. Paul doesn't call or text when the
clock strikes midnight.

I text Paul.

Happy New Year. Ben sends his love.

JANUARY

The future looks French

Paul is moving out tomorrow.

I have mixed feelings. Part of me thinks, *Hoo-fucking-ray*—because the atmosphere is starting to make the house feel miserable—as though our anger is rebounding off the walls around us. And I want to brighten the place. And a part of me is sad. Because I feel—I know—Paul won't be coming back.

I think it's pressure from Sarah. Or perhaps it's a good idea after my impromptu Christmas Day trip to the seaside.

Whatever the reason, I'm quietly relieved.

Rather than move to live with Sarah, he's moving in with his parents, to be close to Ben, but I think it's more to do with the fact that Sarah, for some reason, won't live with him and he wants to be with his mummy. Could be wrong. Perhaps Sarah knows about the farting.

The day he leaves the house, his father and brothers take out his furniture. I make them tea and toast. Without the use of a teapot.

As most of his furniture fills the house, and most of mine is in the attic, the house now looks pretty empty.

And I love it. I never liked his reproduction antique furniture. Nor the watercolour paintings of ships going in and out of harbour. Nor the black and white line drawings and architectural prints of obscure buildings. I bring all my stuff out of the loft and spread it about. Admittedly not much. But it softens the place. Ben is only upset when he notices Paul taking away the television in our bedroom.

Ben—tearful—'Don't take the TV away, Daddy.'

Paul—tearful—'Daddy's going away.'

Ben—'That's fine. But don't take the TV away.'

I phone Gemma to keep her updated on the latest.

'Hi, Gemma. Paul's packed and gone.'

Gemma—'Good. That's good for you.'

Sarah—'Thankfully he's left the main TV and the DVD player, some chairs and one table, and he took his clothes, which is rather good, really, because I'm now able to spread my clothes out for the first time and do a really good rummage. Chuck out the old stuff—stuff that wasn't me anymore. Not that I know who me is anymore. But I feel so relieved he's left, and I think Ben does, too. I feel for the first time in months that I'm able to leave the confines of my study and walk about the house, let the walls ring again with laughter and games. And make noise. And run about the garden naked with Ben—albeit not on the days the gardener is here.'

Gemma—'Are you going to stay in the house?'

Sarah—'Not for long. Too many bad memories. I'm staying here for now. I would really like to keep the house in France as well. We will see.'

Gemma—'Where are you thinking of moving to?'

Sarah—'Possibly Richmond. It's very expensive, but has all the qualities I need and Ben needs now. A wonderful park, a green, cinema, theatres, the river, easy access in and out of London and to the airports, good schools, and it's safe and has good shops. Perfect. I'll probably rent for six months and get to know the area, rather than have some estate agent seduce me into buying a place which is too large or too small or totally unsuitable. And that phrase *with potential*. Which translates as having possible subsidence or at least another £100,000 of work on top of the asking price. That sort of thing.'

Gemma—'And you need to be central for work.'

Sarah—'And not too far for Paul to see his son. So, I need to know—when am I allowed to put *the marital home* up for sale?'

Gemma—'You can't do that yet, Sarah. You don't know if it's yours yet.'

Sarah—'When will I know?'

Gemma—'You've got to wait till next month. Then you can put it up for sale. Otherwise you'll antagonise Paul unnecessarily.'

Sarah—'He's done his fair share of antagonising me unnecessarily, Gemma.'

Gemma—'That's his problem, Sarah. Not yours.'

Sarah—'Okay, then. And how about the house in France?'

Gemma—'We've got to speak to Jeremy about that. We're having a meeting with him next week and will see what he says. He now has all Paul's files. What's the house like?'

Sarah—'It's two buildings, actually. On two acres of land, in a little hamlet near a "*plus jolie ville de France*" in the South of France. It's a former convent, looking down over a valley. There's a gite as well. Paul and I fell in love with it the minute we saw it. The pool is being built, but nothing else has been done. Everything has been put on hold since the divorce petition. Paul doesn't want to spend any more on it in case he doesn't get it. I want it and he wants it. But I need to make sure how much I want it so I've booked flights to take Ben to see it next week. It may be the last time I ever see it, but I want to take one last look.'

Gemma—'Tell Paul you want to go there and see what he says.'

Sarah—'I've already asked. He says he doesn't mind me going. And that even when it's no longer mine I can still come to visit.'

Gemma—'Fine. Go.'

So the following week I find myself and Ben at seven a.m. at Stansted Airport.

Ben is excited about going on a plane. We wait at the terminal. Ben plays with my phone, which is one of the whizzy camera ones, and takes about twenty photos of other passengers—most of whom look as though they've been hit by the ugly stick. And more of me and him, and me and the chair, and the carpet, and a few of the ceiling, and his teddy. He's happy. I phone Jane.

Jane—'Hi, Sarah—where are you?'

Sarah—'Off to France. Where are you?'

Jane—'In the States. New York with my sister. Spending loads of money. Why are you going to France?'

Sarah—'To check out the house and see how much I want it, and how hard I'm prepared to fight for it. Maybe this is the last time I will see it.'

Jane—'See what happens. Never know. You may get it. Fingers crossed.'

Sarah—'I hope so. The house doesn't have any furniture, so I can make my mark on it rather than just accept or change everything Paul has chosen.'

The flight is short and painless, and Ben sleeps most of the way. The hire car is large, and Ben likes it because it has more space than the GTi. The French drivers are forgiving. Perhaps because some of them don't seem to mind which side of the road they drive on either.

The journey is mile upon mile of narrow country road. Each corner reveals another fabulous landscape of fortified villages on hilltops—which always look more beautiful from a distance than close up. The most beautiful of all of these is Najac.

I'm enchanted by this little village. As I drive into the square I recognise all the locals. It's like a scene from a musical set, where the locals all come together at once as if to do a song and dance number centre stage. Everyone knows everyone else's name and seems to be content with their lot. Most of the locals remember me, as I made it my mission when we bought the house to introduce myself to everyone—making sure they weren't hostile to English neighbours. I get *bonjours* and hugs from the chemist, baker and grocer, and flirtatious whistles from the waiters in the restaurants.

Najac's crowing glory is its castle. A wonderful castle on top of a hill, which Ben loves to run to through the narrow cobbled streets, up to where the views are spectacular.

In the evening we visit the local restaurant serving rabbit and *foie gras* and *cassoulet* and river trout.

Ben practises his three French sentences on François, the owner.

'*Comment ça va?*' How are you?

'*Je m'appelle Ben.*' My name is Ben.

'*La vache est brun.*' The cow is brown.

François—'Ah, Monsieur Ben. *C'est tres bien.* You are verrry clevar.'

Ben grins. He realises these are all phrases of vital importance in making new friends in a rural community.

Thankfully my A level French is helping me to understand and be understood by Monsieur Gascon, who is handling the plumbing and bathrooms, Monsieur Bizou, who is the gardener, and Monsieur Vincent, who is managing them all and making sure they turn up the week they say they will and not one month later.

Monsieur Vincent—'It is verrry difficult, Sarah. Zeeze men verrrry good craftsmen, but they do not always understand me.'

Sarah—'I understand. I will talk to them. But we don't know yet who is getting the house. Unfortunately Monsieur Paul and I are divorcing, and the house may go to him or may go to me. But we both want you to continue the work, whatever happens.'

Monsieur Vincent—'Ahhhh, no. That is verrrry sad. And the poor little boy.'

Sarah—'He is fine. He knows that his mummy and daddy both love him very much and he will always be able to come and play here with his friends. That's why we want you to continue the work.'

Monsieur Vincent—'*Pas de probleme. Pas de probleme.* Will the monay still be in the *banque?*'

Sarah—'Yes, it will still be in the bank. No problem. The house and garden look wonderful. When should it be completed?'

Monsieur Vincent—'I am tould by July. *Juillet.* Yes, July.'

Sarah—'That's fine. Summer here—hopefully with Ben. That's fine.'

Ben and I stay at the house for three days. Walking into each room, rubbing our fingers along the tall stone walls, laughing very loudly and playing chase and hide 'n seek. Relaxing completely, taking long walks in the surrounding hills, and breathing in the clean air. Whoever described the countryside as 'quiet' has obviously not lived near Najac. At night a combination of voracious bonking frogs and screeching ducks echo into the early hours, and the church clock chimes at dawn. Bliss, but not quiet bliss.

I feel quite pagan and want to mark my territory, so pee in the grounds surrounding both houses and get Ben to do it as well. He thinks this is hilarious, and asks if we can do it around our house in England. I say yes, if he likes. But only in the back garden.

I pay Monsieurs Vincent, Gascon and Bizou their *monay,* and visit the nearby town of Villefranche to choose lights and get more ideas about furniture and colour schemes. Ben and I go to the local cinema and watch *Shrek* in French.

I meet some of the neighbours. One of whom is a farmer and says he's happy to provide us with free-range eggs and homemade bread if Ben is happy to walk his dog when we are there. Ben needs little encouragement to walk a large Labrador puppy with big brown eyes, floppy ears and a penchant for chocolate.

Last night here, we lie on the grass and watch the stars and the bats dance in the sky. And I decide the house is worth fighting for. I know I'm happy here because in three days I've managed to put on weight, feel healthier and a little stronger and more positive about life. And I haven't thought about the court case or Paul or Sarah at all. And Ben's grinning from ear to ear.

Returning to *the marital home,* as Gemma and Felicity now always refer to it, makes me realise how much I like the French house by comparison.

The house in France, with its stone walls and large windows, is always filled with light. Even on a grey Jan-

uary day. I can sit on the toilet and look out over mead-
ows and brown cows. It's an inspiring house and a house
to be inspired in. Even when sitting on the loo.

The marital home, by contrast, has a view of a busy
road—though admittedly the view from the back is
lovely. A long, lovely garden with vagina-shaped bushes.
Makes me think of Simon. Perhaps I can get Monsieur
Bizou to have a go at the bushes in the French garden
once I know if it's ours or not. I've grown rather fond
of those bushes.

WINTER INTO SPRING

FEBRUARY

Moving on

Phone call to Jane.

Sarah—'Jane, I've just received a huge legal bill from Wearing, Shindley and Strutt. Hopefully they are worth it. Paul is paying, but this divorce business is very expensive. No wonder he wanted to do it without solicitors.'

Jane—'Sarah, he didn't want solicitors involved because he didn't want to give you as much as he is going to have to give you.'

Sarah—'The court case is being heard next month. I'm meeting the barrister again this week, to decide what we're going for and what we're not. Want to know where I'm going and move on from this.'

Jane—'You will. I managed to do it. I've managed to move on and meet a lovely man, who is kind, with a very big willy and an enormous sex drive. Not that that's important to me, of course.'

Sarah—'Of course.'

Jane—'He's divorced and has three wonderful children. His ex-wife is a bit odd.'

Sarah—'Careful, Jane—I'm the *odd ex-wife* as far as Sarah is concerned.'

Jane—'Then don't be odd. Be nice. Be so fucking nice she won't know what's what.'

Sarah—'I will. But can't stomach it at the moment. Just came back from France.'

Jane—'How did it go? What was the house like?'

Sarah—'Fabulous. Wonderful. Hope I get it.'

Jane—'Well, we're thinking of buying a house in France. So you *must* get yours.'

Sarah—'We could be neighbours, eh? If I get it. Wish me luck.'

Jane—'Good luck, girl. You'll be fine.'

I must phone Kim and find out how she's doing. I call her mobile.

Sarah—'Kim, it's me. How are you?'

Kim—'Hi, Sarah, I'm fine. Well, not fine, but okay. Coming to terms with everything—and we're going to try again. Jamie has been very supportive. So I think it will all work out. But these things happen for a reason, and it's made us think about our relationship and what's important and what isn't.'

Sarah—'I know. But having children isn't a panacea. It doesn't save a marriage or make one. It's about you and Jamie and that's it. The fact you want a kid and he wants a kid is fine. But it's not everything. I've got a friend who was on IVF. Tried it many times. She was an infant school teacher and it must have killed her every morning, going in and working with children—especially of that age. She was a changed woman when she finally became pregnant, and it was nothing to do with the IVF. She gave up work. She just chilled. You give up work and *click*—you'll be pregnant again in no time.'

Kim—'I know. It stresses me out. I need to use the old grey cells but I'm thirty-eight now, so no spring chicken.'

Sarah—'But you're a fit thirty-eight. A fit thirty-eight is different from an unfit one.'

Kim—'Fertility reduces by some fifty per cent, I think, after thirty-five.'

Sarah—'So have fun trying.'

Kim—'I will. How are you?'

Sarah—'Fine. Busy. Court case next month. Meeting dishy barrister this week. Finding out what I will get and what I won't. Think I need a new car. I've had the green Golf for five years. Paul bought it for me when I wrote off his Lotus and he refused to let me drive his new one.'

Kim—'Which is understandable.'

Sarah—'Totally.'

Jane—'But you want a new start. New house, new life, new man—hopefully—and new car.'

Sarah—'Correct. So I'm going to the garage nearby to look at the new Mini Cooper S. Fancy a yellow one with a white top, so I can call it Buttercup or Daisy or something. Or something light blue, perhaps, so I can call it Bluebell.'

Jane—'Sounds just right for you, Sarah. Go for it, girl. Got to dash. Bye.'

I drive to the car showroom after dropping Ben at nursery.

Man, five foot nine, with dubious blond hair, big grin and shiny eyes approaches me, like a lion stalking his prey. His name-tag says he calls himself Steve Smith.

Steve Smith—'Good morning, madam. Are you looking for a car? A Mini Cooper S, perhaps? You look very Mini Cooper S-esque, if I may say so. I think a subtle blue or roaring red one would suit you well. Something a little racy, perhaps? Racing green, even?'

I think, Steve is wasted here. He should work in a designer boutique in the West End.

Sarah says—'Really? Do I? Hope that's good. Anyway—yes, good guess.'

Steve—'My name's Steve.'

Sarah—'Then you can call me Sarah, Steve. I haven't been a madam in a long time.'

He smiles. Loosens up a bit.

Steve—'I will—Sarah. Would you like to have a closer look at the car?'

Sarah—'Yes—test drive, please.'

Steve—'Okay, follow me.'

He shows me to a metallic blue Mini Cooper S, gives me the keys, and I settle into the driving seat.

Steve—'Drive where you want to, then. This car, may I say, is a great little mover. Moves really well. Nice and tight. Really tight. Feel that clutch. Feel it, Sarah. Very, very good to handle. But fast and sexy. Good shape. Your hand feels natural on it. You've got to give it just the right pressure.'

I think—Is this man for real?

Sarah—'That's good. I want a fast and sexy car.'

I start the car. It stalls. I try again. It stalls again. I feel stupid.

Sarah—'That was me, not the car.'

Steve—'I know. Keep the touch gentle. The clutch control is very sensitive.'

Third time. Please fuck be lucky.

Yessssss. It goes.

Steve—'Great. Now, where do you want to go?'

Sarah—'Oh, along leafy lanes, motorways, dual carriageways—see what it can do. That sort of thing.'

Steve—'Sounds good to me.'

We drive in silence for two minutes. From the corner of my eye I can see his eye is on my knee, not on the road. But I say and do nothing. I love the car. Then:

Steve—'So what's your story? Why a new car?'

Sarah—'I want a new start. New life. I'm getting divorced. Want a change.'

Steve—'Silly man. Why is he divorcing you?'

Sarah—'Found a new model.'

Steve—'What? Why swap for a Fiat when you have a Ferrari?'

Sarah—'Because he couldn't handle the Ferrari and thinks he can the Fiat.'

Steve—'Give me a Ferrari any day. You're definitely a Ferrari girl.'

Sarah—'Alas, I'll have to be content with being a Mini Cooper S girl, which is all I can afford. If you can convince me I should buy one.'

Steve—'You should. You would look lovely in anything you drove.'

I think, Where does this guy get his lines?

Sarah says—'You're good for the confidence.'

Steve—'That's my job. And I sell cars.'

Sarah—'Does that help you sell cars?'

Steve—'Only with lovely soon-to-be divorcées.'

Sarah—'Well, this one's different. Have to try harder than that.'

Steve—'We're giving a two grand discount if you order one this month.'

Sarah—'Better.'

Steve—'Interested in seeing my package?'

Sarah—'Could be.'

Methinks the wonderful thing about talking to salesmen is that they are professional flirts. And therefore completely harmless. They are good at it, and know when to back off. They are not compulsive, but it comes naturally to them. They can turn it on and off like a tap. They know exactly when the line is crossed and how far to go with each customer. It's fascinating to watch. It's their job. You know it. They know it. So communication is great, and if they're lucky they can sell a car in the process and make a commission. And if they're *really* lucky they get laid.

But, looking at Steve, I think, Hey, not today. Want to have fun, but not today. Still not completely over Paul yet for some reason. Not out the other side emotionally.

Perhaps in a month or two months' time I'll be game for a little more with a car salesman. But then again, noticing the tattoo of a dragon on Steve's right arm, per-haps not.

MARCH

Drawing battle lines

I have a meeting with Felicity, Gemma and Jeremy. I'm meeting them at Jeremy's chambers. At nine a.m. prompt. I'm at the offices half an hour early.

We sit in a cold white waiting room.

Jeremy walks in. Smiles and sits.

Jeremy—'Right, I've had a look at your files. And his counsel has sent us Paul's financial statement for the year. Very interesting. He has had a large bonus this year. In excess of £800,000. This means I think you will definitely get the house in Chelmsford. And perhaps even the house in France.'

Felicity—'I don't think Sarah will get that.'

Jeremy—'Well, if the numbers are right, he has over two million in the bank—and five hundred of that is in cash. Doesn't like to take risks this man, does he?'

Sarah—'Very careful with money always.'

He reads more of the file while I sit in silence. Then:

Jeremy—'According to the numbers, you could get both houses. We will try for you. Are you attached to that house in France?'

Sarah—'More than to the one in England.'

Jeremy—'Would you keep it?'

Sarah—'Yes.'

Jeremy—'Okay, then. We go for both houses.'

There is ten minutes of calculation and strategy about maintenance between Jeremy, Gemma and Felicity— what we will and will not be prepared to accept—then Jeremy turns to me.

Jeremy—'Sarah, first thing to remember—this is a game. Your husband plays this game for a living. You don't. That's why we are here for you. Listen to what we say and what we think you should accept as settlement and it will be over quickly. Become too emotional about material possessions and money and it won't. With regard to the items in the house, don't waste money—his or potentially yours—fighting over antique fish knives or a yellow chair. Court history is full of stories about tens of thousands of pounds spent fighting over something of sentimental value, and in the end the victory is a hollow one—only we, the lawyers and barristers, win. Neither party wins, though one may think they have. So listen to what we say and you'll be fine.'

That night I don't sleep. I sleep with Ben in my bed and cuddle up to him. And I feel for the first time that I'm cuddling up to him because part of Paul is in Ben and I want to hug Paul, too. Tonight I want to hug him and tell him it's going to be all right. Because I know this is horrible for him, too. And he has everything to lose. And he may have only just realised this now.

At six a.m., I'm tired of not being tired and get up, take a shower and get dressed. Something simple and black.

I feel as though I'm going to a funeral. And perhaps in a way I am.

I tidy the house a few times. Not that there is much furniture to tidy now. When we moved here it was so busy and bright and needed so much work done to it. We had fun doing it. Laughing at our mistakes and hiring and firing builders and decorators who wouldn't turn up when they promised. I remember gutting the kitchen. Paul hired a sledgehammer and knocked down the wall and almost killed himself. I had hugged him and we kissed in the dust, surrounded by rubble.

And how we laughed at the highly patterned carpet in all the rooms. And I remember the housewarming, and how everyone enjoyed themselves. And the happy moments. And the laughs. And how we slept in each room as we decorated each in turn. And how the main bedroom and our bed moved from room to room, until the last was done and Ben was born. How the kitchen saw so many highs and lows. So many tears and so much laughter. And so much happiness and genuine love. And I mourn the memories. All of them. The good and the bad and the ugly. I mourn silently.

My mobile buzzes with three messages.

Message received:
Hi, its Kim. Good luck today. Be strong girl. Love you.
x
Message received:
Good luck Sarah. Remember Paul's feeling it too. You have everything to win, he has everything to lose.
Jane. X

Message received:
Thinking of you Sarah. You'll be fine. So will Paul.
Samantha. X

Nine-thirty a.m. Outside Charter Lane Courts, Central London. Gemma, Felicity and Jeremy are there waiting for me. They smile and we walk in together.

I see Paul. He looks grey, overweight and tired. He is by himself. I look at him. He looks at me. Neither of us know if we are meant to smile at each other at this stage. So we both half smile.

Gemma—nodding to Paul—'It that him?'

Sarah—'Yes, that's Paul. That's my husband.'

Gemma—'He looks older than his years. Thirty-six, you say?'

Sarah—'Yes, he does look older. But I think I do as well.'

Gemma—'Not as old as him. He looks about forty-six.' Then looking at me. 'You still love him, don't you? Can tell by the way you look at him.'

Sarah—'Everyone tells me he's done me a favour, but I just feel very sad. And, yes, I think I do love him still. And I need to love him for Ben, really. So that we can bring up our son believing that he came from love. Although he will never remember us together.'

We enter the courtroom. A very bland room, with a central desk slightly higher than the surrounding desks, and a very gruff-looking judge, about fifty, looking sternly at everyone. As though he doesn't want to be there.

Paul arrives with his female counsel, Andrea Smart. Suited, roman-nosed (do all barristers have roman noses?), and blonde. Looks stern, like a schoolmarm. Jeremy sits in front of us.

Gemma—'Sarah, you don't say anything. The barristers talk.'

For five minutes Andrea gives Paul's side of the story. And offers the house in England with small maintenance.

For five minutes Jeremy gives my side of the story, saying I am entitled to both the English marital home and the French house and much bigger maintenance.

The judge speaks.

Judge—'I've heard both sides and I think the husband is being more than fair by offering the marital home.'

Methinks, So do I, but I would rather live in the French house with Ben than the English one.

Jeremy stands and starts detailing a case which, from what I gather, resulted in the wife getting half.

Judge scowls at Jeremy.

Judge—'I know the case, and it isn't relevant here.'

Gemma—whispers—'It's important we try to resolve financial issues now. Otherwise we have to wait another six months to go to the High Court. Financially this may cripple Paul—although it ultimately comes out of the pot for you and Ben—emotionally another six months of uncertainty could be very stressful to both of you.'

I think, Another six months of not knowing what is happening, whether I can settle in a familiar home in Chelsmford or France, or need to start a new life for myself somewhere strange and new. That sounds horrible. Paul can't want that either.

Sarah—'We must try to resolve this now. I don't want another six months of this. And neither will Paul.'

The judge speaks again.

Judge—'I suggest you go away and see if you can agree. But I think the husband offering the marital home and maintenance is more than fair.'

I can feel Paul smiling. I don't look. I just go to the

little room we've been assigned and sit down and look at my counsel.

Felicity —'The judge is wrong, of course.'

Gemma—'Unfortunately, he's the judge, and the opposing counsel will be spurred on by his comments. As will Paul.'

Jeremy—'But he's wrong. I suggest we wait to see what they offer. If Paul behaves like most banker husbands in this situation he will want closure as soon as possible. We will wait for him to up the offer. I will speak to his counsel.'

Gemma—'Do you know Andrea?'

Jeremy—'Yes, I have worked against her before.'

Gemma—'What's she like?'

Jeremy—'She's a litigator.'

Gemma—'So she knows her stuff?'

Sarah—'Is that bad or good?'

Gemma—'Good, because she won't waste her client's money or time. She knows what is a good deal to strike.'

Jeremy leaves the room. We wait. Drink tea and coffee. Everyone is thinking hard so no one talks.

Jeremy returns after five minutes.

Jeremy—'They won't budge on anything. They have been bolstered by what the judge has said, which is understandable. I recommend we stand firm.'

Sarah—'I agree.'

I'm thinking about the house in France. About the views. And about how Ben could run about the rooms with his friends and how it could ring with laughter. I think about that and I don't want to let it go. And I think about Sarah, *the new Sarah,* being the new lady of the house. And I get angry, then realise it's just jealousy. Then realise it's not. I want to keep it. It's not her being with Paul. It's her having my house. Fuck that. I want my house in France. So I say it again.

Sarah—'I agree.'

Jeremy looks at me and smiles.

Jeremy—'You like that house, don't you? As I mentioned before, I have a house in France, not far from Toulouse. So I can understand why you love the area.'

Sarah—'Yes, well. It is special.'

Knock on the door. Andrea Smart asks to speak to Jeremy.

Gemma—whispers to me—'This is a good sign.'

Sarah—whispers back—'Why is it?'

Gemma—'They are now ready and willing to negotiate. Paul wants closure. Think Jeremy was right about that.'

More tea. More coffee. Small-talk to distract ourselves.

Felicity—'Has anyone seen the film version of *Chicago?*'

Sarah—'With Catherine Zeta-Jones?'

Felicity—'Yes. Was prepared not to like her, but she really is very good.'

Sarah—'Haven't seen it, but would love to go.'

Felicity—'Good film.'

Sarah—'Have you seen *The Matrix?*'

Felicity—'No. What's that about?'

Sarah—'Reality not being real, and we're being run by machines.'

Felicity—'Sounds like a documentary to me.'

Gemma—'What are you doing at the moment job-wise, Sarah?'

Sarah—'Interviewing celebrities about their travels. And travelling—but obviously not as much, because of the situation.'

Gemma—'Who have you interviewed?'

Sarah—'Loads of people. Most interesting for various reasons was Lord Linley. He was very sexy. Didn't keep his eyes off my eyes. Even when I stuck the microphone up his nose by accident.'

Jeremy returns just as I'm warming to my subject. Big smile on his face.

Jeremy—'You've got the French house.'

I feel relief. In spite of the fact there's still so much more work to do on the house I am thrilled, and he can see it in my face.

Jeremy—'You are pleased. I can see. This is a different Sarah now.'

Gemma is smiling, too. Somehow I feel this team are rooting for me. Even the formidable Felicity manages a warm smile, as if to say, I'm happy for you, Sarah.

Jeremy—'He wants your endowment policy. And he has prepared a list of chattels he wants.'

Sarah—'Oh, he can have that. Chattels—what's that in layman's terms?'

Jeremy—'Furniture—stuff in the house.'

Sarah—'Hah! He's taken most of that.'

Jeremy—'Well, I have the list here. But first we have to sort out maintenance.'

Sarah—'Oh, don't worry about that. I can work.'

Jeremy—'You will take some time to get back to work, and what with looking after Ben you will never be able to earn as much as you could without him.'

Sarah—'So what do you think I should ask for?'

Jeremy—'You've already drawn up your monthly outgoings. It's likely he will want to separate your maintenance from Ben's maintenance. That way, should he fight for custody at a later stage, it's much more clear-cut. And it sounds, from what I've seen and heard of him so far, that this is what he'll do. The question is, do we accept their offer so far or go for more?'

Sarah—'Well, I…'

Jeremy—'Sorry, that was purely rhetorical.' Smiles. 'I recommend we go for more. Now, look through the chattels and see if there's anything you disagree with.'

I look at the list. Paul has typed and ticked everything he wants to keep. He's already taken most of the furniture from the house, but he's now also ticked most of the things that were our wedding presents. They were mostly from his friends, and as mine weren't invited it seems churlish to say I want them. So I'm content. He's asked for the yellow chair and the fish knives. I like both, but think of what Jeremy said yesterday.

Sarah—'All okay—apart from the microwave and the large TV. Think he can buy his own. He's asked for all the wedding presents. He can have those.'

Another knock on the door. Andrea again.

Jeremy—'They want to know if we're happy. Round two. Ding-ding.'

Jeremy leaves. We resort to more tea. More coffee. Rich Tea biscuits. More of what at any other time would seem like normal girl-talk.

Felicity—'So the affair you had before you got married? Out of interest, are you still in touch with the guy?'

Sarah—'No. Think I broke his heart—or his ego or something. I was totally smitten at the time. If I saw him now, don't know if I'd feel the same way. Don't want to spoil the memory and meet him and think, Yuck.'

Felicity—'Understandable. Though equally you may still like him.'

Sarah—'Possibly, but I don't want to go there. And I don't think he would want to speak to me.'

Felicity—'Have you tried to call him?'

Sarah—'Yes, and that's what his PA said. So actually I know.'

Gemma—'How about the journalist in Australia?'

Sarah—'He knows the situation. And he wants to meet up, in fact. But I don't think it's right at the moment.'

Gemma—'No, you're right. Focus should be on Ben. Though you have a life as well…'

Sarah—'I know. I'm gradually getting one back.'

Gemma—'Sounds as though you are starting to move on emotionally.'

Sarah—'Well, yes. Sometimes I think I am, and sometimes not. I used to cry every day, which was exhausting as well as boring. Then I would cry about once a week. Now it's about once every two weeks, and it will be less as the months go on, I know. It's not just people telling me it will be better with time; now I'm realising it, too.'

Gemma—'It's interesting how Paul found out about your affair. Reading the e-mail. So many of our clients now are getting found out because of e-mail or text messaging.'

Felicity—'I would say about fifty per cent of our business now results from infidelities discovered in this way. Business is good. Mind you, September 11th added plenty. So many men deciding that life's too short and looking at their wives and going, *Yuck, I want out.* Women, too. Looking at their men and going, *Yuck, I want out.*'

I visualise men and women all over the world waking up simultaneously to their spouses and looking at them and in one synchronised phrase all going *Yuck.* Very odd, but maybe it happens like that. Just like babies all being born at the same time.

Sarah—'I find that thought kind of comforting. I somehow don't feel so alone any more. So, how many people get divorced every year? What are the statistics?'

Felicity—'We have an increase year on year.'

Sarah—'What's the busiest time?'

Felicity—'Usually after Christmas. Everyone tries very hard for the family—bit like you did, Sarah—then the realisation hits that they can't make it work, and then they come to us.'

Sarah—'Very sad.'

Gemma—'It is. I have a boyfriend who wants to get married, but I think my view has changed on marriage.'

Sarah—'Do you love him?'

Gemma—'Yes—but the sex isn't great.'

Sarah—'That's only part of a relationship. But when you don't have any it becomes all of it.'

Gemma—'Yeah. And he's small and—well, I like big. They say size doesn't matter, but, as most women know, it does.'

It strikes me that this is a very unusual conversation. Are they chatting like this to take my mind off matters at hand? Or is this what they usually talk about? Whatever, this is a very unusual day for me. I try just to take it in my stride.

Sarah—'Paul is quite small. But I think width is more important than length. And some men are wider at the top than they are at the bottom, and that's better than the other way round. It allows deeper penetration and you feel more.'

Gemma—'Really? I must have a good look at my boyfriend next time we have sex.'

Sarah—'And they've got to wiggle it about in the right way.'

Gemma—'What way is that?'

Sarah—'You know—like a belly dancer.'

I get up and sway my hips.

Sarah—'Don't know if I'm doing it quite right, but I read it in a magazine somewhere and told the journalist I had an affair with about it. He was quite large anyway, but when he did this it was amazing. And—well, try it when you get home.'

Gemma—'I will. How does it go again?'

Gemma gets up and has a go at copying me until she's satisfied she's got the technique right.

Gemma—'Okay, I'll try it tonight.'

Sarah—'Plus, I'm told if men take zinc penis size increases.'

Gemma—'Really?' Pause.'Where can you buy zinc?'

Sarah—'Any good health shop.'

Gemma—'Thanks.'

Sarah—'Anyway, are you going to marry him?'

Gemma—'Nope, I think living in sin is better.'

Felicity—'Not financially. Better for the woman if she is married. Get nothing for common law marriage.'

Sarah—'Do people know that?'

Felicity—'I want to write a book entitled *You Won't Get Half* for every woman, and another for every man— *Don't Screw Around*. Would save a lot of heartache.'

Sarah—'Perhaps I can ghost-write it?'

Felicity—'Okay. Perhaps we should talk after all this has finished.'

Jeremy returns. Almost forgot about him. Almost forgot where I was. Hope he doesn't ask what we've been talking about…

Jeremy—'Right, then. He's agreed to everything, Sarah. You give up your endowment and you get both houses and £3000 in maintenance net a month. Not bad. Not half—I'd say about thirty per cent of his net worth—but not bad. And it's a good thing it's over as quickly as it is. Saves on more legal fees, which is all money that could be going to Ben for his future and education. So good all round.'

Sarah—'Really? Has this been a good case?'

Gemma—'Nearing a model one, Sarah. If all clients behaved this reasonably it would always go well. It's bad when you have clients who have unrealistic expectations and want to fight for—well, the yellow chair.'

Sarah—to Felicity—'Perhaps you should write a book called *The Yellow Chair?*''

Felicity—'Indeed. Maybe next year.'

Jeremy—looking slightly puzzled—'So, are you pleased, Sarah?'

Sarah—'I'm not *pleased*. I feel *relief*—that one part is over. But I feel I've so much more to go through. *Pleased* isn't the word. I feel emotionally exhausted, more than anything else. And a sense of loss. I've lost my family. This was never about money for me, so in a way this bit was the easy bit for me. I had nothing to lose and everything to gain, really. As he told me all those months ago, it's *his* money and *his* house. And that's how I felt about it, too. Now I've got two houses I feel were never mine in the first place. And money that was never mine to spend. My focus is more to do with preserving a home for Ben and me. The house in Chelmsford I will sell, because if I stay the happy memories will haunt me more than the sad ones.'

Jeremy—'Mmm. With reference to seeing Ben, are you happy to deal with this between yourselves? Custody of a child is always a difficult issue.'

Sarah—'Yes. I know Paul should see as much of Ben as he is able. I think that would be good for Ben. Not for me, as I don't want to see Paul, and I think the healing process will be better if we don't see each other for some time. But as far as Ben is concerned it's good he sees his daddy.'

Jeremy—'I agree. And the fact he is probably going to make lots of money is also a good thing. For Ben and for you.'

We walk back to the offices of Wearing, Shindley and Strutt. I hug Felicity and Gemma and shake hands with Jeremy.

Sarah—'Thank you. Thank you very much.'

Then for some inexplicable reason I burst into tears.

Sarah—'This isn't supposed to happen. I've just walked away with two houses and good maintenance and my son. I shouldn't be in tears.'

Felicity—'You should. It's relief—and you still love him. You've lost your family and this is a complete change of life for you. But you will be fine. Why don't you call a friend?'

They leave me in the room I was led to the first time I came to Wearing, Shindley and Strutt. It seems only yesterday I trundled in here with my boxes of papers, meeting Felicity and Gemma for the first time.

I call Jane.

Sarah—'Hi, Jane. Well—it's done.'

Jane—'How'd it go? I expect you have mixed feelings.'

Sarah—'I do. I still love him, Jane.'

Jane—'I know you do, but you will be fine. This is a big step towards moving on.'

Sarah—'I know it is. I know it is.'

Jane—'And you *will* be fine. And you have little Ben, who is wonderful.'

Sarah—'I know…'

Jane—'And Paul will be fine. He's full of anger at the moment, but he will be fine.'

Sarah—'I know. I want to call him.'

Jane—'Why don't you, then? That's a good idea.'

Sarah—'Do you think he will listen—or curse me?'

Jane—'Call him. He's probably feeling as wretched as you. But remember he's lost everything.'

Sarah—'Okay.'

So I call. Mobile. He answers.

Paul—'Hello?'

Sarah—'Hello, Paul. It's Sarah.' Pause. 'It was horrible today, wasn't it?'

Paul—'Yes.'

Sarah—Bigger pause—'I just wanted to call you to tell you that I still love you, but you broke my heart, Paul. You broke my heart.'

Paul—'I know.'

Sarah—'And I…I hope you will be Okay.'

Paul—'I will be fine.'

Sarah—'And Ben will be fine, and I will be a good mother to him. I know you love him.'

Paul—'I do. Very much.'

Sarah—'I just wanted you to know that.'

Paul—'I know. I know.' His turn to pause. 'Are you okay?'

Sarah—'Not really. I will be, though. Take care of yourself.'

Tears are streaming down my face as I'm talking to him. I can't stop crying. I try to compose myself because I want to speak to Kim, too, and tell her how it went. And ask how she is.

I feel good about calling Paul. However cool he sounds, I know he is burning up inside. I know that much about him. There is still a corner of his soul that hasn't been eaten up by the City life. It's embodied in that little bundle of our love—Ben.

My mobile rings.

Kim—'Hi, Sarah—how did it go?'

Sarah—'Okay. Just spoken to Paul.'

Kim—'He will be feeling it badly, Sarah. I think ironically he will start to think beyond the financial issues now. Which you've been doing all along. Did you get the house, though?'

Sarah—'I got both.'

Kim—'Fuck. Good girl. The house in France! Great.'

Sarah—'Yes, but that wasn't what it was about for me. The French house will hopefully be the house where I eventually settle.'

I sit in the offices of Wearing, Shindley and Strutt by myself and look outside into the street. I feel the way I did when I'd just given birth to Ben and went out for the first time into the High Street to do some last-minute Christmas shopping. Only I knew I'd done this wonderful thing. Had this special little boy. Had been given this gift, this opportunity, this responsibility. And it set me apart from everyone else. And I feel like that now. I feel I've been given a responsibility, yet an opportunity to shine, and that I'm on an incredible learning curve. And that I've been treading water emotionally for a long time but I'm not any more.

My mobile buzzes with a message.

Message received:
Thank you for calling me. I forgot to tell you. I still love you too. Paul.

APRIL

Clearing the cobwebs

Table booked for one p.m. I arrive at twelve-forty-five. I've invited the girls—Jane, Kim and Samantha, to Circle. This is my celebratory '*Coming Out*' party. The *coming out* being my coming out of Chelmsford. I've left Chelmsford and found a flat in Richmond, south-west London, and am officially house-hunting for a home for Ben and me. I've been so manic I haven't seen the girls together for ages, and soon I'm flying off to Canada for work. So lunch it is.

Duncan greets me at the front door.

'How are you, Sarah? You look beautiful.'

Sarah —'Thank you, Duncan. I feel a lot better than the last time I came here. But it was nothing to do with the service or the food.'

Duncan—'You looked painfully thin. Divorce?'

Sarah—'Yes. You guessed it.'

Duncan—'In this business one gets to know these things. You looked a little—well, a little damaged, Sarah. Beautiful. But damaged and rather vulnerable.'

Sarah—'I am a little. Damaged and vulnerable. On the mend now, though.'

Duncan—'Well, we'll see what we can do for you. What I suggest, Sarah, is that you bring every suitor you meet to the restaurant. Ideally lunch—then they can't hide behind the candles. I will check them out. Give them marks out of ten. Advise you if they have gay tendencies. Gay men can tell another gay man even when he's married with children or looks completely straight. I have a sixth sense about it. And it's important to be clear about these things, Sarah. If they score below five, don't bother again. Six to seven, use them for sex. Above seven, they have potential. If any of them deserve ten— well, perhaps I should take their number.'

Sarah—'Thank you, Duncan. You would really do that for me? You are a sweetie. See what you can do.'

Duncan—'Of course, *I* would have you, darling. But Angus would be very upset.'

Sarah—'How long have you been going out with him now?'

Duncan—'Seven years. It's wonderful. Emotional side good, and the sex is fantastic.'

Sarah—'I found anal sex a bit—well, painful.'

Duncan—'All in the position, darling. Lubrication is key. And position. Got to get the position right. Problem with straight men is they don't get enough practice.'

The girls approach the table.

Duncan—'Argh! Your friends.' Then, whispering: 'Are they all little piggies?'

Kim arrives first. Then Jane. And lastly Samantha. All before one p.m.

We all air-kiss and butt-kiss about how everyone looks very beautiful today.

Duncan brings the menus and wine list.

Duncan—'We've run out of tuna today. I'm very sorry, Sarah. But the cod is lovely. And there is also halibut. Neither include dairy in the ingredients—as I know you're allergic to dairy.' Turning to Kim: 'Ah, the lady who loves her food.'

Kim—'Yes, the one with the curly tail.'

Duncan—'May I suggest the steak?'

Kim—with a twinkle in her eye—'That would be fine.'

Samantha orders the lamb.

Kim—'So, how's life been?'

Sarah—'Interesting. Lots to tell. Last night had a mini row with Paul.'

Kim—'What about?'

Sarah—'*Other* Sarah's now living with him at his flat. He's rented one in London, to be closer to work. He didn't tell me Sarah had moved in.'

Kim—'Well, you knew it would happen eventually.'

Sarah—'I did. But as Ben is now with his dad every other weekend, it also means he's with *her* every other weekend. Which I don't like.'

Kim—'You're onto a win-win situation there, Sarah. Paul adores Ben. Sarah knows Paul adores Ben. She wants Paul to adore *her*. So she's going to be nice to Ben. Even if she doesn't want to be. If she's not nice then Paul will see it, and judge her accordingly. Plus, Ben's not exactly a shy child, is he? If there are any problems Ben will come back from his weekend either subdued or upset. Has that happened?'

Sarah—'Well, last week he came back and asked if I wanted Daddy to die. I said of course not, and that Daddy loves Mummy and Mummy loves Daddy and we both love Ben very much.'

Kim—'You're doing the right thing, Sarah.'

Sarah—'I just thought Paul would have told me himself that Sarah had moved in.'

Kim—'He was scared of how you would react.'

Sarah—'It was worse, of course, finding out this way. Just phoning the flat. It was the shock of it. I wouldn't have rung in the first place if I'd known.'

Kim—'How were you with her?'

Sarah—'Fine. I remembered your advice about being super-nice, so I thanked her for taking Paul off my hands.'

Kim—'Good. What did she say?'

Sarah—'She was a bit stunned. Didn't say anything.'

Kim—'Excellent. Anyway, you can do better than Paul. Have you been seeing anyone?'

Sarah—'Not really. I've had my hands full with selling the house, finding a flat to rent in Richmond and house-hunting. That and finding a school for Ben. And for some reason I've been given lots of commissions, all of which involve travel and very tight deadlines and overnight writing. I'm living off coffee and guarana pills at the moment.'

Kim—'Off *what?* What's guarana?'

Sarah—'Oh, caffeine—but natural caffeine. So it's healthier for you. Or supposed to be.'

Kim—'Sounds bollocks to me. Stick to the unnatural stuff. But all work and no play, and all that, Sarah. You've got to go out and party, girl. You know what? You look so much better since the divorce. More relaxed. Your hair's grown. You've got to get a sex-life back.'

Sarah—'I'm due to go skiing with Ben in Canada in a few days. It's work, of course, but it's more fun if I'm with Ben. So that's a break of sorts. I haven't had time to party, Kim. But I'm okay. I'm thinking less of Paul each day—which is good. And much more about what's happening in my life.'

Jane—'Well, Pierce says Paul talks about you a lot at

work. He started off by saying you were a money-grab-bing bitch. You sent a shock wave through the office. He's told everyone you *took everything.*'

Sarah—'I didn't take *everything.*'

Jane—'We know that. But they don't. Anyway, it's made the other guys in the office twitchy about their flings. But lately, according to Pierce, he's telling people he has more respect for you now you're divorced than he did when you were married.'

Sarah—'Really? Strange. I respect him less now. I found his behaviour through it all—well, disappointing.'

Jane—'Think he's probably going through what you went through last year. The sadness. The wanting to know what you're doing all the time.'

Sarah—'Yes. He wants to babysit for Ben.'

Kim—'Don't let him do that. It's a control thing. He wants to know what you're doing. Plus, when he comes to drop off and collect Ben don't let him linger.'

Sarah—'I don't—instinctively. He usually wants to chat. I just want him to take Ben and go. I don't want him in my flat.'

Samantha—'What's your flat in Richmond like?'

Sarah—'Two bedrooms, garden flat—very central. I'm still looking for a house, though. Something with three beds and lots of character, lots of natural light, close to the town centre, with a garden and parking space. All I get sent, though, are details for flats which are double my budget, in the middle of nowhere, and which need loads of work. You know—usual estate agent bollocks.'

Kim—'Any good nightclubs in Richmond?'

Sarah—'If you're asking about talent, yep—plenty of handsome men. A lot of whom look about twelve—and the ones who don't look twelve act twelve. But, well, they're generally more handsome than in Chelmsford, I'd say. Especially around the rugby season. You get these men with amazing toned thighs running up and down Richmond Hill in their training gear. It's wonderful to watch. Ben plays 'watch with Mother' in one of the bars that has outdoor tables on their routes.'

Kim—'Have you tried that speed-dating?'

Sarah—'No, but I know someone who has. She says you get some real geeks on it and the women are a hundred times better than the men. She thinks there's probably a high percentage of serial killers in there as well, staking out their prey.'

Jane—'How about the soulmates columns in the nationals? Sure you would meet professionals through those. Doctors, lawyers, dentists and such.'

Sarah—'Not interested. Again, I know someone who did it, and she ended up with an arrogant twat who told her that he wasn't surprised she had to use something like that because she was so ugly. Not realising, perhaps, that the argument could also be applied to him.'

Samantha—'Nice. How about the Internet?'

Kim—'That's no good. Friend of mine tried that one. She got this guy, liked him, and dated him for six months. Then she became a bit suspicious when he couldn't meet her on Friday nights. Went on the Net again, under a different name, and asked if he'd go out with her. The bugger said he'd love to, as he was single.'

Sarah—'At least she knew, then.'

Kim—'I know, but what a way to find out.'

Jane—'Of course you could try going to one of those ceroc or salsa classes. You can get nice and intimate with someone there. All sorts go.'

Sarah—'You're right. All sorts *do* go. I went last week. I can dance, so it was okay. But I obviously haven't learnt to say no yet. Ended up dancing with the weirdest-looking people around. And they kept looking into my eyes and doing moves that involved rubbing their hips against my hips and stroking my body. Horrible.'

Kim—'There's always the old faithful. A bar.'

Sarah—'Why not? Worked for Paul.'

Jane—'Have you ever been approached by a married man in a bar? You know, one that isn't *understood* by his wife?'

Sarah—'Don't think so. I don't tend to look at their hands, anyway, when they're chatting me up.'

Jane—'I always look at the hands. Not just for a ring, but—well, you know.'

Samantha—'Is that true? Is penis size related to hand size?'

Jane—'Well, I think it's an indication. Feet are better. But you can't really ask them to take their shoes off, can you? Not the first time you meet them anyway.'

Samantha—'I suppose not.'

Jane—'I was approached by a married man once. Said his wife *understood* him but he realised he needed entertainment elsewhere…'

Sarah—'What did you do?'

Jane—'Told him that was fine by me, but perhaps I should contact his wife, just to make sure she was okay with the fact I was fucking her husband.'

Sarah—'Did you?'

Jane—'Contact her? 'Course not. The guy went white and told *me* I was a tart.'

Sarah—'Don't you think men look weird when they're having sex?'

Samantha—'What do you mean? The position?'

Sarah—'No, the faces. The faces they make when they're inside you. I suppose they're concentrating.'

Kim—'On coming.'

Jane—'Or not coming.'

Sarah—'Whatever. But they twist and contort their faces. Bit disconcerting. Reminds me of when I had Ben. I must have been making faces likes that. That's why I used to close my eyes with Paul sometimes, or ask to be taken from behind—because his face made me laugh.'

Jane—'Not very sexy. Pierce used to sometimes wear a mask, or ask to blindfold me or me to blindfold him.'

Sarah—'Oh, that sounds good. I've got furry handcuffs. Purple ones.'

Samantha—'You never told me that!'

Sarah—'Well, somehow I feel more open now. I can talk more openly with you all. When I was married to Paul there was so much I had to keep secret about our relationship, and—well, it seeped into other bits of my life.'

Kim—'So do you like being tied up, then?'

Sarah—'Depends who by.'

Jane—'I have one of those pink bunny vibrators. You know—the ones with the little ears.'

Sarah—'Any good?'

Jane—'Makes it last longer. Not as intense, but still good. But nothing like a real man. And that's what we've got to find you, Sarah. Or *you've* got to find you. A genuine, full-blooded, heterosexual, highly-sexed male.'

Duncan arrives with the food.

Journey time to the Canadian ski resort of Big White is nearly ten hours from London Heathrow. Ben and I are exhausted, but once we arrive it's wonderful. Powder snow. Blue skies. Minus five degrees. English-speaking ski instructors for Ben and me.

Mine is called Howard. He's tall and blond and handsome and tanned and Australian. And I keep falling down and he has to pick me up and it's a real bummer. And he says I have a nice butt. And I say he has a nice butt, too. And we have a quick snog at the top of a red run. Well, we have a quick snog at the top of a lot of runs. But that's it. No sex. Firstly because there's no babysitting for Ben in the evening, and secondly because it takes such a long time to get through the layers of clothing when we're on the piste. I also suspect he thinks I'll write about his sexual prowess—or lack of it—in the travel article I'm working on. I joke about it, but I think he thinks I'm serious. But lots of snogging in the snow is nice. For now.

Ben, of course, learns to parallel turn in the first few days, and is happy copy-catting the instructor down the red runs. Howard tells me to try putting my brain in my pocket, because only then, he says, can I get really confident, go faster and move on.

And the penny drops. It drops midway down a red run when I think I'm just about to crash.

Sarah, put your brain in your pocket and go for it. This is what I should be doing in life. I should be going for it. Having confidence in myself and my abilities. I have the energy to do it, and the initiative. So why not go for it? Allow myself to be happy and enjoy life rather than be scared of it. Cut the cord with Paul. And with the other Sarah. And with any of those cronies who called themselves our friends. They're not worth thinking about or hating or mourning.

This is good. It feels as though a weight has been lifted from my shoulders. It's almost like an awakening, realising that I can do it alone. By myself. I've taken legal counsel, got two houses, sold one and am buying another—hopefully soon—all by myself. This is the woman who thought she could do nothing towards the end of her marriage with Paul O'Brian. Who was told by her husband she could do nothing. That she was a liability. A negative on the balance sheet. And she's starting to feel good about herself again.

The trip is productive in all respects. I get a two thousand word commission from a major national, Ben is now a decent skier, and I'm getting happier and more confident with the red and even some black runs. And on the last day I discover Howard's favourite number is sixty-nine.

SPRING INTO SUMMER

MAY

The mating season

House-hunting is the most boring occupation on the planet. I start off excited, full of energy, hope and inspiration, then after a while all prospects start to look exactly the same. Bit like dating men, really.

I have viewed more than fifty houses and garden flats in three weeks, and still haven't found what I'm looking for. Some look too lived-in, or smell musty; others lack character. Most do have incredible potential. That is if you want to knock them down completely and start from scratch. But nothing catches my eye. So very much like the men I'm dating.

That is until I find *the* house. Number 69 on the prettiest street. It's a little three-bedroom cottage, large picture windows at the front. It has a garden, garage—and character. Formerly owned by a member of the Royal Shakespeare Company. As I walk into the hallway I'm stepping over piles and piles of first editions. The estate agent has listened to me this time. It needs nothing done to it. I'll see what the survey says, but I feel right about this house.

Ben comes round to survey what he describes as his

house. He tells me I will only live there to look after him. He sounds more like his daddy each day.

Ben—'I want a cat. Can we have a cat?'

Sarah—'Do you really want a cat?'

Ben—'There is a cat flap. Yes, I want a cat, and I think the house wants a cat. House, do you want a cat?'

Silence.

Ben—'The house says yes.'

Sarah—'I didn't hear anything.'

Ben—'Only I can hear the house talk. The house also says I should have the biggest bedroom and some Maltesers, because I have been a good boy.'

Sarah—'The house knows that, does it?'

Ben—'Yes, it does.'

Sarah—'Sweetheart, would you like to live here?'

Ben goes upstairs to survey the bedrooms and bathrooms, and then out into the garden.

Ben—'It's not as big as our house in France.'

Sarah—'No, it's not. But it's close to the park and the trains.'

Ben—'Then I like the house, and I think the house likes us.'

I hand in my notice on our temporary rented flat. It's looked after us well. We'll be able to move almost at once, and then I'll be spending the summer with Ben in France—or I'm planning to, at least.

I'm excited, and want to tell the world I've found Ben and me a *home*.

So I do. Kim, Jane, Samantha, Pierce. Everyone, it seems, except Paul. I don't want him to know about the house. Not just yet. It's my house and Ben's house, and if I meet a significant other who smells good, with character and fulfilled potential, we might move and rent it out, but number 69 will always be our home. Sarah and Ben's.

★ ★ ★

First day in number 69. My mobile rings.

'Hi, it's Joe.'

It takes me a second to place him. Joe…old friend of Paul's and mine…

Sarah—'Oh, hello, Joe. Haven't heard from you in ages. How are you?'

Joe—'I'm fine. More importantly, how are you? Don't you live in Chelmsford any more? I went round to the house yesterday and this woman answered the door and said you'd moved away.'

Sarah—'Yes, last month. Actually, Joe, Paul and I are divorced.'

Joe—'You're *what*? No way. Good God. Not you two. You're the perfect couple.'

Sarah—'No, we aren't—and weren't, Joe. There was lots wrong with our relationship. Paul is fine. He's met someone else. Where have you been?'

Joe—'Working in New York. Just come back and—well, wanted to come round and say hi to both of you.'

Sarah—'You can still say hi. I'm sure Paul would love to hear from you, too. Ben is fine. He's living with me and has settled in well.'

Joe—'That's good. But where are you now?'

Sarah—'Richmond. I've just bought a house. It's perfect. Number 69—'

Joe—'I like the number.'

Sarah—'Yes, well, I chose it for that reason alone—as you can imagine.'

Joe—'You haven't changed. You sound surprisingly upbeat.'

Sarah—'Oh, it's been bad. But I'm on the mend now.'

Joe—'Do you want to meet up?'

Sarah—'That would be good.'

Joe—'How about Mezzo in Soho, tomorrow night?'

Sarah—'Fine, I'll get a babysitter for Ben.'

As usual these days, I arrive early. I'm looking forward to seeing Joe. Haven't seen him for nearly nine months now, and he always makes me laugh. He's a reporter for the BBC World Service, handsome and broad, with a wide, easy smile

I get myself a drink at the bar. Turn round. He walks in the door. And smiles. It's so good to see him, and we hug for a few minutes without saying a word. I want to cry. Think I do a bit, because Joe reminds me of some of the fun times with Paul and that makes me a little sad.

Joe—'Well, all things considered you look wonderful.'

Sarah—'Thank you. So do you. New York treat you well?'

Joe—'Yes, great. Great city. Lots of opportunity. Back here for six months, then they're sending me off to I don't know where. But it's fun and challenging.'

Sarah—'Do you want to eat?'

Joe—'Sure. You look as though you could do with some food inside you.'

Sarah—'You should have seen me three months ago. I was *very* thin then.'

Joe—'Then we better fatten you up. But you do look good. Very beautiful.'

Sarah—'Thank you.'

I like the way he says I look beautiful. He's a good friend. He's a friend of Paul's as well, but after so long with no compliments from Paul, it's nice to start getting them in spadefuls.

I choose salmon. He chooses lamb. Strangely, neither of us seems to be hungry any more. I haven't seen

him for such a long time, and I feel I'm a totally different person from the one he knew when I was with Paul. A totally different woman. And he talks to me in a different way. I suppose because I'm not Paul's wife any more.

Joe—'It's been a lovely evening, Sarah. It's good to see you, and you've done brilliantly. The journalism and everything. You're quite a woman.'

Sarah—'Don't know about that. But I would like to go out a bit more than I'm doing at the moment. I've been concentrating on all the basic stuff—selling and buying houses, sorting out Ben, that sort of thing. And I do want to have some fun. So if you're short of a stalwart for an evening, perhaps on a weekend I don't have Ben, I'd love to be your stalwart.'

Pause. Joe looks down, then looks up again.

Joe—'Yes, that would be nice.'

I can tell he's not thinking about what he's saying.

Sarah—'What are you thinking?'

Paul—'Oh, nothing, really. Just that—well, I think I'd like you to be more than my stalwart, Sarah.'

I think, How do I feel about this? A friend becoming something more. Someone who knows Paul as well as knows me. And am I ready for a relationship? Can I trust this man? Can I learn to trust again? Am I ready?

Sarah—'Would you? What do you mean by that?'

Joe—'You know what I mean.'

Sarah—'That you don't want to be friends?'

Joe—'We're that already, Sarah.'

Sarah—'So you want to be more than friends?'

Joe—'Perhaps.'

Sarah—'Don't play games.'

Joe—'Then don't *you* play games. Who is Ben with tonight?'

Sarah—'My mum has him. He's staying round at hers for the night.'

Joe—'Right. Well, I'd better see you home, then.'

Sarah—'Yes. See what you think of the house.'

He pays. We get up and walk to the door. There are no taxis, so we walk towards Piccadilly Circus where there are loads. Then he stops. And he turns me to him, his hands firmly round my waist, and kisses me on the lips. Very firmly and gently, and for a very long time. After what seems like an eternity I pull away and smile, and look at him.

Sarah—'Shall we get that taxi now?'

Joe—'Think we should.'

We get in a black cab. Holding hands. Kissing occasionally. He lives in Kensal Rise, which he assures me is up and coming and has potential.

I smile, because that is what the estate agents said to me about so many places I visited when I was trying to find a house I could call home. And they were all crap.

Richmond isn't a long drive away. I invite him into the house and show him the sitting room. He takes my coat off, but leaves his on. And he kisses me. This time his hands are not round my waist. They are pushing down into my knickers.

Sarah—'You're impatient. Don't you want to see the rest of the house?'

Joe—'Bedroom would be good.'

So I lead him upstairs to my bedroom.

He kisses me and pulls me onto the bed. I pull away. He tries to take off my top.

Sarah—'No, undo it properly. Undo the buttons. One at a time.'

He does. Very slowly. He's still fully dressed. Even his coat on. I feel this is slightly unfair, but am still

turned on by it. I can't wait to see him naked. He slowly undoes all the buttons and then pulls the blouse aside. Gently touching me, he kisses my nipples. Gently sucking, then gradually harder, until I start to feel myself pushing against him and begin undoing his trousers.

Joe —'I should take off my coat.'

Sarah—'No, leave it on for now.'

I undo his flies and gently kiss and stroke his trunks. Black. I kiss and gently bite, and run my fingers up his chest. I can't wait any longer and pull his trunks down with my teeth, nuzzle with my nose and start to suck. He tries to push me away and I don't let him. He's now half lying on the bed, resting on his elbows, watching me. I'm standing, leaning over. He pulls my skirt up so he can see the tops of my stockings. And he tries to reach me. Inside my knickers. But I'm too far away. Out of his reach. I can feel he's being turned on, and I stop and push him on the bed and start to kiss him on the lips. My hands are around him while I do this. Then I go down again. Slowly kissing his chest. Licking. Starting again. More slowly and firmly, and I can feel he's coming. And I don't want him to. I want it to last. And he comes, and I feel pleased and at the same time disappointed, because I wanted that moment to last longer. That anticipation. That first time. With him. With Joe.

He pulls me on top of him and kisses me, breathing in as I'm breathing out. Taking control. And looks at me.

Joe—'Would it be terrible if I fell in love with you?'

Sarah—'It would be very inconvenient.'

Joe—'I'll try not to, then. I keep having these…these Sarah Giles moments. You know—I've known you as a friend for nearly twelve years, and now you're almost naked and I'm almost naked, and you're lying on top of me and have just had me inside your mouth and I'm about to make love to you. And it's just a surreal moment.'

Sarah—'You're just about to make love to me, are you?'

Rubbing his nose very gently into mine, he whispers.

Joe—'Yes.'

While I'm lying on top of him he undoes my skirt. Zip at the back. Obviously he checked that out before. He pulls the skirt down. Leaves the top.

Joe—'I prefer it when women have some clothes on. I like your top.'

As I move up and down his body, very slowly, my nipples play peek-a-boo. Now you see them, now you don't. He slowly moves his hand into my knickers and starts to stroke. All the while kissing me on the lips. He swings me around so that he is on top of me, and pulls my knickers to the side and starts to lick and kiss. Then up again. Kissing me and holding my hands in his. Pressing them into the sheets and moving my legs apart slowly with his knees.

He is large.

Not painfully so, but large. I let out an involuntary sigh. Nothing false about it. No false flattery. I feel all of him.

Joe—'You're very wet. You're becoming very wet, Sarah.'

Sarah—'Perhaps you're turning me on.'

Joe—'Perhaps you're right.'

He kisses me, then pushes my legs up to his shoulders, so he can reach deeper. I start to moan. I've never done this with Paul. Never felt this aroused with Paul. Despite the fact I loved him, wanted him, had a child with him, I've never been this turned on. Then, as I feel Joe is about to come, he stops and turns me over again, and starts to take me from behind.

This feels much deeper, and I start to moan loudly. Very loudly. I start to lose track of time. I think I must have lost track of everything, because I hear myself suddenly getting very loud indeed. I'm somewhere I've never been before. I've never reached this place before. As he holds my thighs he pushes me onto him. And it's so deep and intense, and he just keeps going, and I think I'm going to pass out. And I can't work out if I'm in pain or if this is pleasure. Or both. And all I know is I'm getting very wet. And he keeps going. And I start to cry.

Sarah—'Stop!'

After a few seconds he does, and holds my tummy and pulls me up to him so that my back is against his front.

Joe—'Are you okay?'

Sarah—'I think I nearly came.'

Joe—'I think you nearly did. Why did you tell me to stop?'

Sarah—'Because I've never been there before.'

Joe—'And did you enjoy it?'

Sarah—'It was wonderful—and scary.'

Joe—'You don't need to be scared with me.'

I somehow feel very vulnerable and small again, but this friend is still a friend, and whatever happens he will always be that. Because he is there for me. When I need him. I have tears in my eyes, I think because of the combination of pain and pleasure and the moment, and he kisses them away.

Joe—'I want to make you come. I get really turned on when you are really turned on.'

Sarah—'Believe me, I'm very turned on. I'm extremely wet.'

Joe—'I know. I can tell.'

Sarah—'That could be you as well as me.'

Joe—'It's you.'

He moves his hands very slowly over my tummy, down between my legs. He's very gentle. Paul was rough. Fine with his tongue, but too eager with his fingers. It always hurt. And I would tense my bum so that I wouldn't have to keep saying, Be gentle, be gentle.

But with Joe I don't have to say, Be gentle. Because he is gentle. He keeps kissing me while he strokes me. Teases me with his fingers. Reaching inside me, then out again. Gradually working me into a state of frenzy until I come. Violently and long.

I'm relieved. I'm relieved I can come at all after the past months. I'm relieved I can lust after someone without feeling guilty or confused or angry, or thinking about Paul or Paul with Sarah. I'm pleased with myself, and with Joe, and pleased I'm here and naked with him. And, looking at Joe's face, I know he's pleased, too.

Joe—'That felt unexpectedly natural. As though we were meant to do it. I didn't feel guilty or weird. As I say, I had one of those Sarah Giles moments when you were on top of me earlier. But now I just look at you and see a beautiful woman with a beautiful body, and I feel lucky to be lying here with you and making love to you.'

Sarah—'What a wonderful thing to say.'

I lean over him and kiss him. He kisses me back, cupping my head in his large hands. I look at him as we pull away. Look deep into his eyes.

Joe—'Are you falling under my spell? Falling into my magic?'

Sarah—'That's a rather arrogant thing to say. I don't know yet.'

Joe—'I fancy a bath. Do you want a bath? Do you have a bath big enough for two?'

Sarah—'At a squeeze. We can always lie on top of one another.'

Joe runs the bath and I watch him and his gorgeous butt lean over to pour baby oil into the warm water. Five minutes later we get in. Legs entwined around each other. Lathering each other with soap. Paying extra-special attention to the crevices and the neck.

Joe pays extra-special attention to my nipples and between my legs, because he says he feels they need that extra-special attention. And I lean onto him. And kiss him. And his hands move down my spine, soaping and rinsing my back, squeezing my bum while kissing my back.

Joe—'We'd better get out before I get too wrinkled.'

Sarah—'I could stay here all night.'

Joe—'So could I. But I want to make love to you again.'

Sarah—'We could do it in the bath.'

Joe—'We could. But I want to make love on the bed. Just for tonight. The bath is for another night. The bed is for tonight.'

We make love another three times. I feel very at ease with him. Leaning over the base of the bed, with him holding my hips again, pushing himself onto me, then resting just above my face. Resting himself so that I can take him and just about breathe at the same time. And at times we become so passionate he looks at me and says:

Joe—'This is not supposed to happen this early in the relationship. We are not supposed to feel this intense. This close.'

Sarah—'We've known each other for twelve years. It's understandable.'

Joe—'Perhaps. Perhaps.'

At three o'clock in the morning, Joe wakes me by fondling my breasts and going down on me. What a wonderful way to start the day. I come three times before dawn. Each time more intensely. I sense he loves that he turns me on so easily, and that I so obviously enjoy being with him.

In the morning I dress. This seems to turn him on even more, and he undresses me almost immediately. Wonderful and impractical.

Joe—'I love watching you dress. It turns me on to see you put on clothes I've ripped off you the night before. I want to take them off you again.'

And he does. So we make love again. By which time it's just gone twelve.

I have to collect Ben. I drive Joe to the station and he kisses me hard and won't let me go until I say my mother will be worried if he doesn't, and I will get a parking ticket—which I do.

As I drive to fetch Ben, my mobile buzzes.

Message received:
You are amazing and wonderful and I want you in my life always.

This stings me a bit. This is what Paul said to me the first time he met me all those years ago.

You don't forget something like that, when someone you care about says something that sensitive. And Joe has used the same phrase—word for word. I freeze. Perhaps Joe is too much like Paul. Perhaps I'm falling for the same type. Perhaps I should slow down. After all, it was just one night. So I send one back.

Message sent:
You're amazing too. I wish you were in my bed tonight.xx

Which is true. Just more short-termist than *always*.

I see or speak to Joe every day of every week for the next few weeks. He's a lucky man in more ways than he realises.

By some fluke I'm given commissions to romantic destinations. The Seychelles at a new resort, the Banyan Tree. We enjoy a week of unbridled passion. I get out the furry purple handcuffs and he uses them on me and I on him. Thank goodness I manage to explain them at Customs.

Good. We trust each other. Two fit, long, lithe expectant bodies together, trusting each other. Liking each other as well as lusting. Laughing. At all the right times. Having fun. Chasing each other round the villa. Splashing water. Sex in every conceivable place. And position. I love his smell and touch, and the way he looks at me when he's inside me, and as he's about to go down on me. That look. Must take a photo of that look—his eyes staring at me as he gazes along my body when he's about to go down on me. Very slowly lowering his head. That moment captured. Best holiday snap of them all. But how the fuck am I going to get that one developed?

The *al fresco* shower, the *al fresco* Jacuzzi bath sprinkled with rose petals, the *al fresco* sunbeds where we receive a massage at the same time, after which he comes so violently he almost screams as loudly as me. (Real sense of achievement here.) In the swimming pool, which is a mere four steps away from the end of our bed, he pushes into me from behind as I look out over the side through the palms to the beach. The sun on my back and Joe inside me. Over the basins with large mirrors so that he can see the expression on my face and I can see the expression on his when he comes and takes me from behind. And the bed. Diagonally, vertically, horizontally, upside down, splits, on his face, on my face, hanging slightly off. Legs in the air. Splayed. Every position gymnastically possible we try.

We wear very few clothes. He brought too many. I knew we wouldn't need many. We try to make love on the beach, but there are too many people about (four others), so we return to our villa and make love again. On a bed of frangipani petals spelling out HAPPY HOLIDAYS. Joe rearranges the petals to say I LOVE YOU.

We eat very little. Drink a little. Bathe a lot. Have lots of mutual massages—from the spa masseuse and also from each other. Have lots of fruit—but don't always take it orally. The sun beats down on my back as I make love to him, and the sun is on his back when we change positions. We catch very odd suntans—bits tanned, others not. It's a perfect, perfect, perfect holiday, and I give the resort and the Seychelles the best fucking review they have or will ever receive. My review reads:

The Banyan Tree is not a place for honeymoons, second honeymoons, husbands and wives. It is for lovers. Lovers who have known each other for only a few weeks, been friends for a lifetime, and want to get to know each other intimately and passionately for a few more lifetimes.

I think, I hope Paul doesn't read this. Then think, Not my problem any more. I'm not his wife any more.

I receive a thank-you note from the owner, who hopes I enjoyed it. And that perhaps next time I would like to sample their extensive DVD collection if I have time. I say thank you, but I don't think so.

I've been asked to write about more romantic breaks. I've been asked to visit a hotel in Lake Windermere, allegedly one of the most romantic hotels in the UK. I take Joe.

We have the hotel to ourselves. Just us and the staff. In the sitting room, log fire blazing, I try to get Joe to make love to me. Almost manage. He pulls my dress down to just below my nipples, then gets cold feet and puts the straps up again—fearing the waiter will return at any moment with coffee and liqueurs.

Joe—'I want you so much, but not here. Just in case. Plus, you're here for work. You don't want people talking, do you?'

Sarah—'At this moment in time, I don't give a fuck.'

Joe—'Yes, you do.'

Sarah—'I don't. All I want is to be with you. Here and now.'

Knickers don't make it to our room. Neither does the dress. He is inside me before he gets a foot in the door. When the weekend is over he drives us back to London. I don't want to leave him. The weekend has been wonderful and heady, and I haven't slept or eaten or drunk much, but feel full and empty at the same time.

Joe—'I will call you.'

Sarah—'When?'

Joe—'In about an hour. And then again when you're home. And then again when you're in bed, half naked, and can play with yourself while I talk phone sex. Okay?'

Sarah—'Okay.'

This man speaks my language.

Next day I arrange to meet Samantha over coffee, and tell her about Joe.

Samantha—'It sounds wonderful. Special.'

Sarah—'I like him. I feel it's too early to say I love

him. I've known him for a long time, but as a friend, and this is—well, this is different and it's still too soon.'

Samantha—'It is. But it's what you need. You've been working on autopilot for a long time, and you deserve to give yourself a break and a few bloody good orgasms—which it sounds as though you're getting.'

Sarah—'*Sound* being the operative word! He's taking me to parties. Last week we went to one at his friend's, just off the Fulham Road. The cheap end. We drank a lot of champagne and he led me upstairs into one of the bedrooms and undid my top. Almost stripped me naked. We had sex there and then, while they were partying downstairs. We could hear people walking by outside and they could have walked in at any time. It was very sexy. He made me count to ten and said I would come before I got to eight.'

Samantha—'And did you?'

Sarah—'By five. Paul would never have done anything like that. I feel alive and excited each time I see Joe. Or hear his voice. His phone sex is inventive. He is the butler. I am the maid. Sometimes I'm the butler and he's the maid which is—well, interesting, too. It's silly and funny, and still sexy, and as we're both journalists we're good with words. I love the fact he likes wearing black and dotes on me. And he looks at me as though he can see through my clothes and absolutely loves what he sees. I love the fact he finds me funny and that I find him funny, and that I'm as happy watching TV with him as I am going off to the Seychelles. Well, maybe I'm a bit more happy going off to the Seychelles…'

Samantha—'You sound as though you really like him, Sarah.'

Sarah—'I do, Samantha. I do.'

Samantha—'Have fun. Enjoy yourself. You deserve it.'

Sarah—'How is Edward?'

Samantha—'I don't know, Sarah. I've called off the wedding. I didn't feel he was committed. I was making all the arrangements and he didn't involve himself with anything.'

Sarah—'A lot of men are like that.'

Samantha—'This is different. Your experience has made me think about what I want from a man and a relationship, and if I want to compromise, and—well, this isn't good enough. So I'm waiting to see what happens. I love him, but these are warning signs, I know they are. And I'm learning from your experience that nothing is ever as it seems.'

Sarah—'Good to learn from someone else's fuck-ups. I only ever learn from my own. And not even then, sometimes.'

My mobile rings. It's Joe.

Joe—'Hi, my lovely. I've booked that restaurant you say you always like. Circle. For lunchtime today. Is that okay? One p.m.'

Sarah—'That's lovely. See you there.'

I turn to Samantha.

Sarah—'That was Joe.'

Samantha—'I know. I could tell by your voice. Went all soft.'

Sarah—'He's arranged lunch at Circle. I want Duncan to meet him. See what he gives him out of ten.'

Samantha—'Do you care?'

Sarah—'Well, I'll see what he says. I've known Duncan a long time. And he'll also be able to tell me if he's got gay tendencies!'

★ ★ ★

Twelve-forty-five. Circle. Duncan gives me a big hug and says I look lovely.

Sarah—'Thank you, Duncan. So do you. I have a man. Name is Joe and he's sweet. He's a friend who's become more than a friend.'

Duncan—'Don't mess with words, Sarah. Does "more than a friend" mean you are having sex with him?'

Sarah—'Er, yes.'

Duncan—'Is it good sex?'

Sarah—'After twelve years of pretty much nothing, I think anything would seem like good sex. But, yes, I think it is good sex. And we make love. We don't just have sex.'

Duncan—'Mmm…well, table number nine. Your voice softens when you talk about him, which is a good sign. Women who get very defensive about their choice sound as though they're trying to convince themselves. I will tell you when he goes for a pee. They always go for a pee just before dessert.'

Sarah—'Fine.'

Joe arrives on time. Duncan leads him to the table. Start off with Kir Royales. I have the tuna. Joe has lamb. Chardonnay. Sunshine beaming through the windows. I don't watch anyone except Joe. Pre-dessert pee, Joe disappears and Duncan approaches.

I anticipate praise.

Sarah—'Well? What do you think?'

Duncan—'Square.'

I'm surprised.

Sarah—'Square? He works for the BBC World Service. He's a reporter. Very adventurous. Well-travelled and kind and considerate and…'

Duncan—'Square. 'Scuse the pun—but, Sarah, you're

a *circle*. You're not square. When he settles down he will be a pipe and slippers man. You don't do square, Sarah. You don't do pipe and slippers. Not even when you're absolutely in love with them. Perhaps when you're in your eighties, perhaps then. But you'll be the one smoking the pipe and expecting the slippers. Perhaps it's something you're giving off at the moment, Sarah. You seem to attract men who don't so much want to look after you but—well, *control* you. Perhaps that's what you want at heart—to be controlled? You're not all free spirit—but when you meet a square, Sarah, that's what you become. Hate to say it—but you need someone with a bit of oomph. Someone who has had a life and has a life, who challenges you. What do you talk about?'

Sarah—'Everything. Well, not much, actually—but we're still in the throes of looking into each other's eyes and just being happy with that.'

Duncan—'Sex is good?'

Sarah—'Yes. Phone sex is good.'

Duncan—'And the real thing?'

Sarah—'Well…'

Duncan—'Do you think of Paul when you're with him?'

Sarah—'No. Well, sometimes.'

Duncan—'I feel sorry for this guy. He's nice. He's obviously good for you in some ways. You look glowing, but—well, it's too soon, Sarah. Too soon for you, and I think he knows it. I've been looking at the way he looks at you, and he dotes on you. But do you know? He looks sad as well. As though he knows you still love Paul. That's sad. Because he knows it and in spite of it still loves you. I would give him eight. Keep him as a friend. Was he Paul's friend, too?'

Sarah—'Yes.'

Duncan—'That would piss Paul off. He's chosen you above Paul's friendship. He seems a nice guy, but you need something different.'

Joe returns, not knowing his fate has been sealed by a gay worldly maître d' who has somehow managed to see inside my head to the thoughts I haven't yet allowed myself to admit.

Joe—'I love this restaurant. Perhaps we should come here again.'

Sarah—'Yes, that would be nice. I'm off to Tuscany next week. Press trip. Going for four days.'

Joe—'I'll miss you. I'm going to the States soon, too. Bit earlier than expected, but we can keep in touch.'

Sarah—'We can indeed.'

Joe—'I love you, Sarah Giles.'

Sarah—'I love you too, Joe.'

Joe—'And I always will.'

Sarah—'I know you will. You will always have a huge place in my heart.'

I somehow don't think I will have to say anything to Joe. To explain how I feel. Because we're that close. I think he knows. I *know* he knows. He senses that it's still a bit soon, and we stare at each other, our silence speaking volumes.

I'm pleased about the press trip to Tuscany, for myself and four others.

The group are from the *Daily Post,* the *Manchester Echo* and *Scottish Solutions.* And one from *Posh Times.*

Posh Times get the best bedroom, followed by the *Post,* then *Manchester* then *Solutions.* They have all brought partners and I'm the only single. I get the single room, just to rub in the fact I don't have a man.

Paolo is our host. He owns this villa and will be cooking for the group. He looks and sounds like the actor Timothy Dalton. And he smells of musk. He has muscular arms and body, and wears a white linen shirt. I think I have a fettish for white linen shirts on men. Especially when they're tanned. And his smell… His smell reminds me of the way John, my former lover, smelt. It's a very potent smell. A very *I want to rip your clothes off right now* smell. But I need to be careful, because I don't want to end up sniffing his chest—which, as I drink more Chianti, I start to want to do.

I notice he has large hands. And no wedding ring.

I mellow with the wine and the afternoon sunshine, and sit next to him under the olive trees.

Paolo—'So, who are you writing for?'

Sarah—'A glossy magazine.'

Paolo—'Have you been to Italy before?'

Sarah—'Yes—many times. It's wonderful.'

Paolo—'I 'ave lived 'ere for many years. It's very romantic and special.'

Sarah—'I can see why you like it. My idea of romance is either something like this, or somewhere completely different. Like Cornwall. Somewhere very rugged—cold, with storm clouds and huge waves and strong winds on the coast.'

Paolo—'You are a verry passionate woman. Italy can be passionate, too, you know. Tuscany can be passionate, too.'

Sarah—'I'm sure it can.'

We have eye to eye contact for thirty seconds. Say nothing and smile.

Paolo—'Are you married?

Sarah—'I was.'

Paolo—'You look a little sad. Did you love him?'

Sarah—'Yes—still do, I think.'

I tell him a little about the background, but I don't really like talking about my relationship and divorce any more. I feel I've moved on from that. Whereas all I wanted to talk about a few months ago was my relationship, it's irrelevant now. A past which is painful, but which is past. And from which I feel I've learnt a lot. So recounting it has no meaning for me now. No cathartic purpose. But Paolo seems interested.

Paolo—'You are hurting still. That is to be expected. But you are a beautiful woman. You need time for yourself and your son. And to find yourself.'

Sarah—'Yes. And I'm happy I've found myself in Tuscany this week. Very lovely it is, too.'

We look at each other again for thirty seconds. Until the rest of the table goes silent and looks at us. And then we all giggle, drink more wine and go to our rooms.

My room has a single bed with white Egyptian cotton sheets. The room looks Oriental—the walls decorated in colours of ochre and red, with what look like huge war masks hanging at intervals, somehow managing to look both intimidating and provocative. The windows allow views overlooking the hills and onto the city of Cortona.

As my mind has been full of buying houses, I keep mentally putting a price on every property I'm in, and how I would describe it. *Idyllic villa in the heart of Tuscany, where every room has a view. Price on application.*

Knock on the door.

'Hello?'

'Hello—it's me. Paolo.'

'Oh, hi, Paolo. Come in.'

Paolo—'I just thought you would like to have a look

around the vineyards. The others seem too tired at the moment, but I thought you might be interested.'

Sarah—'Yes, why not? I'd love to.'

I follow him into the hallway and down some steps into the courtyard. It's empty. But we can hear the sound of squeaking. I smile because I think it's beds. Paolo hears the noise too, turns around and smiles at me.

Paolo—'This place is for lovers.'

Sarah—'Yes. I'm sure it is.'

I follow him into the vineyards and through the vines.

Paolo—'I have a little surprise for you. I was going to ask the whole group to this, but they seem…well, they seem otherwise occupied.'

An opening in the vines reveals a table laid with wine and a variety of black and green shiny fresh olives, at least fifteen different types of cheese, and various long and round and square-shaped breads.

Sarah—'How lovely! Pity the others can't see this.'

Paolo—'Would you like some wine?'

Sarah—'That would be lovely.'

I sit, fully aware that this may be my *Room with a View* moment. Where the man may or may not pounce and seduce me in the middle of a vineyard. But perhaps it's the romantic in me. Wishful thinking. I may have mis-read the signs.

Paolo—'Have you ever had a Latin lover?'

I think, Nope. Definitely not misread the signs. This is definitely a seduction line—in whatever language. This man wants to fuck me.

Sarah—'No. Are they any good?'

Paolo—'From what I hear, English men are not ver-rry passionate.'

Sarah—'Some are.'

Paolo—'Do you have a lover, Sarah?'

Sarah—'No. I did, but—well, he was a wonderful friend, but the timing wasn't right. Lovely person, wrong timing.'

We sit and drink, and nibble at olives. I feel a bit self-conscious, so drink a little more wine. I'm aware he's invading my body space by leaning close to my face when he talks to me. Sometimes our lips are almost touching, but he doesn't kiss me.

Paolo—'So, where do you live, Sarah?'

Sarah—'Just outside London. A place called Richmond. I've just bought a house.'

Paolo—'That's good. Would you like some more wine?'

Sarah—'No, I think I've had enough.'

Paolo—'This is too good to waste, Sarah.'

And he drinks some and kisses me, blowing the wine into my mouth.

Paolo—'Tastes good, doesn't it?'

Sarah—'Mmm, yes. Tastes good when you put it that way.'

Paolo—'Would you like some more?'

Sarah—'That would be lovely.'

Paolo leans towards me and kisses me very slowly on the lips. No wine this time.

Sarah—'You forgot the wine.'

Paolo—'This tastes better.'

He kisses me gently on the lips. Runs his fingers through my hair, pushing me against the table, sending olives flying. But I don't want to be taken. I want *to take.* So I kiss him back hard. And push him away. Then, as he stands there watching me, I undo my skirt. And let it drop to the ground. I take his hand and push him back against the table. He holds me tighter and kisses me back. Hard. We're almost having a battle of who can kiss who the most hard, the longest and most passionately. And I start to get turned on by his strength, because he's having to be very strong to control me. Or try to control me. And he picks me up effortlessly—without me feeling he's going to drop me—and sits me on the table.

I think I've sat on the olives, but he doesn't seem to care, and increasingly neither do I. He starts to kiss down my body, but doesn't take off my clothes. Kissing through my blouse and working his way down, until…

Methinks, Fuck he's good. Christ. Talk about Latin tongues.

And he stops. Just as I'm about to come. I am under the Tuscan sun in the middle of a vineyard, with an amazing lover called Paolo who, as far as I'm concerned, is the king of oral sex.

Paolo—'I think someone is coming.'

Sarah—'You bet the fuck someone is coming. Why are you stopping?'

Paolo—'No, my sweet, no. I think someone is coming.'

I'm extremely dazed. Dazed and frustrated and aching to come. I know Duncan would have wanted this guy's number for himself. I am mellow with wine and not much food, my knickers are covered in green olive juice, and my skirt is somewhere in the environs. I can't see exactly where. And I am so close to coming, very hot and very horny.

Paolo—''Ere is your skirt, Sarah. We will continue this later, perhaps?'

Sarah—'Yes.'

I whimper.

I get up and put on my skirt, which at least hides the green, moist marinated knickers. I straighten heavily tousled hair, try to compress nipples, and look as unravished as possible. It's the couple from *Posh Times,* Lucinda and Francis.

Sarah—'Oh, hello. How are you both?'

Lucinda—'Fine, Sarah. We thought we'd wander through the vines—it's such a lovely afternoon. We were reading and just freshening up. What have you been doing?'

Sarah—'Oh, wandering. Lonely as a cloud and all that.'

Lucinda—'Ah, right. Well, what's this?'

She pointed to the table of food and wine—much of which is now scattered on the floor.

Sarah—'Oh, I think Paolo organised it for us. Perhaps the birds got at it. You never know. Anyway, it looks good.'

Lucinda goes to the table and takes a piece of cheese. Hope she doesn't go for the olives.

Sarah—'I'd better go. Better get ready for this evening. I think they're laying on fireworks for us, with fire-eaters and dancers.'

Francis—'That sounds very good.'

Francis is looking at me as though he knows what I've just been doing, which is disconcerting.

Sarah—'Well, better go. Nice to see you both. Bye.'

I walk quickly through the vines, hoping I will find Paolo. But he's nowhere to be seen. He's not in the courtyard, or in the dining room or the library. I can't find him anywhere. At last I give up, starting to calm down, aware that the moment has passed and he's probably gone to the market.

I return to my room alone. Where I find my Paolo. In my very own room with a view.

Paolo takes the pleasure of my company every night. And every afternoon, while the others take their siesta.

He gently and progressively unravels my anger and frustration, and my fear of not feeling loveable for such a long time. He's a very gentle, passionate lover. I never thought the two could go together, but somehow with Paolo they do. He's clever and considerate. Fun without being intense. Powerful without being controlling. I feel he's awakening in me the woman Paul beat down over the years. The sexual being who craved, who screamed for affection. And ultimately felt and still feels she doesn't deserve it. Paolo makes me feel I do. And that I'm worthy of this. And much more.

At Pisa airport I am checking in—standing at the back of a queue that has not moved for the past hour. The other journalists are whingeing because they are not in first class, but I'm still mentally with Paolo, making love amongst the vines, and in the olive grove, and on my bed, in my bath, in my shower, on the windowsill. I am still half heady with romance, and half stifled by the crowds of Italian families saying goodbye and hello to their relations very vocally, in the way only Italians can.

I have honed my baggage down to one piece of hand luggage. Years of hardened travel journalism have made me realise less is more, especially if your clothes for the trip get lost *en route*. Not that clothes would have mattered that much during my time with Paolo. Clothes are irrelevant with that man.

I'm still fantasising about *that man* when another handsome face appears in front of mine.

'Hello, Sarah. Long time no see. Hope you're well. How are things going with Paul? Where are you living now? And how's the house in France doing? Have you done much to it?'

I look at the face. No, no. Don't recognise it. Who can this be? But he seems to know a lot about me. Perhaps if I let him speak a bit more I will eventually get who he is. Handsome face, so it's not too painful looking into his big blue eyes and listening to his oh-so English tones. He's invading my space, but as he's good-looking and smells nice I'm happy to be invaded.

It's Jeremy. Jeremy the barrister—Jeremy. Shit, he looks different in casual gear. White linen shirt hanging over jeans. Very tanned, hair slightly ruffled. Looks very different. Amazing, actually. Thought he was dishy when we met in his chambers and in court, but he really looks rather splendid now.

Sarah—'Wow, hello. You look different.'

Jeremy—'I know. This is more me. What are you doing here?'

Sarah—'Oh, I've been on a working trip. Tuscany with some other journalists.'

Jeremy—'Hard life, then. But someone's got to do it.'

Sarah—'It *was* hard, actually.'

I think of Paolo and smile. Perhaps noticing, Jeremy says:

Jeremy—'Meet anyone nice, then?'

Sarah—'Yes—guy called Paolo.'

Jeremy—'Oh, God. Not another Paul?'

Sarah—'Ah, yes, I suppose so. But very different. He didn't seem to have the same hang-ups as my husband of seven years. But then he didn't have any of my baggage either.'

Jeremy—'Talking of which, you don't seem to have a lot. You always travel this light?'

He looks down at my hand luggage.

Sarah—'Years of travel journalism. Everyone always takes too much. This is ideal. And what are you doing here?'

Jeremy—'Oh, I've been on holiday. Taking a break from it all. I've just got divorced myself.'

Sarah—'So sorry to hear that.'

Jeremy—'These things happen.'

Sarah—'Yes, so I'm told.'

Jeremy—'So, I've been sorting stuff out about that in Italy. I have a house in France myself. I may have mentioned it. About an hour from yours, I think.'

Sarah—'Oh, yes, I think you said. In Gaillac? Fabulous wine.'

Jeremy—'Yes. How are things going with your house in France?'

Sarah—'Okay when the builders turn up. Having problems with the *crépie* man at the moment.'

Jeremy—'I may be able to help with that. If you want to give me a call.' He hands me his card. 'Or I can call you—think I've still got your mobile number on file somewhere. I will be delighted to help.'

Sarah—'That's very kind. Thank you.'

We exchange cards and kisses on each cheek. He disappears amongst the throng of chatting *mammas.* My tanned knight in blue jeans and white linen shirt.

I arrive home to number 69—warm with the memories of Paolo and the sunlight. And for the moment I'm even able to watch Helena Bonham Carter and Daniel Day Lewis in *Room with a View* without getting tearful or cynical or soppy about love and romance.

JUNE

Brief encounter

My brief meeting with Jeremy at the airport slips my mind until four days later.

I'm in the bath, waiting for a call from work. Something that should have been written yesterday and was needed the day before. The usual. I have filled the bath with lots of bubbly, highly coloured oily stuff, which claims it's soothing and good for the skin and sanity, but is bloody awful to clean off the bath afterwards. Sink in and lie back. Five minutes relaxing, then mobile rings.

Sarah—'Hello?'

Jeremy—'Hello, there. It's Jeremy. Where are you at the moment?'

First thought—Jeremy who? Then remember. Oh, yes, barrister Jeremy. Airport. Linen shirt. Handsome. I think, Shall I tell him exactly where I am at this very moment? I think yes. Tease him.

Sarah—'In the bath.'

Jeremy—'Oh. Right. Bad time, then.'

Sarah—'No, no—don't worry. Just got back from the gym. Hot and sweaty and all that.'

Jeremy—'Oh. Take your phone to the bath, do you? I keep the bath sacred. That and the toilet.'

Sarah—'I was expecting a call from work—something urgent. Anyway, how are you?'

Jeremy—'Fine. Just wanted to know if you are free for lunch next week?'

Sarah—'I can't do lunch at the moment, Jeremy. Because of work commitments and Ben. I can do a drink after work.'

Jeremy—'How about making it supper, then?'

Sarah—'Fine.'

Jeremy—'Somewhere in the City? Club Gascon?'

Sarah—'That sounds good.'

Jeremy—'Very French, and does a lot of the food you'd get in our region of France. You know—*cassoulet* and *foie gras.*'

Sarah—'Oh, I don't eat meat and I don't eat dairy, and I don't eat *foie gras.*'

Jeremy—'You've chosen the right part of France to live in, then, haven't you?'

Sarah—'They do have vegetables there, too, you know.'

Jeremy—'Pity—it's a good restaurant. You could always watch me eat, then. No, seriously, I'll choose somewhere else. Is there anything in Richmond?'

Sarah—'There's a place called the Green Table. It's not organic or vegetarian, so don't be misled by the *green* bit.'

Jeremy—'Okay, I'll book there. Must be in the phone book. About eight on Monday? If that's okay with you?'

Sarah—'Yes, fine. See you then.'

Jeremy—'Bye.'

I think, That's kind. Nice man. Perhaps I can get

some free legal advice over supper. Now back to the bubbles.

Mobile rings again.

It's Jane.

Jane—'Hi, there, Sarah. How you, girl?'

Sarah—'I'm good. Tuscany wonderful. Had wonderful lover called Paolo. Gave me back my sexual confidence and I didn't think about Paul once.'

Jane—'That's great. Particularly as he's got the same name as your ex.'

Sarah—'Yes. Never thought of that, really. But I suppose that's the way he probably thinks about his new Sarah. Same name, but totally different person and experience.'

Jane—'Yes, but rather confusing for those with him. Pierce said he saw him the other week and he kept talking about Sarah. He had to keep asking Paul which one he was talking about. Anyway, point is you had a good time, a *better* time, with the Italian version.'

Sarah—'Most definitely. Plus I met my barrister at the airport on the way back. Don't know if I mentioned him before. He was very helpful and may be able to get me some more legal advice. Plus he's got a house about an hour from mine in France.'

Jane—'Sounds promising. What's he like?'

Sarah—'Oh, it's not a date, Jane. Just to talk about how to get on in France and some legal stuff. You know—if Paul starts to be funny about Ben—access and all that.'

Jane—'He sounds interesting. Is he handsome?'

Sarah—'Yes, but…'

Jane—'Does he excite you when you think about him?'

Sarah—'Yes, but that's not the—'

Jane—'Do you find him interesting and stimulating?'

Sarah—'Well, we haven't really talked much. Mainly about the case. We're meeting to talk about France. I think he can help me with some stuff there, also about some issues with Paul and my custody of Ben. That's why we're officially meeting. Unofficially, Jane, I'm curious about this whole divorce process. I think it's the journalist in me coming out. I'm curious to find out what he thought about my case. Whether Giles vs O'Brian was normal or out of the ordinary. It was a very out of the ordinary experience for me, but he must see so many of them. I find that fascinating.'

Jane—'Well, have fun. Have you got time for drinkies tonight?'

Sarah—'Yes, sure. What's up?'

Jane—'Will tell you when I see you.'

Meet in the bar at Circle. Buzzing with people doing business. Duncan is there to greet us.

Duncan—'Not eating today, Sarah?'

Sarah—'No, just a drink this time.'

Duncan—'You look tanned. Have you been away?'

Sarah—'Yes—Tuscany. Had a lovely time. Met a *ten*.'

Duncan—'Surely not? Not a *ten?* You must bring him.'

Sarah—'No. Only a ten for four days. Not a lifetime.'

Duncan—'Well, take a pew, ladies, and I'll get two Kir Royales—will that do?'

Sarah—'Wonderful.'

Jane—'No—can I have some apple juice?'

Sarah—'What? Jane no alcohol? What's up?'

Jane—'I'm pregnant.'

Sarah—'Oh, Jane. Congratulations! Well done, well done, *well done.*'

I hug Jane, crying with happiness. She hugs me back.

Jane—'Shut up, *shut up*. Don't get me started with tears. Bloody fucking hormones. I'm getting tearful in meetings now. Have to keep excusing myself to go for a pee when really I just want to cry when I'm shouted at. Normally I'd just tell them to sit on it.'

Sarah—'Are you pleased?'

Jane—'I'm very pleased. Wasn't planned. Well, actually it was. I'm a complete fascist with contraception. As with life in general. But I stopped taking the Pill and—hey presto. My man has got such a huge willy he popped my egg.'

Sarah—'Well, that's one way of looking at it.'

Jane—'Anyway, I'm expecting in November, and want you to be godmother. I know you believe in God and not the Church, and I think that's the right way round. So will you be godmother?'

Sarah—'I would be honoured. Thank you, Jane.'

Jane—'And—well, another thing. I've already thought of names. And if it's a girl we're going to call her *Sarah*. I like the name but you may have reservations now.'

Sarah—'I don't mind. What's another one in this world? All the *Sarahs* I know are totally unique. All a little bit off the wall. Potential to be naughty.'

Jane—'Yes, well, we like the name. And there's more. I'm buying a house in France. My new man and I are buying a house! About five minutes from Toulouse. I've been thinking about it for a long time, and when you got your house I thought, Hey, fuck it, go for it. So I've found this huge barn. Bloody massive thing, it is. Of course it needs complete renovation, but I've done all the plans, found an architect, so I know exactly what's needed and what isn't.'

Sarah—'New family, new home. Wow, you've decided to go for it, Jane.'

Jane—'Well, *you* do, don't you? I think when I divorced Pierce I started to re-evaluate everything and put life into perspective. What was important and what was urgent. And a lot of my life is full of stuff that really isn't either—I just think it is. Or someone tells me it is. What's important to me is my health and happiness. And my friends are so much a part of that for me. Work is stimulating, and it gives me focus and drive and purpose—but I've seen how you are with Ben and think I'd like to be a mum. And Harry—well, he's so different from Pierce. And then there's the quality of life in France. What with the Internet and all, I can work from anywhere—supposedly. And you'll be just up the road—or a two-hour plane and taxi journey away.'

Sarah—'I'm very happy for you. But you're taking on a lot. New house and new baby all in one go? And I thought you were buying in England?'

Jane—'Estate agents are fucks, aren't they? Got the house I wanted, negotiated hard—but when it came to exchanging I looked at it and thought, Hey, this isn't worth the money. Whereas this place in France is worth ten times what I'm paying for it. That's the difference, Sarah. And I just felt it was the right time—the right time for me to move on. It's been nearly two years since I split from Pierce, and that's the time it usually takes after you divorce, and—well, it's just my time. And I've found the right man, I think. He's a wonderful, caring man—but a complete animal in bed. You so often get them the other way round. Aggressive everywhere except where they should be.'

Sarah—'You never know—we might both end up

living out there permanently. My babysitting rates are very reasonable.'

Jane—'So are my divorce consultation and counselling fees, Sarah.'

I smile. And think, Yes, Jane has been there for me during a challenging year.

Jane—'Anyway, that's my news. I'm spending some time there in the summer, and I think you said you were going to be in France then, too. So we can meet up, and you can check out my place and I can check out yours. Deal?'

Sarah—'That would be great. Perhaps I can get the others to come down as well. Samantha, and Kim—if she's in a fit state. How would you feel about Pierce coming down?'

Jane—'Doesn't bother me. I know he's got a number of sex kittens on the go at the moment. Might make for some light entertainment if you invite him down. You've got to have someone to talk about in a group.'

Sarah—'We'll see.'

We pause to drink and contemplate life for thirty seconds, as you do. Then:

Jane—'I like the sound of Paolo, and I like the sound of the barrister. He sounds—well, more *you*. Intelligent. Challenging. Sexy. Intelligently sexy.'

Sarah—'As I said, it's not a date. Perhaps I'm just into white linen shirts.'

Jane—'Perhaps. As long as you're yourself now, Sarah. You were always trying to be something you weren't with Paul, and the more you know yourself and respect yourself, the more respect you'll command from others. Truth is, you never respected Paul. And he knew it. And you know it now. It sounds as though you respect this guy. Anyway—big kiss. Got to fire and hire someone to-morrow. If they piss me off I might just throw up all over them and blame it on morning sickness. Busy, busy, busy.'

And with that Jane wafts off through the glass doors, air kissing Duncan and turning heads.

Monday at eight. Mum babysitting for Ben. I meet Jeremy at the restaurant. Square room, small square tables, dimly lit. Complete opposite to Circle. Even the maître d' is straight.

Jeremy is already sitting at the table. I'm on time.

Jeremy—'Hello, Sarah.'

Sarah—'Hello, Jeremy.'

He's wearing a white linen shirt again, and dark trousers. He looks a little nervous, which I find rather charming. I've never seen him nervous. Doesn't strike me as the nervy type. Surely not Jeremy the barrister, the man who can stand in front of terrifying judges and juries and witnesses and intimidates the intimidators? Surely not Jeremy? But this evening he looks a little unsure of himself.

Jeremy—'I like the restaurant, but I think we may have trouble seeing our food. They don't believe in light here, do they?'

Sarah—'I think it's all in the name of romance.'

Jeremy—'Ah, is that what it is? Oh, well. How are you? You're looking well.'

Sarah—'I'm fine. Happy to have a home now, and Tuscany was glorious. It brought back my sense of romance and my thirst for adventure. And you?'

Jeremy—'Oh, as I mentioned, I got divorced around the same time as you did. I was handling your case when I was getting divorced.'

Sarah—'Must have been challenging, representing a

divorcing wife when you yourself were a separating husband.'

Jeremy—'You have to be professional in cases like that, Sarah. If you can't, then you shouldn't be practising.'

Sarah—'Was my case unusual?'

Jeremy—'Not really. Paul behaved the way every City banker behaves in situations like this. They seek closure quickly and want to move on. They don't have the emotional capacity to stretch out the proceedings, even if they have the financial capacity. And, unless they particularly enjoy litigation, they resent involving solicitors—mainly because their spouses do rather better out of it than they would if we weren't involved.'

He pauses to think, then continues:

Jeremy—'I must admit, I read your file again before I came out. I think your case stuck in my mind because of the no-sex issue. Being able to cope with a sexless marriage for so many years. That is different. That and the fact you say you very nearly didn't get married.'

Sarah—'It wasn't loveless. Just sexless. And I also had a self-worth issue. So I felt I deserved his treatment. And everyone told me what a good catch Paul was. I knew instinctively it wasn't right. I just didn't have the emotional strength or intelligence to get out of it before I got into it. And I did love him when I married him.'

Jeremy—'I think that's rather charming.'

Sarah—'Why? Didn't you marry your wife for the same reason?'

Jeremy—'No, she was pregnant.'

Sarah—'So you believe you did it out of duty?'

Jeremy—'I don't *believe* that Sarah. I *know* it.'

Sarah—'How did you meet her? At the *bar?*'

Jeremy smiles.

Jeremy—'No, she's not in law. I met her in a previous incarnation—before I entered the law. I'm not a conventional barrister.'

Sarah—'No, you don't strike me as a conventional barrister. But then I don't know what a conventional barrister is.'

Jeremy—'Someone who has really studied the law, straight from school. Bit square. I've done a few other things. I'm a bit of a…'

Sarah—'Circle.'

Jeremy—'Yes, I suppose you could put it like that.'

Sarah—'What were you before you were a barrister?'

Jeremy—'I was in travel—public relations.'

Sarah—'Really?'

Jeremy—'Yes, really. Seemed like a good way to travel and get paid for it. Plus I slept with a lot of journalists.'

Sarah—'How gallant of you.'

Jeremy—'Then I went into a rock band. Very successful we were, too. Called Urban Pods.'

Sarah—'Weird name. Did you get into the charts?'

Jeremy—'We got to number two. I played the drums. That's how I met my wife—Annie. She was a guitarist in another band. She was due to get married to another guy, but was having an affair with me. She married him, then two weeks into the marriage told him that it wouldn't work—she divorced him after three months, and married me.'

Sarah—'Sounds a little like my story. Doubts till the last. I was torn between two men. I should have walked away from both. But I chose Paul because I loved him more than I loved myself.'

Jeremy—'At least you're aware of it now.'

Sarah—'Yes, I'm aware. Now I must act upon that awareness—not ignore it and go and happily get into the same rut again.'

The waiter arrives at the table and hands us menus.

Sarah—'I'll have the salmon.'

Jeremy—'I'll have the lamb.'

Methinks, What is it with men and lamb and me? Some sort of analogy there?

Jeremy—'They don't do Gaillac wine here. Chardonnay do?'

Sarah—'Lovely.'

Jeremy—'Would you like a drink to start?'

Sarah—'Kir Royale would be good.'

Jeremy —'Good idea. Two of those, please.'

The waiter nods, smiles and leaves.

Jeremy—'Man of many words.'

I smile.

A slight pause.

Jeremy—'How is your house in France coming along?'

Sarah—'The pool is nearly complete. Just needs the water. The main house is being painted a bright yellow with blue shutters, but I need some help with the man handling the *crépie*. If you have any ideas, that would be great.'

Jeremy—'Yes, I do have some contacts. I'll text or e-mail you the numbers when I get home.'

Sarah—'Thank you. The gardens are being finished. I've bought an outdoor chess set and it's going underneath a big cherry tree just by the big house. Lots of drystone walling and a stone arbour by the pool. It should be lovely when it's finished.'

Jeremy—'What have you done for furniture?'

Sarah—'I bought six-foot cherrywood *bateaux-lit* beds for each bedroom. The rooms are huge, with incredibly high ceilings, so everything needs to be oversized. The kitchen's been made by a local guy, and all my bits and bobs have been taken there. I wanted it very much as a home for Ben and me.'

Jeremy—'Everything seems to be working out for you, Sarah.'

Sarah—'Well, yes. It's taken some time, but it has worked out okay. My personal theme tunes at the moment are the Sugababe's "Stronger" and Christine Aguilera's "Fighter," so sort of both along the same lines. The more crap I get, the more crap I can take.'

Jeremy—'You do seem very strong at the moment.'

Sarah—'I'm okay. How about you?'

Jeremy—'What about me?'

Sarah—'Your divorce. What happened? Do you want to talk about it? You know my stuff, but I don't know anything about you. And it must have been strange—being a divorce barrister and getting divorced yourself. I should imagine you were the worst person *to* divorce.'

Jeremy—'On the contrary. When you're personally involved in a case, all reason goes out of the window to make way for raw emotion. I was in a similar situation to you. I should have never married in the first place.'

Sarah—'Why not?'

Jeremy—'As I said, I didn't love her.'

Sarah—'How long were you married?'

Jeremy—'Fourteen years.'

Sarah—'You mentioned your wife was pregnant. How many children do you have?'

Jeremy—'Four girls.'

Sarah—'So you were married to a woman for fourteen years, had four children with her, and didn't love her. That either makes you very stupid or very weak or both. But you don't strike me as someone who puts up with something that easily.'

Jeremy—'I'm not usually. But in this case I think I was probably weak. I stayed out of loyalty and duty.'

I freeze. And I say what I'm thinking as I'm thinking it.

Sarah—'I can hear Paul's voice in yours. I feel as though Paul is talking to me about our marriage. Explaining to the new Sarah why he left me. Did you petition for divorce or did she divorce you?'

Jeremy—'I petitioned her. She was having an affair.'

Sarah—'Why was she having an affair?'

Jeremy—'She was unhappy. She said I was cold and aloof and didn't communicate with her.'

Sarah—'And did you?'

Jeremy—'I'm very English, I'm told.'

Sarah—'Is that an excuse or a disease? Do you mean you are *emotionally anal?*'

Jeremy—'I suppose I do.'

Sarah—'So she had reason, perhaps, to feel unloved—especially if she was, as you say, married to a man for fourteen years who now claims never to have loved her. I'm sure she was miserable. But then, how come you had four children?'

Jeremy—'Oh, these things happen.'

I think, I can't believe I'm hearing this bullshit from an intelligent, worldly guy like this.

Sarah—'What do you mean, *these things happen?* You sound as though you turned your back for a second and they suddenly appeared out of thin air.'

Jeremy—'Well, not quite like that. But I was a different person then.'

Sarah—'Did she want the divorce?'

Jeremy—'No.'

Sarah—'But she had the affair?'

Jeremy—'Yes.'

Sarah—'It sounds *very* similar to my situation with Paul, then. It sounds as though, despite what you claim, there was incredible chemistry there—but that you took her for granted. *Being English* is a cop-out. You're worldly, you've done stuff. She went elsewhere for attention, got it, and got found out. Your pride was hurt, you got angry and cold, and sought and found closure quickly. Filed for divorce. She was and probably still is devastated, and reeling from the pain, and you're in denial.'

Jeremy—smiling—'It's not that simple.'

Sarah—smiling—'Sometimes it is.'

The food arrives. The waiter pours the wine.

I look at Jeremy. He's looking at me. I'm not sure about him. He's very bright and talented, and he's had a life. Many lives in one lifetime. A bit like me in some ways. He's got his own baggage, but that makes him more interesting than the rest. Than those late thirty-somethings who have stayed single either because they're workaholics or commitment phobes, and who lack the same emotional depth and experience. I wonder if his wife broke his heart or just his pride?

I drink a glass of wine as though it's water.

Jeremy—'I've brought pictures of my house in France. Would you like to see them?'

Sarah—'Would love to.'

He brings out some photos and a typed A4 sheet advertising the rental. As I look through five photos and read the description he talks.

Jeremy—'I bought it about ten years ago. Fell in love with it. That's why I understood your desire to keep your house in France. I understand the passion you have for it. I have the same passion for this house.'

I look through photos of a kitchen with a long, large oak table. Bedrooms with whitewashed walls and what

looks like Egyptian cotton sheets on four-poster beds.
A swimming pool overlooking a valley of vines. Everything is on a much larger scale than my house, but then
he's had his a lot longer.

Sarah—'It's beautiful.'

Jeremy—'It is. The kids have always had a wonderful time down there. My wife, Annie, has custody. But
I see them every weekend.'

Sarah—'Paul only sees Ben every other weekend.
And some holidays.'

Jeremy—'Yes, but my wife is a recovering drug addict.'

Sarah—'Did she become a drug addict during your
marriage? Or was she like that when you married her?'

Jeremy—'I didn't make her turn to drugs, if that's
what you're implying.'

Sarah—'So you knew she was a drug addict when
you married her?'

Jeremy—'We both dabbled. I could control it. She
couldn't.'

Sarah—'Did you try to help her?'

Jeremy—'Yes, but like anyone with an addiction they
have to admit it to themselves before they can be ef-
fectively treated.'

Sarah—'That applies to lots of things. Awareness is
half the battle.'

Jeremy—'Yes. And pride often gets in the way.'

Sarah —'I think you loved her and still do. You knew
she was capable of betraying a man because you'd seen
her do it to someone else. You knew what you were getting into.'

Jeremy looks at me.

Jeremy—'Does one ever know what one's getting
into in a relationship? Can one ever know everything?

Relationships change over time. If they're healthy they change.'

Sarah—'I agree. But with Paul from the start I was trying to be something I was not. I wanted to be accepted for what I was. And I think Annie probably did, too, and you wanted to change her.'

Jeremy—'Perhaps Paul never saw the real you. Perhaps you never *were* the real you with him. Perhaps you're only now learning to be the real you. Have you ever considered that?'

Sarah—'I have. And I'm enjoying the experience.'

We pause again while the waiter checks on us. How I miss Duncan. Wish we'd gone to Circle.

We sit and stare at each other for a few seconds. Then:

Sarah—'It's very good to see you, Jeremy.'

Jeremy—'It's very good to see you again, too, Sarah. You look much happier and less stressed than when I last saw you.'

Sarah—'I've been on a vertical learning curve, Jeremy. Sometimes I felt I was going to fall off.'

Jeremy—'Me, too. You know what they say, Sarah. People who've suffered a broken heart are the most interesting people in the world. Far more interesting than those who haven't suffered.'

Sarah—'Yes, I've heard that. And that suffering makes you creative. Well, I must be absolutely fucking fascinating, then.'

Jeremy laughs.

Jeremy—'Are you lonely?'

The man stops me in my tracks again. He's asking me questions I haven't asked myself. Not even Jane or Kim ask me that question. I thought I'd answered all the questions.

But, *Are you lonely?* No, no one asks me that one.

He's making me think. I haven't met a man who's made me think and talk this deeply before. Not like this. Not for a long time. When I first met Paul I talked like this, but that is a distant memory. My life seems to have been full of banal conversations about irrelevancies for such a long time now. And relationships—well, they've made me feel horny or happy or relaxed or sexy, but the men have never made me *think*. Perhaps that's why I do feel lonely. But I can *do* lonely. I'm an only child. I did lonely all through my childhood and all through my marriage, so it's something I can cope with.

Sarah—'Yes. Yes, I think I *am* lonely. I have Ben, but he's a little boy—and I don't want to be his mate; I want to be his mummy. But I do feel lonely. There are times when I've wanted to cuddle up to Ben in bed but realise it's best if he sleeps in his own bed. I've had to handle all of this by myself. I don't really have family who are able to help. I have a handful of good friends. I think realistically no one has more than a handful of good friends. And they've been wonderful and special and there for me. But ultimately I feel lonely because I've become more aware. More aware of how people manipulate one another and how they don't hear their own voices any more because they get suppressed by so many other voices. And that makes me feel very alone. And I realise I've been alone for a very long time, Jeremy.'

I think I want to cry. *Tony Blair. Tony Blair. Tony Blair. Tony Blair.* Good. Done it. He still works.

Jeremy—'This loneliness is all part of healing. It makes you a whole person. Paul needs someone else because he isn't complete as a person. He needs someone else and I think, at least subconsciously, he realises that. Awareness of your limitations as well as your strengths is important. Self-awareness is important. He'll never be as strong as you. But knowing that will help him. He can either accept his limitations or try to stretch himself and become more of a person. But most people—not just men—are quite lazy. Sarah, I think you're slightly different. I don't think it's your limitations you are not aware of. I think it's your strengths.'

Sarah—'My strengths? Well, they've been tested—but I knew they would be. Yes, I do feel stronger. But I knew all this would make me strong. I wrote Paul a poem about things which at the time I hoped wouldn't happen. It was about the divorce. But it's all come to pass. As for Paul, I feel pity for him more than anything these days. Compassion—because he's lost everything and I don't think he realises what he's lost. He sees it all in monetary terms, but that's the tip of the iceberg.'

Jeremy—'Those who work in the City see everything in monetary terms. It gets into their blood, Sarah. It dominates their lives. They think they control it, but ultimately it controls them.'

Sarah—'I know. When I see him now, which is rarely, he always pleads poverty—and I know he's making loads of money. He makes me laugh. It's never been like that for me. Money has always been the focus for him.'

Jeremy—'Some would say you've had the luxury of his money so you're able to say things like that.'

Sarah—'Ah, but that's the opposing counsel's case, Jeremy. Remember? You told me yourself—it's not *his* money. It was *our* money. I do realise I got what I was legally entitled to, not necessarily what I deserved.'

Jeremy—'Yes, Paul should have read the small print. But he will get married again. His type always do. They need a mummy. They say they want an equal, a partner. But they don't. He'll be back in the divorce courts in ten years' time.'

Sarah—'Whether he is or he isn't is totally irrelevant to me. I'm happy being single, but I want a lover. Someone who's a grown-up. I don't want a child.'

Jeremy—'All men are children.'

Sarah—'That's a cop-out, too. Men think just because they admit it, it's okay to be that way. Bit like saying, "I'm a serial killer. Deal with it."'

Jeremy—'Well, not quite.'

Sarah—'Well, you know what I mean. Men only behave like children because women allow them to.'

Now I stop him in his tracks. He looks at me.

Jeremy—'Would you be upset if he married again?'

Sarah—'It's not an issue with me any more. I want him to move on and find someone else. If Sarah isn't the one, I want him to find someone else and make a life for himself—but be there for Ben and support him. I don't want him in my life because—well, to be blunt, I don't like him. I did initially, when we married, but the more I've grown to respect myself, the less respect I feel for him.'

Jeremy—'You've gone on a voyage of self-discovery, haven't you, Sarah?'

Sarah—'Doesn't everyone when they go through something like this?'

Jeremy—'Not always. You get those who are bitter twenty years down the line. Others who are—what did you call me?—in *denial,* and others who use up all their energy in vengeful spite and hating. And those who bonk themselves into oblivion. I tried to do that—the bonking bit—but I think sex without love ultimately makes you feel more lonely. But it's good for releasing tension.'

He pauses again. The waiter arrives to take the plates and ask if we want dessert.

Jeremy—'I usually ask for two. I've a sweet tooth.'

Sarah—thinking of Kim—'I know a woman you would get on with. Me, I'm not a dessert person.'

Jeremy—'I'm not hungry tonight, for some reason. Ms Giles, you've taken my appetite away.'

Sarah—'Sorry about that.'

Jeremy—'That's okay.'

He looks at me and smiles.

Jeremy—'So, what have you been doing with yourself apart from healing after the divorce?'

Sarah—'Me? Writing lots. House-selling and buying. Getting Ben into a good school and getting a life for myself and—well, getting myself back.'

Jeremy—'A lot of women would like to be in your shoes.'

Sarah—'Yes, one in particular did. Her name's Sarah, too.'

Jeremy—'You know what I mean.'

Sarah—'No—what? Having supper with you here, tonight?'

Jeremy—'Well, that as well.'

He avoids the issue.

Jeremy—'I would like to do this again some time soon.'

Sarah—'That would be lovely.'

He drives me to number 69 and kisses me three times on the cheeks. I can see my mum twitching the curtains in the sitting room to see who the man is.

Jeremy—'Thank you for a lovely evening. You're—well, you're not what I expected.'

Sarah—'Are women ever?'

Jeremy—'Sometimes. But you're not. Next Monday? Can you do supper next Monday? In Soho this time.

Promise no *foie gras.* I know a good restaurant. A guy called Duncan is the maître d'. He knows me.'

I say nothing. Just smile.

Sarah—'Okay. See you then.'

I'm walking on air. I haven't walked on air for ages; haven't known this feeling for at least twelve years. Almost forgotten what it felt like. I'm curious about this man. Over the past year it's felt like I've been climbing across wet concrete which has been slowly setting, dragging me deeper and deeper. I thought I was safe when all along I was just suffocated. I'm sure Paul felt the same way about our relationship. Relationships are not about setting things in stone. They are moveable feasts. They grow or die. Easy to say. Less easy to do.

Supper Monday week. At Circle. Duncan smiles and kisses me. Then he greets Jeremy.

Duncan—'Hello, Jeremy—how are you? Good to see you. Where have you been?'

Jeremy—'Busy. Work and personal life.'

Duncan—'And you have the pleasure of the lovely Ms Giles tonight?'

Jeremy—looking surprised—'I didn't know you knew Sarah.'

Duncan—'But of course. She brings all her lovers here.'

Pause.

Jeremy—'Oh, I'm not her lover. I'm her barrister. Or was.'

Duncan—'Pity. You make a nice couple. Well, give you time, give you time. Which table would you like? Something in the corner?'

Jeremy—'That would be good.'

Duncan—'Table nine, then.'

He leads us to the table.

Jeremy—to me—'I didn't know you knew this place. And Duncan.'

Sarah—'Yes. Know it quite well. I bring my lovers here and Duncan gives them marks out of ten.'

Jeremy laughs.

Jeremy—'He does the same for me.'

Sarah—'Churlish to ask what he's given us.'

Jeremy—'I don't think we will on this occasion, Sarah. Let's make our own minds up.'

Duncan doesn't ask what we want to order. He just brings two Kir Royales, followed by chardonnay, seared tuna and lamb. Followed by two desserts for Jeremy and none for me.

Jeremy—'You look lovely tonight, Sarah. But I expect you get that all the time, so it sounds a bit clichéd.'

Sarah—'Depends who's saying it.'

Jeremy—'You are also, if I may say, looking extremely horny.'

I redden.

Sarah—'I am. Extremely. Think it's the humid weather. It's making me tetchy.'

Jeremy—'I'm only your barrister, but I may be able to help you.'

Sarah—'How do you think you can do that?'

Jeremy—'Oh, I can find a way. I'll take care of the bill. My chambers aren't far away. I need to get some papers, and then perhaps I can take you home.'

Sarah—'That would be nice.'

Jeremy pays and thanks Duncan. He doesn't say anything to me. Just gives me a hug and tells me to have fun.

Jeremy—'I haven't brought the car. I've brought the bike. Are you okay with that? I've got a spare helmet.'

He leads me to a Harley-Davidson.

Sarah—'Why have you got a spare helmet? Do you always carry one, just in case?'

He smiles.

Jeremy—'No, not usually. Just thought you'd like to ride on the bike.'

I look at him, then at the bike, and smile.

Sarah—'You're right. You're not a conventional barrister.'

Jeremy—'Are you happy to ride on the back?'

Sarah—'Yes—fine. Fine. Do I have to wear a helmet?'

Jeremy—'Absolutely. You'll be breaking the law if you don't. Trust me. I'm a barrister.'

Ten minutes later and we're at his chambers.

It's dark, and I remember all those months ago. The first time I came here. Stressed and thin and desperately unhappy. And now look at me.

Jeremy opens the door and keys in a security code. Which he seems to have forgotten because he curses a few times until the buzzer stops beeping. I step inside the main entrance hall and walk towards where I remember his offices to be. The building is as I remember it. Wonderfully grand and ever so slightly formal—with very high ceilings. The place oozes an elegance which struck me even in my misery six months before.

He turns me round, takes my bag, and drops it onto the floor beside me. He then goes into the reception room—I think to turn on some lights.

Sarah—'Can I look around? I'd like to see the meeting room again.'

Jeremy—'Of course, Sarah. Just upstairs to your right. Second door.'

I go upstairs. It's as I remember it. Tall white walls. Cornicing. Large, long oak table with red velvet-covered chairs. A clock above a formal Adam fireplace, which looks as though it's one of those gas ones but has never been lit.

I think I'm alone in the room, but:

Jeremy—'What's your fantasy, Sarah?'

He startles me. I turn round and see him standing in the doorway. Smiling.

Sarah—'What's my fantasy? What do you mean? Sexual fantasy? Or romantic fantasy?'

Jeremy—'Both.'

Sarah—'You really want to know?'

Jeremy—'I really want to know.'

Sarah—'Okay. I will tell you.'

As I talk I walk around the table, and he slowly follows me.

Sarah—'Very simple. Inspired by the film *Ryan's Daughter,* really. The bit in the wood with the bluebells. I'm riding a horse through a wood. I'm with a soldier. Bluebells carpet the floor. I feel I've been riding a long time with this man. And I'm tired, but excited—and hot because the weather is humid and close. My horse stops and refuses to take another step. The soldier appears by my side on his horse. And we're standing side by side. The horses nuzzle noses and we watch them. Not touching.'

As I talk I'm still walking, occasionally looking at Jeremy, who is looking at me. Watching me. I continue.

'I get off the horse because it's hot and sticky, and walk my horse to a tree to tie it up. The soldier also gets off his horse. Following my lead. Still not talking. And we tie them side by side.'

Jeremy—'Why tie them side by side? Why not slightly out of reach of each other? So they can smell each other? But they can't touch each other. Just out of reach.'

Sarah—'It's my fantasy, that's why.'

I continue:

Sarah—'And I walk deeper into the wood. I don't know if the soldier is following me, but I just have this urge to keep on walking. I feel his breath on my neck. I sense his presence, but he says nothing and I say nothing. He's like my shadow. A shadow I fear yet which excites me. And I stop and turn round.'

At this point I stop walking round the table and turn to Jeremy.

Sarah—'And I see the soldier's there, just behind me, so close to me but not touching me. And I want to be touched, but every time I walk towards him he moves just out of reach. And turns into a shadow again.'

Jeremy's getting into the spirit of things, because as I approach him he moves away. Almost touching me, but not quite.

Sarah—'I feel the only way to persuade him to come closer is to arouse myself. And I lie down in the bluebells.'

As I do so, I sit on the table.

And lift up my skirt.

Very slowly I move my knickers aside and start to stroke myself, until the shadow is looming over me. Still not touching me, just watching me. And he's so close, but he doesn't touch me. I feel his breath and his heat, and I sense he's undressing, but I can't see the soldier any more. Just sense the shadow.

And I want to make him real. And I undo my blouse and let it fall open, and I feel his kisses on me. Like warm raindrops.

I'm lying on the table now, and Jeremy's over me. Kissing me gently. Living my fantasy.

Jeremy—'And then the shadow passes and moves on.'

Jeremy suddenly moves away and stands back from the table.

I'm half cross and half amused.

Sarah—'No, it doesn't. It's my fantasy!'

Jeremy laughs. And walks towards me. And leans very close to me. He opens my blouse so that he can see my nipples, but he's still not touching me.

Jeremy—'And has the shadow become real yet?'

Sarah—'Yes, but it can't decide which part it wants to kiss first.'

Jeremy—'Perhaps the nape of the neck?'

He goes to kiss my nape, but stops short.

Jeremy—'Or the breasts?'

He goes to kiss my breasts, but stops short.

Jeremy—'Or the belly button?'

He goes to kiss it, but stops short.

Jeremy—'Or here?'

He goes to kiss me underneath my skirt, but stops short.

In the dark, in the meeting room at midnight, he's standing by the table. I'm fully dressed, but he can see everything. He hasn't kissed me yet—anywhere. I'm breathing so erratically I think I'm going to faint. Whose fantasy is this anyway?

Jeremy—'Do you want the shadow to become real?'

He stands back and undoes his shirt. Nice body. Toned and tight. And brown. I untie my skirt. Let it fall to the floor.

He doesn't want me to wear anything. I can tell. Not like Joe, who liked me half dressed, half undressed. Jeremy wants me naked—and fast. He's almost feasting on me. This is no shadow.

He pulls off my knickers. Almost tearing at them. I push against him, because I want some of the power back, and pull him over so that I'm lying astride him on the table. I gently ease my body along his until I get to his black pants. And I suck through the cotton and then pull them down with my teeth. And kiss around and above and below, and then long and hard, with long and hard strokes. First with the tongue, then the hand, then the tongue, then the hand. Holding him down and back, so he can watch but that is all he can do.

Jeremy—'I want to taste you, Sarah.'

I ignore him. I don't want him to yet.

Jeremy—'I want to taste you. I want to taste you.'

He pulls me round. He's stronger than he looks. I try to keep my balance and position, but he swivels me round and I'm now in his mouth, and he's touching me, and fingers are flying and stroking and I can't concentrate any more.

Think of something non-sexy. Fuck it. I can't.

He pushes me again. Swivelling me like a top, almost, on top of him, and he licks his fingers, then pushes them inside me and grips. Grips me with his thighs.

First thought: the thighs are very strong, like a vice. It's very sexy. He rides well, I should imagine.

I can't move, and he wants to push himself inside me, but I come down on him again and force him back. His head hits hard against the table.

Sarah—'Are you okay?'

Jeremy—'Fuck it. I'm okay.'

Then he pushes me again, so that he's on top and I'm below him, and pushes himself into me. And then he moves. He moves himself inside me. Christ. This is a first for me. Wonder if it's something they teach them at Cambridge. But he twists his hips and, wahay, this is amazing. I can feel my back arching, and him holding my hips, gripping them tight and moving them to fit his own rhythm, making the sensation inside me feel quite different from anything I've experienced before. And then as suddenly as he started he stops. And he turns me around, taking me from behind and forcing himself into me, nearly anally.

Sarah—'Did you mean to do that?'

I think he did, but he shifts himself and chooses a path—well, more travelled. And all I can think is this man knows what he is doing. And he keeps stopping, because I'm starting to moan and I can tell he doesn't want to come, and then he turns me again and presses down onto me, looks into my eyes and says:

Jeremy—'Are you on the Pill? You are? You aren't, are you? Are you?'

And that sort of spoils it.

Sarah—'I have a coil.'

Jeremy—'Oh, that's okay then.'

And then his hand wanders. And I feel he wants to take me another way. And I'm scared, because I've only done this with Paul, once when we were still going out, and it hurt like hell. But I'm so caught up in the moment, so relaxed, I feel it's natural.

Jeremy—'Don't worry. I'll be gentle. I won't hurt you. Not unless you want me to.'

Sarah—'I don't want you to. Don't want you to hurt me. Physically or emotionally.'

He kisses me, and I feel I'm about to pass out with the heat and the excitement and wanting this man inside me.

I think I may actually pass out or come. I don't know which will happen first. It may be simultaneous. But I know I'm going to do one within the next sixty seconds. And he pushes himself once more inside me, kisses me hard and comes.

He stares into my eyes, his chest barely touching mine.

Not saying anything. And then he lies back with a self-satisfied smile and I sit up over him and look at him.

Jeremy—'Did you enjoy that?'

I think that was a rhetorical question. So I don't answer.

Jeremy—'Did you enjoy that?'

Sarah—'Oh, sorry, I thought you were talking to your penis.'

He laughs. I'm so close to coming, but he makes no effort to make me come. Perhaps this is why his wife thought him *English*. I don't think this is English. I just think this is fucking selfish. But I'm so wired and angry I say nothing except:

Sarah—'I've got to go home now. I've got to take over from the babysitter.'

Jeremy—'Can't you say you are out all night?'

Sarah—'No, I can't, Jeremy.'

This man is a father and asking me to do that. How fucking selfish.

I slowly get dressed while he gets dressed. I go downstairs while he calls for a taxi.

Jeremy—'It will be ten minutes.'

Sarah—'Fine.'

I start to leaf through some magazines about Legal Aid and how to get it, and look at the plaques on his wall. He won a scholarship to get into law school, it seems. I'm sort of impressed, but still frustrated and pissed off. Perhaps it's a public school thing. I have a feeling Pierce would probably be the same as a lover.

He follows me into the reception room and moves up behind me.

Jeremy—'You have lovely slim hips.'

Sarah—'All those years of working out. Plus the gene pool. I can touch my toes, you know.'

Jeremy—'Can you, indeed? Care to show me?'

I'm still feeling extremely horny, so I bend over and promptly touch my toes. My forearms resting on the floor.

He moves my feet apart. Pulls my skirt up and my knickers aside and pushes himself inside me again.

I'm so turned on by this. The spontaneity of it. At least my calves will get a good stretch tonight. He comes again within five minutes. He moves away and puts my knickers back in place, lowering my skirt.

The doorbell goes. It's the fucking buggery bollocks fucking fucking taxi.

Jeremy—'Just in time.'

Sarah—'Yes.'

Now I'm absolutely pissed off that I haven't come and he hasn't offered. I feel used. But, hey, I made my bed, I have to lie in it. Deal with it, Sarah.

We kiss goodbye. Very briefly. On both cheeks— which seems somehow inappropriate in the circumstances. But this whole evening feels surreal to me anyway.

Jeremy—'I will call you.'

He gives me forty pounds for the taxi.

Sarah—'Thank you. Is that what I'm worth tonight?'

Jeremy—'A whole lot more.'

In the taxi I'm fuming. I like Jeremy. I like this shadow of a man. He is entertaining and sensitive and funny— and fucking selfish. But perhaps that was just the timing. Or lack of it.

I pay and thank the babysitter. Then lie in the middle of the sitting room floor and make myself come. Three times. Within ten minutes.

Next morning Jeremy *e-mails*. I suppose it could be worse. He could have faxed.

E-mail received:
Thank you for a lovely evening. Hope the babysitter wasn't too cross.

I'm annoyed. Is that all he can say? I'm not pussy-footing about any more. My pride is hurt. I try to call his office. I am told he is in court all day. Fuck it. I'll e-mail.

E-mail sent:
Morning. I know, like me, you have loads going on in your life, emotional as well as practical. And you're working like crazy, as I am. I think the decisions we've taken along the way are quite similar—and I hope I can help if you need it. I empathise with you more than you are aware.
It would be a lie to say I did not want to sleep with you on Monday, but if I'm honest I didn't want it to happen that way. I felt I was relieving your tension like some hooker, and I'm worth more than that. I'm not sure what you want from me. I initially thought you wanted friendship, because of the proximity of our French houses, and then thought, Hey, perhaps he likes me, because of the way you are with me. But I am now not so sure. I love being with you, find you very stimulating, and know there's more there. I think you're wonderful, albeit a rather selfish lover, and think you could prove quite entertaining out of the bedroom as well as in it. But I may have completely misread you.

I go out all day and busy myself with work and gym and Ben. At nine p.m. I log on again.

E-mail received:
I am very distressed that you feel this way about last night. If I'd had any idea I would not have taken you back to cham-

bers. On my part I thought it was a very enjoyable and spontaneous act, and am horrified that you felt otherwise. I thought you felt the same. I am very cross that sex seems to have got in the way of our relationship. And I want to redress this. I am miserable at the idea that I will not see you again, and consider our friendship more important than sex. If we can go back to square one, and continue where dinner finished, I would very much like to get to know you and apologise for the hurt I have unwittingly caused.

I feel a bit better now. I wanted to have sex with Jeremy. It's just that—well, fuck it, I wanted to come!

E-mail sent:
I don't think you could have written anything more eloquent. And thank you for that. I would very much like to get to know you, and would like you to get to know me better (the file notes, believe it or not, don't have everything about Ms Giles!). Let's see what happens.
I would love to see you again—both here and in France. Jeremy, there's so much more to me than a pretty body. And, yes, I would have loved to have stayed all night, but I have Ben and it was too soon and, as I said, I'm a romantic. And if I didn't care, I wouldn't have told you.
Take care.
Sarah
xxx

Next morning:

E-mail received:
I look forward to seeing you next week. Circle again?

E-mail sent:
That would be lovely.

I don't think about Jeremy for the next few days, then get a call on my mobile.

Jeremy—'Hi, it's Jeremy.'

Sarah—'Hello, there. How are you?'

Jeremy—'Well, not good, actually. Bad news. Very bad news. Annie took a drug overdose last night. My eldest called me and managed to stop her. I've got custody of the children and Annie's been sectioned.'

Sarah—'Christ. Jeremy, I'm so sorry. Is there anything I can do?'

Jeremy—'Nothing at the moment. But I've got my hands full, as you can imagine. I would love to see you, but can't. I will call you. I promise.'

I don't hear from him again that month.

JULY

Facing old demons. Opening new doors

Paul has summoned me to the Great Eastern Hotel for lunch. Summoned as in texted me late on Sunday evening. Past 11 p.m.

> *Message received:*
> Can I take you to lunch on Tuesday? Urgent issues to discuss. Paul.
> *Message sent:*
> No. Can do Monday lunch. Sarah.
> *Message received:*
> Fine. I will change Monday meetings. Paul.

'*Urgent issues*' could mean anything. He is getting married. He is engaged to be married. Sarah is pregnant. He has discovered Sarah is a man. Or he is gay. Or she is gay. Or he is moving to Richmond. Or to Australia. Or he's leaving his job and can't pay maintenance. Or he wants Ben to live with him.

The only one that concerns me is the last. Strangely, I don't care about the others. Of course he could be terminally ill, though I hope he would phone me for that one. But I never know with Paul these days. Still think he's an alien. But now I'm aware he always was an alien—it's just that I only realised it a year ago.

As for custody of Ben—well, according to Jeremy he has to prove I'm a bad mother, and I'm not. I'm a surprisingly good one. I'm even surprising myself. Ben is remarkably well balanced. They even say so on his nursery report.

> Ben O'Brian is a very happy, well-balanced little boy. Very confident in class. He is well liked by all his classmates and is a natural leader. Very creative and has excellent communication skills.

Methinks, this is the woman who thought she would completely fuck it up. There is still time yet, of course. There are still the teenage years. But this is why Ben must see a lot of his father. When he rebels, as all teenagers do, I want him to hate his dad as much as he does his mum. Only fair. At the moment he wants to be a builder (Bob the Builder) or Luke Skywalker. I suggest he will earn a lot more money as a builder than a skywalker. Probably even more than his dad does as a banker.

Number 69 now has three additions. Two tortoises—Bill and Ben—and one grey floppy-eared rabbit—Buzz Bunny. Ben still wants a cat, but I tell him if we get a cat, the cat will terrorise the tortoises and kill the bunny. So the cat has to wait.

Monday lunchtime. One p.m. at the Great Eastern Hotel restaurant. Full of bankers. I'm on time.

Paul—'You're on time. You're never on time.'

Sarah—'No, I've been early for the past year. So on time is good for me.'

We're shown to a small square table in the middle of the room. I don't like it. And I say so.

Sarah—'Excuse me? We've got some important business to discuss. Do you have a table that is quieter? Less central? In a corner somewhere? It's just that we don't want to be overheard.'

Waiter—'Yes—over there. Will that do?'

He points to a table by the window.

Sarah—'That's fine. Thank you.'

I walk to the table and sit down. I almost feel like the man. As though I'm taking the lead in a dance. I shouldn't be, because I don't know what Paul is going to say. Hate to say it, but I feel a bit like his mother. Don't look it. Everyone says I look much better since the divorce.

Paul looks grey and stoops more now, and he has put on some weight. Perhaps it's the young girlfriend and all those cottage pies and apple crumbles she's probably cooking him.

It's weird because I feel he's going to ask my permission for something, or that he's been a naughty boy and has to tell me something. So I wait until he's ready to tell me. I expect he will small talk through the first course and get to the nitty-gritty in the main, when he thinks I've drunk enough or he's warmed me up enough. Anyway, I'm hungry. Do they have tuna on the menu?

Paul—'So how are you, Sarah?'

Sarah—'I'm fine, Paul. How are you?'

Paul—'I'm fine.'

Pause.

Paul—'I have something to tell you.'

I look at him. I think he expects me to guess. Best of three. But I say nothing.

Paul—'I'm getting engaged to Sarah.'

Sarah—'Okay. When are you planning to get married?'

Paul—'September.'

Sarah—'If you can let me know the dates that will be helpful. I presume you will want Ben as a page boy?'

Paul—'Well, yes, that would be nice.'

Sarah—'Fine. Let me know when you need him for clothes fittings.'

Paul—'Probably some time next week.'

Sarah—'Fine. Lots of notice, then. Okay. As long as he's not taken out of school.'

Paul—'Great. Well, that's it, really.'

Sarah—'Where do you plan to live?'

Paul—'Don't worry. Not near Richmond, but not too far out.'

Sarah—'Good. Well, now that's over, is there anything else you need to tell me that's urgent?'

Paul—'No, don't think so.'

Sarah—'Okay. As long as you never forget your commitment to Ben, that is all that concerns me. That you never forget him and always support him—emotionally and financially. I wish you well, and I am very pleased you are not moving to Richmond. I am sure Sarah is, too.'

He smiles.

Paul—'Yes, she is. She's rather intimidated by you, actually. She thinks she has a hard act to follow.'

Sarah—'She does? Hope she doesn't have to take the crap I did. She sounds arrogant on the phone, so she probably gives you as good as she gets. Let's hope she can sustain it. And that she's kind to Ben when you have him.'

Paul—'She is.'

Sarah—'Good.'

I finish my fish in silence. Say goodbye. No kiss. And depart.

I'm not upset or disappointed. I'm actually questioning why I'm feeling the way I am. Or rather why I'm *not* feeling the way I think I should be feeling. I feel as though I have a shield round my heart at the moment. That nothing can get through. But perhaps there's a delayed reaction. Perhaps I'll start sobbing on the way to the Central Line.

But as I leave the restaurant and walk down the stairs all I feel is numb. Indifferent. I'm more concerned about the practical issues rather than the emotional ones. I'm so concerned about my distinct lack of concern I call Kim on the mobile.

Sarah—'Hi, Kim, it's Sarah. Where are you?'

Kim—'At home. I'm fine. Where are you?'

Sarah—'Just had lunch with Paul. He's getting married to Sarah. In September. Wants to have Ben as page boy.'

Kim—'Really? Well, how do you feel about that?'

Sarah—'Surprisingly okay, I think.'

Kim—'Taking it well, then?'

Sarah—'That's just it. I'm concerned that I'm not more concerned. Surely I should be crying or angry or sad or something? But I'm just numb. Perhaps it's a delayed reaction.'

Kim—'No. I just think you've moved on so far that Paul's in the past. Of course he's Ben's dad. But Paul as an entity, a husband, is so far in the past that you—well, feel indifference. Which is what you should feel. It's healthy. I don't know if he will feel that. I think it probably pissed him off considerably that you didn't seem to care. Men are so arrogant, after all, and Paul was always one who appreciated a strong reaction. And for a time that's exactly what you gave him. But he doesn't get that reaction from you any more, so he will behave differently towards you—which is good for you and for Ben. And if it annoys Paul—well, that's not your concern any more. It's his, and now it's hers.'

Sarah—'Quite. Must try to get Ben to stop calling Sarah "*nasty Sarah*"—I don't think that will go down well at the wedding.'

Kim—'Where did he get that from?'

Sarah—'Erm, may have let that one slip a few times. Possibly heard me saying it months back and it stuck. Or he's so diplomatic—maybe that's what I'm called in their household.'

Kim—'You're probably right.'

Sarah—'But I'm his mummy and will always be his mummy.'

Kim—'You're right there, too. And, talking of being his mummy, I've got some news. I'm pregnant again.'

Sarah—'Oh, Kim. That's wonderful news.'

Kim—'Yes, we're delighted. But I'm going to take it easy.'

Sarah—'Why don't you come to France this month? I'm going down there with Ben for the whole of the summer. I'm collecting my new car, my little yellow Mini today, and I'm sooo excited. I'm inviting Jane, who's bought a house nearby, and Samantha, and I might invite Pierce with one of his squeezes. And you never know—Jeremy might be at his house in Gaillac. Come— you'll enjoy it, and you haven't seen the house yet.'

Kim—'I would love to.'

As I click off I feel something. A sadness that I can't give Ben a brother or sister. Not for the moment any- way. But I'd rather be a mother than a wife.

The sadness doesn't last long as I'm excited about seeing my new car. It seems an eternity since I met Steve Smith. I wonder if he remembers me?

I phone the number.

Sarah—'Hi, there. Is Steve in?'

Steve—'Hello—that's me.'

Sarah—'Sarah Giles here. Woman who ordered the yellow Mini Cooper S with a white roof?'

Steve—'Ah, yes, I remember you well. Divorcee. Sexy.'

Sarah—'Er, yes—that one. A very gay divorcee, actually, at the moment.'

Steve—'Pleased to hear it. The car is ready, Ms Giles. When would you like to collect it?'

Sarah—'Today, if possible.'

Steve—'Good. See you about two p.m. You sound good.'

Sarah—'I think I am.'

As I drive round the M25 in my little old car, I remember all the things I've done and seen in it. How it's served me well, and hasn't broken down too often. How it's seen some horrendous and hateful arguments, loads of tears and lots of laughter. Mine, Ben's, and even Paul's in happier days. But it represents one less material possession to tie me to the past. A green door closing as another door, a yellow one, opens.

I can see my new car as I drive in. It's beautiful. Shiny and yellow and perfect. It's mine. Paul has nothing to do with it. Style, colour, interiors, accessories. The lot. He has nothing to do with it. Like number 69, it's mine. And as I sit in it I feel good. Liberated. Happy.

Steve—'What do you think of it?'

Sarah—'It's perfect.'

Steve—'Want to take it for a spin with me?'

Sarah—'Okay.'

I get in the car and start the engine. I don't stall it this time. It purrs, and I decide where we're going.

Steve—'Where to?'

Sarah—'Southend, I think. Last time I was there was at Christmas. Christmas Day, if I remember rightly. Got to confront my demons.'

Steve—'You have demons in Southend?'

Sarah—'Someone has to.'

Steve—'So how have you been, Ms Giles? How's your son?'

Sarah—'Good. He wants a *mini* yellow Mini. Do you do those?'

Steve—'I think we can rustle up one for you.'

Sarah—'Thank you. And how are you?'

Steve—'Fine. No girlfriends. Looking for an older woman. More experienced, sexy, elegant.'

Sarah—'With good taste in yellow Minis.'

Steve—'Yes, that sort of girl.'

Methinks, I'm a free agent. I can seduce this Essex man in the car and no one would know about it. Except a few hundred of his friends, perhaps. I look at him.

Sarah—'How old are you, if I may ask?'

Steve—'Twenty-nine—but I look older.'

Mmm. Paul's Sarah is probably in her twenties. Paul isn't the only one who can pull a younger model. But do I want to pull this one? Do I really want to sleep with Steve just because I can and because he's got me a good deal on a car? And will it be like saying to Paul, *Anything you can do, so can I?* Haven't slept with anyone since Jeremy, and he hasn't called, but am I that desperate? He's handsome. It's an adventure. But…I look at him again keenly, while trying to keep an eye on the road and oncoming traffic. No, he's not right. But nice to know I can if I want.

We drive along the seafront. I remember my night

ride to Southend and how I felt, and although the memory is painful I'm not pained. Not hurting this time.

Steve—'Do you like Southend?'

Sarah—'Yes, I do. People are always drawn to the sea, I think, when they're troubled or just want to think.'

Steve—'I just like it because the girls are easy.'

Sarah—'Right.'

Driving back to the garage, I say goodbye to the Golf for the last time.

The house is gone. The car is now gone. I only have one thing from my previous life that I want to keep. And that's Ben.

I hand Steve the Golf car keys.

Steve—'I'm a bit disappointed. Thought I was gonna get lucky there.'

Sarah—'Oh, well, you never know. Perhaps you have. Perhaps I would have broken your heart. And you can't sleep with them all, Steve. I'm sure there are many more divorcees in the sea. Even in Southend.'

Steve—'It's always the ones you want that get away.'

Sarah—thinking of Jeremy—'That's often why you want them in the first place.'

Drive home in my new Mini. *My new Mini.* I keep saying it out loud. Sarah Giles is the owner of her own new Mini. I love it. Nothing like a new car. And I've never had one before.

I drive out of flat Essex into colourless Kent and to the lush green hills of Surrey, then up into London and very slowly through Richmond Park, with the deer grazing or daring to cross the road. Sun shining. Warm afternoon. Cyclists, children playing, joggers, *al fresco* Tai Chi classes. Wonderful. Jazz concerts by the bridge. And only Ben to come home to, to smile at me and demand Maltesers with a prompted please. And a hug. In that order.

★ ★ ★

French leave. Summer in the house in France, with friends, lots of wine and food, and sunshine. Kim and Jane with their respective partners and respective bumps. Samantha now happily single, but still looking.

And Pierce, who is bringing one of his sex kittens. Clarissa, I think he said her name was.

And Jeremy? Well, he has his own house, and I haven't heard from him since the phone call about his wife. All the bedrooms will be filled for a week, which is how long I'm told they all want to stay.

Two double beds in the gite. Three in the main house.

I book ferry tickets to France, and plan to drive down with Ben. I wonder if Jeremy will be in France at the same time. He's still impossible to reach by phone, so I e-mail.

E-mail sent:
I'm in the house in France for the next few weeks. If you are about it would be good to see you. Hope all is okay with life. Been thinking about you.

Doesn't sound too desperate. I hope.

E-mail Jane and the others with directions, ferries and airlines offering the best discounts.

Everyone is flying out except Pierce and his kitten, who are driving down in his new TVR. I hear nothing from Jeremy. Oh, well. As Steve said, *It's always the ones you want that get away.*

I take the Mini to Portsmouth, and Ben and I board the first ferry at six a.m. Then we speed down the autoroute at a hundred to Paris, stopping off at service stations, filling up on extra-strong espresso and buzzing for another twenty-four hours.

I reach the region of the house in just over ten hours, still buzzing with caffeine. But it's dark and foggy and reminds me of the time I got lost *en route* from Slough to Gatwick, when I was trying to give Paul space. Or rope. Or both. But that experience seems such a long time ago now. This is an adventure. A challenge to be met, not feared.

I think, Hey, I'm lost in the middle of France. No road signs. No streetlights. No unhelpful policemen. No one to ask the directions to my house—*my* house—somewhere in the middle of deepest southern France. Now, doesn't that sound fucking amazing?

We're running out of petrol and still can't find our way. Ben starts humming "Show Me the Way to Go Home" which makes me laugh, then bewilders me—because how does he know that song? *I* wasn't even born when that was written.

I give up. Petrol is so low I give up. We end up sleeping the night in a car park outside the only hotel in a village. There are other cars, and it's well lit. Ben sleeps in the back and I curl up in the front seat, leaning across the gearstick, trying to convince myself it's a particularly well-endowed lover sticking me in the back causing me this pain. Doesn't work.

I sleep intermittently. For some reason I dream of a man trying to have sex with a giant spider. I'm told it's usually yourself in your dreams—so am I the spider or the man? I think I'm the spider. But then who is the man? And why the fuck does he want to have sex with a spider? All I keep thinking is, Poor spider. But with eight legs she can move bloody fast. I hope the spider kills the man. Which she probably will if he tries to have sex with her. Perhaps I think Paul's the man and I'm the spider, and he should stick to his own kind. And then I wake up because I can hear tapping, and think I should go to see a shrink or something, because that was the weirdest dream I've ever had.

A little wizened woman is tapping on my window and scares the shit out of me. She looks like the Wicked Witch of the West. Or was it the East? Well, the one with the crooked nose who nearly killed Toto the dog. Anyway, she looks horrible.

Woman—'*Allo? Allo? Q'uest que vous fait ici? Eh? Eh? Eh?*'

Translates as—What the fuck are you doing here?

Sarah—'*Je ne peux pas trouver ma maison. C'est pres de Najac.*'

Translates as—I wouldn't be here, I'd be in Najac if there were any fucking signs.

Woman—'*Ah. Vous êtes anglaise. Bien sur. Bien sur. Je pense que qui.*'

Translates as—Ah, you stupid English cow. Thought so. Not telling you. Bugger off.

Then she walks away.

Okay, bitch. You could have told me where it was. The French are supposed to like children, and I've got a gorgeous four-year-old in the back.

The fog has disappeared and I drive along the same roads I'm sure I drove down last night at least ten times. I find the house within five minutes. Happy, exhausted, with severe back- and neck-ache. Ben is unimpressed about arriving at our French house. Mainly because he hasn't yet spotted the climbing frame, the tree house, the swing and slide, or the swimming pool. Plus there are no dogs.

Ben—'Where's my room, Mummy?'

The main house looms over a small hamlet like a benevolent mother looking over her cherished family.

The family consists of a schoolhouse, a farmhouse, a cattle and tractor shed, seven cottages and an oratory, which is owned by an English couple—Frederick and Marguerita. Marguerita is German, but they haven't told the locals because the Resistance is still strong in these parts, or so Monsieur Vincent tells me. No one would sell her anything if they knew. Or they would charge her double.

Monsieur Vincent—'Some vamilies avern't spoken to each ozer for years.'

Ben and I look very English, so we are okay. And I speak passable French, and Ben speaks enough to ask for sweets and the toilet.

Everything looks wonderful. Pictures and mirrors are all in place. Everyone has worked very hard and it shows. I hug Ben, who has now spotted the tree house and disappears for the next hour. I feel I've found home.

'Hello? Hello? Hello—anyone at home?'

English voices. The sound of Jane and Samantha and Kim shouting at the tops of their voices. *The English have arrived*.

Kim—'We've bought lots of *jus de pomme* for us, and the boys have bought lots of wine. We hired a minibus for the lot of us, and went via Gaillac. Think that's where you said that barrister lives. Anyway, we bought about five cases of wine. Do you have a cellar?'

Sarah—'No, unfortunately not.'

Kim—'Don't worry. The boys will probably drink it. Do you have a bucket? Think I'm going to be sick. Baby-induced, not drink-induced—unless OD-ing on apple juice causes nausea.'

Sarah—'I'm sure we can provide you with a bathroom.'

I lead the way to the bathroom in the gite and leave Kim to throw up. Very noisily.

Jamie and Harry hug me; Samantha opens a bottle of champagne. I pour and start a tour of the buildings and grounds. Ben is still playing in the tree house.

Sarah—'Are you okay, Ben?'

Ben—'Yes, Mummy. I'm fine.'

He's alive. This is a good sign.

I can hear a car in the distance. A racing green TVR scaring the cows and the locals growls into the drive. Hidden behind dark shades, Pierce steps out with Clarissa—also wearing dark shades. Clarissa is six foot, drop-dead gorgeous, with long legs and long body and long arms and long black hair. She also has a long face. She looks longingly at Pierce.

Jane—whispering—'Pierce tells me he met her two weeks ago in a sex shop in Soho. They are *in sex.*'

Sarah—'Ah, right. Is that what it looks like?'

Pierce greets his ex-wife with a kiss on both cheeks.

Pierce—'Hello, Jane, you look blooming.'

Jane—'I am. I am. Might throw up over you at any moment. And there's another girl here who's pregnant, too. So if I don't get you, she will.'

Pierce—'Lovely thought.'

Pierce turns to Harry.

Pierce—'You must be Harry.'

Harry—'I must be. Good to meet you.'

Pierce—'Good to meet you, too.'

I don't get the impression either of them mean it.

Sarah—'Well—right. Pierce, this is Samantha. Samantha—Pierce.'

Pierce and Samantha kiss cheeks.

Kim has just emerged from the gite toilet, looking a bit grey.

'Pierce, this is Kim. Kim—Pierce.'

Kim—'I don't suggest you kiss me. I will probably throw up again.'

Jane—'He had that effect on me when I was married to him.'

Everyone laughs except Clarissa, who pouts.

Clarissa—'I don't throw up over Pierce. But he likes it when I pee over him.'

Everyone stops laughing.

Sarah—'Er, right. This is Clarissa, everyone. That's Kim, Jane, Harry and Jamie.'

The group look at Clarissa, but no one offers to kiss her cheek.

Sarah—'Right—I will show everyone their rooms. Pierce and Clarissa, you are in the gite. Samantha, you are in the other room in the gite. Kim and Jamie, you are in the main house. Jane and Harry, you are also in the main house. All rooms have double beds. Ben is in my bedroom for the duration.'

Jane—'Well, it's the first time I've ever slept in a convent.'

Everyone oohs and ahhh over the house and the grounds. Jane and Kim play garden chess, because they're both afraid their brains are going soft with pregnancy. They're plied with jugs of apple juice by doting dads-to-be Harry and Jamie.

Pierce pushes Clarissa into the pool and jumps in after her. She twines her long arms and long legs and long body round him like the alien did to John Hurt in *Alien,* when he first arrived on the spaceship. But I think Pierce is enjoying it. I'm sure she's trying to get down his throat into his stomach as well. Long tongue, probably, too.

Samantha helps me in the kitchen. We prepare cold

sausage and salami and bread and olives, and it reminds me of the time in Tuscany, when Paolo took me on the table and everything went flying. I tell her my dream about the spider and she tells me I probably should go and see someone.

Samantha—'This is lovely, Sarah. You look very happy here.'

Sarah—'I am. I'm very happy. I think Ben will be happy here, too.'

Samantha—'Now all you need is a man to share it with.'

Sarah—'I have my friends, and they're very special to me.'

Samantha—'I know, I know. But I also know you're lonely, Sarah. You're a lovely woman and you deserve to find love, and you will.'

And my friend gives me a long hug and I cry—because I'm happy and relieved, and I feel I'm the happiest I've been for a very long time.

As well as my Mini, I've invested in two Vespas, which I suggest people can use as and when they like.

Kim—'Oh, we want to do a market, Sarah. We've got to do a market while we're in France. That's what France is all about. Market days. Is there a market near here? Where you can find—you know—locals selling everything at ridiculous prices? And fabulous quality?'

Sarah—'Yes, we've got quite a few of them.'

Kim—'Let's go tomorrow. Okay?'

Sarah—'Okay. But we'll have to be up early.'

Clarissa—'We don't do early.'

Everyone stops talking and turns to Clarissa.

Jane—'Is that *we* as in you and Pierce, or is that the royal *we*?'

Clarissa—'I mean Pierce and myself. We don't, do we, Pierce?'

Pierce—'No. We'll lie in, if that's okay with you.'

Sarah—'That's okay. We can go in the minibus. Eight a.m. sharp.'

Following morning, everyone is ready. I'm running a bit late.

Journey takes about half an hour, but we have to stop once for Kim's sick break.

Market day in Villefranche is glorious. Set in a medieval market square and narrow cobbled lanes, which are taken over by stalls selling tins and jars of *foie gras,* shiny olives, very smelly cheeses, fruits and vegetables, home-brewed wines, breads, huge sunflowers—dried and fresh—handmade leather bags, hand-carved chairs and tables, orchre and siena-coloured pottery, jam and honey in jars with bright red and orange ribbons.

Everyone takes reams of photos just of the stalls and the sellers. Ben gets a toy castle with knights and horses and wizards bought for him by Harry as an early birthday present. Very early, as Ben's birthday is in December.

Laden with food and local crafts—the latter which I know Kim, Samantha and Jane will probably never find space for—we head back to the house.

Sarah—'No sign of Clarissa and Pierce.'

Kim—'They've probably gone off to scare the cows.'

Everyone helps to prepare the food, while Ben watches *E.T.* on DVD with Samantha, who sobs uncontrollably.

Ben—'Don't worry, Samantha. He's going to be all right in the end. You just wait.'

Pierce reappears with Clarissa, and offers to help opening some wine bottles. Offer is gratefully accepted.

* * *

Each day, I prepare breakfast *al fresco,* then the group
swims or reads or plays chess, or plays with Ben, or hops
on the Vespas and tours the nearby villages. We eat well
and intermittently, and drink lots of wine and apple juice.

Second evening, Samantha approaches me.

Sarah—'Having a good time?'

Samantha—'It's wonderful.'

Sarah—'Everyone seems to be getting on well.'

Samantha—'Yes. Everyone is bonding through a mutual misunderstanding—rather than loathing, because
that would be seen as jealousy—of Clarissa.'

Sarah—'Really?'

Samantha—'Yes, really. She has the most fucking
awful voice. She squeaks rather than speaks.'

Sarah—'Well, she does have a rather high pitch.'

Samantha—'I found it initially rather cute, but it gets
annoying after a minute. I'm in the room next to them
in the gite. They have sex all the bloody time. And she
crescendoes like a pressure cooker when she reaches cli-
max. Honestly, its fucking annoying, Sarah. You can tell
when it's going to happen. Pierce lets her off the boil,
then on again, then off again, then on again, then off
again. At one stage I screamed out, "Will you put the
girl out of her fucking misery and just make her come?"'

Sarah—'And did she?'

Samantha—'Well, no. There was silence. Then Pierce
knocked on my door and said that I'd put both of them
off their stride and thanked me very much.'

Sarah—'At least you got some sleep.'

Samantha—'Exactly.'

Fourth day—endless sunshine, wine, and we're so relaxed we spend most of the day being horizontal. No sign
of Jeremy. Perhaps he didn't get the e-mail. Hey-ho.

Last day. Last supper. Everyone pleasantly pink. Everyone has drunk and eaten a lot and swum a lot. Samantha has had a snog with Monsieur Vincent in the garden, but refuses to tell me if she got any further. We all look healthy, happy, shiny people.

Everyone hugs me.

Kim—'It's been wonderful, Sarah. I've even stopped throwing up. The baby likes it here. We'll be back next week. Or soon anyway. You planning to stay all summer?'

Sarah—'Planning to. I've got the Internet here, so I can work from the house, which is good.'

Jane—'We're heading off to look at our house, Sarah. Not in as good nick as yours, but maybe in six months or so. We will pop by next week. I'm going to be here for the next fortnight. Harry's back and forth from the UK, but I'll be here, sorting stuff out. Big kiss. Love you lots. You look wonderful.'

Sarah—'So do you.'

Clarissa and Pierce emerge from the bedroom to drive off in the TVR, and join in the hugging.

Pierce—'Thank you, Sarah. We've had a wonderful time. Thank you.'

Sarah—'It's my pleasure, Pierce. Have a safe journey back.'

Clarissa—'Thank you, Sarah. It has been good.'

Sarah—'My pleasure.'

Clarissa's wearing a short black dress that looks as though it's been painted on. Looking more closely, I think it has.

They both get into the car while everyone stands in a line, ogling Clarissa's painted body. Clarissa's legs are too long for the car and her knees crush up against her firm, pert, obviously silicone breasts. But she looks happy enough. Probably been in that position many times before that week. In and out of the car. As they drive off into the distance Jane says:

Jane—'She is *so* right for Pierce, don't you think?'

Everyone agrees.

I hug Harry, Jamie and Samantha, and Ben and I wave them all off in the minibus.

As I watch the dust settle, I realise for the first time in a week I'm alone again. But I don't feel lonely. Ben looks tired. Thumb in mouth. Eyes half closed.

Ben—'I'm going to lie down, Mummy, for a little snooze. Is that okay? I will be in my bedroom.'

Sarah—'That's okay, Ben. Big kiss.'

Ben—'Big kiss, Mummy. Love you.'

Sarah—'Love you, too.'

He lifts his arms to be carried, and I pick him up and take him to his bedroom—which he kindly vacated for Kim and Jamie.

His legs twine round my waist and his little arms wrap around my neck. I wonder how long I am going to be able to do this, and how long he is going to want to do this. But I'm just cherishing the moment.

As I bed him down I hear a car pull into the drive. Doesn't sound like a TVR. But perhaps they've forgotten some furry handcuffs or something. I look out of the window. It's a blue BMW. I don't recognise it. A voice calls out.

'Hello, there?'

Recognise voice.

Jeremy. It's Jeremy.

I smile. And run down the stairs. Then slow myself down so I don't look completely out of puff.

Sarah—'Hello, there. How are you?'

Jeremy—'Well. It's very good to see you, Sarah. I'm sorry I haven't been in touch.'

Sarah—'I expect it has been horrible. Since your wife…'

Jeremy—'It has. I've had a horrible time. What with the police interviewing the children, and me hiring a new nanny and moving house. But everything happens for a reason.'

Sarah—'I know. It's very good to see you, too.'

Jeremy—'Is Ben with you?'

Sarah—'Yes—asleep in his room. And your children?'

Jeremy—'My mother has the three eldest. I've got the youngest. She's in the car—asleep, too.'

Sarah—'Ah, so we have two sleeping beauties? Well, I've got a spare bedroom. We can put her in there.'

Jeremy opens the car door and cuddles up a little girl, slightly shorter and smaller in frame than Ben. Dark curly hair, long eyelashes.

Jeremy—'Hello, darling. Tired?'

No answer, just a murmur.

Jeremy—'She's tired.'

Sarah—'Take her upstairs—last door on the right.'

Jeremy—'Thanks. Will do.'

He disappears for a few minutes. Then returns smiling.

Jeremy—'Had a little nose around. The house looks stunning.'

Sarah—'It does, doesn't it. The gardens are lovely too. Would you like to see them?'

Jeremy—'Yes, please.'

We walk in the gardens. Monsieur Bizou has worked hard. Fruit bushes, lavender, rosemary and mint all scent and colour this acre of land which was once dense with weeds and bracken. It's now a little garden of Eden. *My* little garden of Eden.

Sarah—'Too late for bluebells, unfortunately.'

Jeremy—'And forget-me-nots.'

Sarah—'Yes, and forget-me-nots.'

Jeremy—'Will daisies do?'

Sarah—'Yes,' (thinking of Joe) 'it can work.'

It's a warm afternoon in July. The cows are grazing in the surrounding fields. Monsieurs Vincent, Gascon, and Bizou are all having siestas. Because in this part of France they still do.

Jeremy walks over to me and kisses me very gently on the lips. And I realise how much I've missed him.

Sarah—'I've missed you, Jeremy.'

Jeremy—'I've missed you, too.'

Sarah—'Good.'

Jeremy—'And you know I wrote that our friendship is more important than sex…?'

Sarah—'Yes?'

Jeremy—'Well, it is. But I want to have sex, make love, too. Can friends do that?'

Sarah—'I don't know.'

Jeremy—'Shall we try?'

Sarah—'I would love to make love. If that's okay with you. If you can be a little more selfless perhaps? That would be good.'

Jeremy—'Mmm—selfish, was I? Last time?'

Sarah—'Yes. You were.'

Jeremy—'I was just very happy.'

Sarah—'So was I. But I wanted to be happier.'

He smiles and kisses me again. I put my hands to his face and stroke his cheeks, brush my fingers through his hair. He does the same. Stroking my hair, kissing me on my eyelids and nose and cheeks and mouth. And down to my belly button, through my blouse.

Jeremy—'If I remember rightly, this is where your shadowy soldier kissed you?'

Sarah—'Yes, but where are the horses and the bluebells?'

Jeremy—'A garden in the South of France, surrounded by lavender? Won't that do?'

Sarah—'For now.'

Jeremy then very delicately kisses the nape of my neck. Very slowly undoing the buttons of my skirt. One by one, but not looking—as though he worked out how to undo each one when he first arrived. Which he probably did.

He doesn't take off my blouse. He doesn't take off my skirt. He pulls it up, very slowly. It's a long white lacy skirt. And he gently strokes my thighs. Only my thighs. Nothing else. I slowly undo each button of his shirt. His white linen shirt.

Sarah—'Is this the only shirt you have?'

Jeremy—'I have about ten of them. I notice you like them.'

I smile.

Sarah—'I do.'

I lift the shirt out of his trousers, but don't take it off. Then I undo his belt buckle and the top button and zip.

He continues to stroke my thighs, just occasionally stroking the sides of my body and my back. The sun is still warm and there is no wind. No bees to distract us. No bugs. Just a wonderful eighty-degree heat. And then he starts to kiss me passionately. His tongue exploring me. Then he gestures that he wants me to stay standing where I am.

Jeremy—'Don't lie down. Just stand. Just stay there. Don't move.'

He kneels down and strokes my ankles. Like Harvey Keitel does to Holly Hunter in *The Piano.* He strokes and blows on my calves and thighs, and pulls up my skirt and pushes my knickers very gently to the side. And he starts to nuzzle and stroke while his other hand reaches up and around my back to the base of my spine, and pushes me gently towards him so that I can't move my hips. Not that I would want to.

And for I don't know how many minutes I stand there, in the sunshine, in the garden, amongst the lavender and rosemary and fruit trees, many, many times on the point of coming, only to be drawn back again. Eased back, very slowly, only to feel the rush again, until I think it's about the fifth, could be the sixth time, and I come.

I feel like that actress in *The Fifth Element,* when Bruce Willis tells her he loves her at the end. I feel as though a shaft of light is entering me. Or leaving me. But I feel so powerful. And I think I cry out. Very loudly.

Sarah—'Have I scared the cows?'

Jeremy—'Fuck the cows. I want you to come again.'

And he kisses me very gently, and I think he's finished but he's still holding me at the base of the spine, refusing to let me move. And he starts again. Soft hand, gentle touch. And I think, Hey, I can't do this. Sharon Stone might have come three times in three minutes in *Basic Instinct,* but I can't do this. And yet he's so gentle and skilful, and I find myself exactly where I was before. The light. The power. And I come again.

I'm getting dizzy now, because I've been standing for I don't know how long in the sunshine, feeling awake and alive and vital and extremely wet. But he doesn't seem to want to come up for air. Because he's starting again. Kissing me again. Gently, in a different way. This can't be for real. No one can do this. *Aghhhhhhhhh.* Fuck, he can.

I try to pull away now. Harder. He stops. Lifts his head from my skirt. Looks up at me.

Jeremy—'I've got a lot to make up for. And you've got a lot of pleasure to take. Don't move.'

And I don't. I don't move. Not because he's told me not to move. I haven't lost the power. I've gained it. Because I realise this is where I want to be. I don't want to move. I want to take it. Just take and enjoy the pleasure. The sensuality of the moment. Of the sensations. And I don't want him to stop and I don't think he wants to either.

He eventually stops. Don't know how many times. I feel my legs will crumble, but as he comes up for air he holds me by the waist, expecting that I might feel faint.

Jeremy—'You might feel faint in this heat.'

Sarah—'How do you know? Have you done this before?'

Jeremy —'That's the first time I've wanted to do it more than once to any woman. But I thought seven was your lucky number. And I felt you wanted to come more than once. And I was right, wasn't I?'

Sarah—'Yes, you were. I just didn't think I could.'

Jeremy—'Well, you surprised yourself. I think you've surprised yourself a lot over the past year, Sarah.'

Sarah—'I think I have.'

Jeremy—'May I ask you something?'

Sarah—'Of course.'

Jeremy—'Have you ever come with someone inside you?'

Sarah—'Almost.'

Jeremy—'You haven't, then?'

Sarah—'Most women can't, can they?'

Jeremy—'Most women don't have your capacity for enjoyment.'

Sarah—'I doubt that.'

Jeremy—'Okay, most women *I've* met don't have your capacity for enjoyment.'

Sarah—'Perhaps. Don't you think we should check on the children?'

Jeremy—'Perhaps. Do you want to stop?'

Sarah—'Oh, God, no. I want to make this last for ever. God, what a cliché. Can't believe I said that. Sorry.'

Jeremy—'I don't want it to end either. And that's not a cliché, Sarah.'

Sarah—'I've got a lot to learn, Jeremy. A lot more about myself. About life. I've got a lot to learn about being a good mother to Ben and becoming a strong woman.'

He stands back and looks at me. Dishevelled, multi-orgasmic me. In my undone blouse and skirt, nipples peeping through, knickers halfway down my thighs, hair as though I'd just had a vigorous Indian head massage. And he says:

Jeremy—'You are a strong woman, Sarah. All women are strong, but you're *really* strong. And you've already learnt a lot. You're a good mum to Ben. I know you're not perfect, and you've had days when you've been angry and sad with Paul and Sarah, but you've done good, Ms Giles. You've handled yourself well. You've handled the situation well. I know this because I've been through it, too.

'I'm on the other side, remember? I'm the angry man. The cold bastard who asked for the divorce because he found out his wife was having an affair. And she loved me, and still loves me. But, well…'

He stops mid-sentence. I think the man who doesn't cry is about to cry. I see the vulnerable man. But I see a man, not a boy. Someone whose heart has been broken and who is trying to learn from the experience. Not repeat it. And now he must be doing what I do when I don't want to cry. Thinking of something unsexy and cold, like Tony Blair. And it works for him, too, because he regains his composure.

Jeremy—'I know you've handled it well. I so want to get to know you better. Not just sexually, but in every way. You will never need a man as much as a man will need you. I know that. I can sense it, and I think you can, too. But you are so deserving of love, Sarah, of being loved, and I think you know that now. You have so much love to give. And so much love to receive. And you've learnt that. You are totally loveable. All I want to do is to show you in every way I can how much I care. It may not be enough, but I will give you all I have to give.'

I stare at him. Gaze at his wonderful tanned face. I'm thinking how this time is for me, for myself and for Ben. And how I don't want to get into a relationship now, because this is *me* time—Sarah time. My time. And I feel sorry for Paul, because I feel he hasn't given himself this *me* time. Not really, for all his boy-toys and nights out. Ironically, he hasn't given himself the *space* that he needed, that he wanted all those months ago. Although I know that was only a ruse because he just wanted *space* from me. And he hasn't learnt about himself. Not really. Not the way you learn when you're alone and can only hear the sound of your own voice and no one else's.

I've never had this time before. And I know that I don't want to get into another serious relationship. Not yet. Not for some time. Maybe not for years, or ever. Who knows? But not just now. Because I am starting to love this freedom and the nonsense we call responsibility, and I am enjoying the challenges we call problems and learning from them. And I'm enjoying experimenting with life, realising I'm living it—not just surviving it.

And then I realise that this is part of the freedom. The choice. Jeremy or no Jeremy. And I choose him. I choose Jeremy now. At the moment. For now. Just for now. For this moment I choose Jeremy. And now I have instinct and strength enough to walk away from this man as well as to walk towards him.

And I smile and kiss him, and realise I'm zooming down the black run of life and loving it. And I'm not afraid any more.

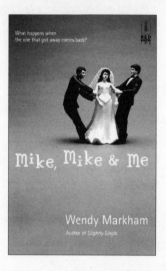

New from Cathy Yardley,
author of *L.A. Woman*

Couch World

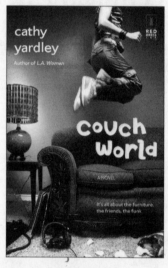

Welcome to COUCH WORLD where life is simple
for the *über*hip P.J., who wakes up at 2:00 p.m.
in someone else's place on someone else's
couch. Showers. Clothes. And goes to work as
a punter—someone who fills in for a DJ who
is unable to make a gig. But life for P.J. gets
complicated when a reporter infiltrates her life
and acts as if P.J.'s life is her own.

**Available wherever
trade paperbacks
are sold.**

RED
DRESS
INK
™

The Last Year of Being Single

Sarah Tucker

Just because he's perfect doesn't mean he's Mr. Right....

Torn between two men—her perfect-on-paper fiancé and an intoxicating and flirty co-worker—twenty-nine-year-old Sarah Giles writes a scandalously honest diary of one life-changing year, and faces the challenge of writing her own happy ending....

RED
DRESS
INK
TM

The Sex Was Great But...

by Tyne O'Connell

A novel about celebrities, sex and secrets

Holly Klein is an A-list celebrity with an army
of assistants. Leo Monroe is a smart-talking DJ
from the streets. She lives on Mulholland Drive;
he lives on...someone else's sofa. But when
Leo rescues Holly from a mugger, their
two worlds collide, literally.

**Wherever trade
paperbacks are sold.**